THE PSEUDONYMS OF GOD

Books by ROBERT McAFEE BROWN
Published by THE WESTMINSTER PRESS

P. T. Forsyth: Prophet for Today
The Bible Speaks to You
The Significance of the Church
    (Layman's Theological Library)
The Collect'd Writings of St. Hereticus
The Pseudonyms of God

THE PSEUDONYMS OF GOD

by ROBERT McAFEE BROWN

THE WESTMINSTER PRESS
Philadelphia

ISBN 0-664-20930-0 (CLOTH)
ISBN 0-664-24948-5 (PAPER)

LIBRARY OF CONGRESS CATALOG CARD NO. 77-178813

PUBLISHED BY THE WESTMINSTER PRESS
PHILADELPHIA, PENNSYLVANIA   ®

PRINTED IN THE UNITED STATES OF AMERICA

Contents

Introduction: "Christianity And..."

The early working title for this collection of essays, "Christianity And . . . ," was meant to convey that Christianity cannot be understood in a vacuum, but only in relation to other aspects of human existence. The theme, if not the title, has persisted in spite of the warning of C. S. Lewis' senior devil, Screwtape, that such thinking serves only to encourage the demonic hierarchy below:

> What we want [Screwtape writes to Wormwood], if men become Christians at all, is to keep them in the state of mind I call "Christianity And." You know—Christianity and the Crisis, Christianity and the New Psychology, Christianity and the New Order, Christianity and Faith Healing, Christianity and Psychical Research, Christianity and Vegetarianism, Christianity and Spelling Reform. If they must be Christians, let them at least be Christians with a difference. Substitute for the faith itself some Fashion with a Christian colouring. Work on their horror of the Same Old Thing.[1]

The present title, THE PSEUDONYMS OF GOD, was finally chosen because it better describes the intent of the essays, even though it may initially sound less clear. (When I queried the publisher about the possible esoteric nature of the word "pseudonyms," I got the reply that in the present climate of opinion the word "God" might seem even more esoteric.) As the essays in Part II make clear, the theme is borrowed from

the writings of the Italian novelist Ignazio Silone, who repeatedly suggests that God is found in unexpected places today,
assuming strange or false names (e.g., pseudo names) and
confronting us where we least anticipate his presence.

Example: On the day on which this introduction was completed, the San Francisco *Chronicle* carried two front-page
stories side by side. In one of them, Daniel Ellsberg was sur-
rendering himself to the federal authorities and facing a
prison sentence of up to ten years for releasing "the Pentagon
papers" to the public, because of his conscientious conviction
that Americans need to know how their Government misled
them into a needless war that has killed hundreds of thousands of innocent people. In the adjoining column, Billy Graham, a Christian evangelist who has never publicly opposed
the expansion of the Vietnam war, was exhorting his followers
to affirm the bumper-sticker slogan "America: Love It or
Leave It," and insisting that we should be praising our nation
rather than criticizing it. In which column was the prophetic
word of God being spoken? It seems to me patently clear that
on this occasion God was speaking through Mr. Ellsberg
rather than through Mr. Graham. The theme of the "pseudonyms of God" insists that God cannot be confined to our
churches, our theologies, or our "religious" actions, and may
be working more through "secular" communities, "secular"
thought, and "secular" actions than we care to admit. To acknowledge this is, of course, to acknowledge that the traditional "sacred-secular" dichotomy has to go by the boards, and
to insist, as a result, that God can work wherever he chooses
to do so.

Since the essays in this volume attempt to illustrate various
facets of the overall theme, they should be able to stand on
their own feet, and a brief rationale for their grouping and ordering will suffice.

Part I, "Adventures in Theological Self-awareness," attempts
to trace my increasing recognition that Christians must listen
to the world as well as speak to it. The first essay offers a fairly

solid 1960 theological statement, and the subsequent essays
show how that position, although basically unchanged, has
been subjected to remolding and reshaping by the events of
the ensuing decade.

Part II, "The Pseudonyms of God," develops the specific
theme of the book in more detail, setting it in the context of
other attempts to account for the remoteness of God from
modern life. It also indicates some of the more explicitly Biblical and Christian overtones of the theme.

Part III, "Discovering God's Pseudonyms Today," offers a
variety of specific examples of the pseudonyms I believe God
is using today. These essays attempt to show how God is
working on the educational scene, in the political arena, and
in such unlikely experiences as death, imprisonment, and civil
disobedience.

The final section of Part III, "Vietnam and the Exercise of
Dissent: A Fragment of History," is slightly different in tone
and intention. From about 1964 to the present, my theological
life has been dominated by the conviction that the American
presence in Southeast Asia represents an almost unmitigated
horror. This book is not the place to spell out the reasons for
that conviction,[2] but it is the place to illustrate some of the
ways in which that conviction has been expressed. I have tried
to show how my theological convictions about war, the state,
and dissent were gradually sharpened and directed by the
course of outer events. My basic position on dissent was clear
long before Vietnam was an issue, but Vietnam forced me into
more specific expression of that concern than would otherwise
have been the case. I offer these papers as a fragmentary case
study of how the world informs and transforms a theological
position, to illustrate my belief that theology is forged
through engagement instead of detachment, on pavements
more than in libraries, and in the midst of ambiguities rather
than clarities.

Since most of these essays originated in response to specific
situations, the source and date of original publication is indi-

cated at the beginning of each one. Minor changes have been made to eliminate overlapping, and to remove slight anachronisms resulting from the interval between original composition and present publication.

If there is any personal debt these pages seek to repay, it is to the one who taught me most about "Christianity and the world," Reinhold Niebuhr. His death, during the time this book was being prepared for the press, has reminded me once again of how permanent is the imprint of this truly great man upon the American—and world—scene. In him, God assumed no pseudonym, but was directly and marvelously present.

NOTES

1. C. S. Lewis, *The Screwtape Letters* (The Macmillan Company, 1943), p. 126.

2. For a more detailed accounting, cf. "Vietnam: Crisis of Conscience," *The Catholic World*, Oct., 1967, reprinted in M. E. Marty and D. G. Peerman (eds.), *New Theology, No. 6* (The Macmillan Company, 1969), pp. 229-242; "Why I Oppose Our Policy in Vietnam," *Presbyterian Life*, Jan. 15, 1968, pp. 14-17, 38-39; and more fully, *Vietnam: Crisis of Conscience* (with Michael Novak and Abraham Heschel) (Association Press, Behrman House, Herder & Herder, Inc., 1967), esp. pp. 7-9 and 62-106.

I
ADVENTURES
IN THEOLOGICAL SELF-AWARENESS

Theology as an Act of Gratitude

GRATITUDE AND GRACE

In the years that I have taught theology, it has become increasingly clear to me that the distinctive word in the Christian vocabulary is the word "grace." That God is gracious to us, that he loves us no matter how unlovable we may be, that he visits us in the midst of our distresses when we have no claim whatsoever upon his attentions, that he identifies himself wholly with us, that he changes our situation by what he does—all of this is the heart and center of the Christian gospel, and all of it may be conveniently summed up under the word "grace." God as revealed in Jesus Christ is a gracious God. This is the gospel we preach. It is also the gospel we teach.

And if grace is the distinctive word to describe God's attitude toward us, there is also a word that describes the nature of the response we are called upon to make. That word is "gratitude." Gratitude is what must characterize our dealings with God because grace is what characterizes God's dealings with us.

If the real test of a theological affirmation is whether or not

Inaugural address as Auburn Professor of Systematic Theology at Union Theological Seminary, given in Oct., 1960, and subsequently published in the *Union Seminary Quarterly Review*, Special Issue, Dec., 1960. Used by permission.

it can be sung—and that may be the most important test—
then the affirmation of gratitude is a particularly resonant
Protestant affirmation. And there is one hymn that, more than
any other, expresses this stance of gratitude. It is a hymn
that seems to be the appropriate one for every occasion
of worship. I find myself wanting to use it at the conclusion
of every sermon I preach, so that it will confirm the fact
of the good news, in case my own proclamation has been
faulty. It is the hymn that seems most appropriate after a bap-
tism. It is the hymn that gathers up our sense of gratitude
after a wedding. It is the hymn par excellence to be sung after
we have celebrated the Sacrament of the Lord's Supper, the
Eucharist, the very service of thanksgiving and gratitude. It is
the appropriate hymn to sing before or after a meal, and was
in fact originally written to be sung as a grace. It is the hymn
that I fervently hope will be sung at my funeral. It is the
hymn that sums up what our reaction to the gospel must be,
and describes what kind of people we must be because of the
gospel. It is the hymn "Now Thank We All Our God."

Now thank we all our God with heart and hands and voices,
Who wondrous things hath done, in whom his world rejoices;
Who, from our mothers' arms, hath blessed us on our way
With countless gifts of love, and still is ours today.

O may this bounteous God through all our life be near us,
With ever joyful hearts and blessed peace to cheer us;
And keep us in his grace, and guide us when perplexed,
And free us from all ills in this world and the next.

All praise and thanks to God the Father now be given,
The Son, and him who reigns with them in highest heaven,
The one eternal God, whom earth and heaven adore;
For thus it was, is now, and shall be evermore.

Why are we people who must be grateful? Simply because
God is the gracious God; because, as the hymn puts it, he has
done "wondrous things"; because in Jesus Christ he has visited

and redeemed his people; because "God was in Christ reconciling the world unto himself"; because the world, this sorry world of ours, is a world into which God has come, a world that he has transformed, a world that is the scene of the victory he wrought over the powers of evil in the cross and resurrection. This seems to me truer and truer every day. The more I read the New Testament, the more I find this the presupposition without which the New Testament would never have been written. The more I read the daily paper, the more I realize that this is the only way in which the chaos and frightful ugliness and terror of modern life can be understood apart from bleak despair.

Now I am quite aware that to say that we live in a redeemed world, or that God in Christ has wrought a cosmic victory over the powers of evil, or that Jesus really meant it when he said not only, "In the world you have tribulation," but also really meant it when he went on to say, "But be of good cheer, I have overcome the world"—I am aware that to say these things is not only to sound naïve but also to involve oneself with a lot of tough theological problems: Why doesn't the world look more redeemed? Why is God's activity so hidden? How can we really believe that "the Lord our God is good, his mercy is forever sure," when all, or at least most, of the evidence seems to point in precisely the opposite direction? All I will say to this at the moment is that I would rather be saddled with problems of that sort, which arise because the gospel evokes confident affirmation, than be saddled with the dilemma of having no more to offer than the hesitant postulate that it may turn out that God will somehow possibly swing the balance of things in his favor more or less, though of course we're not yet sure. On those terms, it seems to me, there would be no gospel to preach. Consequently, the gospel I affirm is the good news that we live in God's world, a world which in Christ he has invaded and conquered. In this world we will surely have tribulation, but we can be of good cheer, for he has overcome the world.

Since this has happened, we can be grateful. All we really can do is to live lives of gratitude. Because God is gracious, we are to be grateful.

> *Charis* always demands the answer of *eucharistia* [writes Karl Barth, i.e., grace always demands the answer of gratitude]. Grace and gratitude belong together like heaven and earth. Grace evokes gratitude like the voice an echo. Gratitude follows grace like thunder [follows] lightning.[1]

Now, there are many ways in which we can be grateful. We can pray. We can engage in politics. We can love our families. We can build buildings. We can be theologians. My particular way of trying to be grateful is to be a theologian. This is what it seems to me the grace of God calls upon me to do—to show my gratitude by trying to think out loud, as it were, about what his grace means. I hasten to add that these ways of being grateful are not mutually exclusive ways. Theology is not an alternative to praying; the more I theologize, the more I am convinced that it is hollow if it does not grow out of the attempt to pray. Theology is not an alternative to loving one's family, though I must add that it often seems to cut into time that rightfully belongs to one's family. Nor does theology exempt one from trying to build buildings to the glory of God. So there are many ways of being grateful.

What attitudes, then, must be brought to the theological task if theology is indeed a response of gratitude for the gift of grace? Let me suggest four things that flow from the basic consideration that theology is an act of gratitude.

1. Christian Theology as a Confessional Theology

First of all, Christian theology will be a *confessional theology*. The one who speaks is himself grateful. Better, I who speak am myself grateful. I do not as a theologian merely describe why other people are grateful. I also try to tell other people why I am grateful. As a Christian theologian, I am a believing theologian, a confessing theologian. I am not so much reporting at arm's length what "they" out there believe, as I am confessing where I stand. And I ought to be able to do this in such a way that the listener could at least respond, "Well of course if I could believe *that*, I would be grateful too." I may not be able to convince him that it is true—and nobody ever argued anybody else into the Kingdom of God—but at least he ought to be able to see why I am grateful, and realize that if grace is real, gratitude is every bit as real, and that both are real to me.

Now this first point may seem very obvious, but I stress it because it seems to be far from obvious to many people of my own theological generation, who apparently feel that it is cheating with the evidence and distorting its academic integrity to indicate one's own involvement in it. Consequently, I feel compelled to take issue with those who say that the theologian can legitimately disengage himself from his subject matter. I am dubious of the approach that says: "Where I stand theologically doesn't matter. I simply lay out the various options for the students." No, this is really to say that the subject matter of theology, while it may be very interesting stuff, isn't really a life and death matter for me, and therefore need not be a life and death matter for anyone else. The alternative is not to sell a particular theological line—a point to which I shall return in a moment. The alternative is to make the student aware that the subject matter of theology really makes a difference. If theology is an act of gratitude, then it must be a confessing theology, a theology with which I as a theologian proclaim my own involvement and therefore my own gratitude.

2. Christian Theology as a Church Theology

But to say this is not enough. For the faith I confess in gratitude is not a faith I have invented, but a faith I have received; not a faith that is the response of my intellect, but a faith to which my intellect must make response. Theology as an act of gratitude is not my solitary act of gratitude, but an expression of the gratitude of the entire Christian community. Theology is not only confessional theology, it is also a *church theology*.

I have no right to teach a faith that is simply *my* faith, but I have every right and duty to teach a faith that is the church's faith, a faith that I have received and appropriated as the gift of God to me through his church. Schleiermacher makes the point in the Prolegomenon to *The Christian Faith*:

> Since Dogmatics is a theological discipline, and thus pertains solely to the Christian Church, we can only explain what it is when we have become clear as to the conception of the Christian Church. . . . The present work entirely disclaims the task of establishing on a foundation of general principles a Doctrine of God, or an Anthropology or Eschatology either, which should be used in the Christian Church though it did not really originate there, or which should prove the propositions of the Christian Faith to be consonant with reason.[2]

The point is that theology is not some self-sufficient discipline of some self-sufficient individual, i.e., me; theology is an activity of the church, an expression of the faith of the church, and therefore—no more but no less—the servant of the church. It is the church being grateful. The church's theology is not an end in itself, but merely a tool to help the church do its job better. So when I speak as a theologian, I am not speaking just for myself, though I must always take responsibility for what I say and for the fact that I may have corrupted what needs to be said because of my own deficiencies as a theologian. What I am called upon to do is to articulate the faith by which the communion of saints has lived, lives, and will continue to live. Since God has been gracious to his community, his community must live in grateful response, and theology is one of the niches within the total life of the church where this grateful response is expressed.

I spent Pentecost in 1960 in East Berlin. On that day, a German-speaking Swiss pastor and I conducted the service of

Holy Communion in a Lutheran parish church behind the Iron Curtain. It fell to me to say before the bread was distributed to people living deep in the East Zone, "Take and eat this bread in the sure and certain faith that Christ died for you, and feed on him in your heart by faith *with thanksgiving*." In gratitude! How could I, R. M. Brown, comfortable, well-fed, much-too-complacent Westerner, tell East Germans who live in constant danger of life and livelihood because they do such reckless things as coming to Communion services, how could I tell them to be grateful? I, of course, as R. M. Brown, could tell them no such thing, but I, as an ordained minister of the church of Jesus Christ, was the appointed means through whom they could be told that because the promises of God are true, and Christ did die for them, they could live in the East Zone—in the East Zone!—with a song of gratitude on their lips. I had no right to say, "I tell you on my authority to be full of gratitude." But I had every right, as the proclaimer and transmitter to them of the bread of life, to tell them that because it *was* the bread of life, they not only could and should, but must, be grateful. In a very special way I know, because of that celebration of the Eucharist, that *charis* is answered by *eucharistia*, that grace is answered by gratitude. But this was not my insight; it was, and is, the very lifeblood of the church.

3. *Christian Theology as a Listening Theology*

Since neither I nor the church invented the faith we are called upon to share, Christian theology is not only a confessional theology and a church theology, it is also a *listening* theology. The theologian earns the right to speak only when he has subjected himself to the discipline of listening. There are at least three directions in which the theologian must listen if he is to be a faithful listener.

a. The theologian must listen first of all *to the Bible*. If we believe that God has acted decisively in Jesus Christ, then our starting point must surely be the place where we learn most

directly that this is so. We always seem ready to admit that
Christ is the Omega, the last, and that all sorts of theological
and even philosophical trails can lead to him, however de-
viously they may wind before they get there. But we must also
be more courageous about affirming that he is the Alpha as
well, the first as well as the last, and that if theology is to be
Christ-ian theology, it must not only end with Christ but also
start with him. This means, the minute we try to be the least
bit specific, that we start with the Bible, since all other materials about Christ are derivative from the Biblical materials. The
Biblical listening may be very sophisticated, and it will surely
make use of all the cultural and hermeneutical tools at our dis-
posal, but it will remain central to our task, unless we want to
end up in a subjectivist morass.

   b. In addition to listening to the Bible, the theologian must
also listen *to the church,* or, just to make it sound very suspi-
cious, to tradition. We must simply face the fact that we read
the Bible in the light of various traditions—Lutheran, Re-
formed, sectarian, liberal, orthodox, or whatever—and recognize that we can never entirely disassociate ourselves from
them. We can no more leapfrog over nineteen centuries to the
New Testament, as though the intervening centuries had not
occurred and conditioned the way we understand the Biblical
materials, than we can be in two places at once. We do *not*
start from scratch in every theological generation. We start as
recipients of all that has come before, and we must examine
critically all that has come before. Our forefathers could be
wrong and frequently were. Sometimes they were brilliantly
wrong, sometimes obstinately so—as useful a distinction as
any, I suppose, between heretics and schismatics. But before
we dismiss them as wrong we must listen to them gratefully,
for at many points they were right. Before we dismiss them as
wrong we must appropriate from them what was right. The
burden of proof is not first of all upon the Christian heritage
to prove itself to me, the burden of proof is first of all upon me
when I reject some part of the Christian heritage that has con-

sistently commended itself to others. This is merely an elaborate way of saying that the corporate convictions of the communion of saints over two thousand years are probably a little more mature than the individual convictions of this particular "saint" after forty years of sporadic reflection.

c. But in addition to listening to the Bible and the church, the theologian must also listen *to the world*. Now to say just how we are to listen to the world would be the subject for another book. I would almost settle here for an overlooked passage in Calvin's *Institutes*, in which he says:

> Whenever, therefore, we meet with heathen writers, let us learn from that light of truth which is admirably displayed in their works, that the human mind, fallen as it is, and corrupted from its integrity, is yet invested and adorned by God with excellent talents. If we believe that the Spirit of God is the only fountain of truth, we shall neither reject nor despise the truth itself, wherever it shall appear, unless we wish to insult the Spirit of God.[3]

We must listen to the world, then, for at least two reasons. First of all, whatever else we are, we are men of the world, and do not cease being men of the world when we become theologians. If I ever have any minimal success in trying to communicate the gospel to twentieth-century man, it will be in part at least because I too am a twentieth-century man, because I too live with the doubts of my contemporaries, because I too keep being amazed at the incredible character of the Christian claim and have to fight the battle of unbelief within myself just as other men do. But this is not the most important reason why the theologian must listen to the world. The most important reason is simply because the world is God's world. Because he has been pleased to act within it in a life and a death and a resurrection, we must be confident that having set his mark upon it, he may also be acting within it at many other places too. Since we have seen him at work in the world of Jesus Christ, we must be prepared to see him at work in other places in the world that Jesus Christ redeemed. We must listen to the world because it is the world that God loved so much that he sent his only begotten Son into it. Our theology does not separate us from the world. It ties us more closely than ever to it.

4. Christian Theology as a Modest Theology

Finally, theology must be a *modest theology*, a theology always subject to correction. Because it is so overwhelmed by the magnitude of what it has heard, it must be humble in its own report of what it has heard. I am aware that there is nothing more arrogant than a statement in praise of humility. But at the risk of inverted arrogance, I must stress the point. Theology must never claim too much for itself. It is not the real thing. It is only the faintest echo of the real thing. Commenting on all the fuss that has been made about his *Church Dogmatics*, Karl Barth says:

> The angels laugh at old Karl. They laugh at him because he tries to grasp the truth about God in a book of Dogmatics. They laugh at the fact that volume follows volume and each is thicker than the previous one. As they laugh, they say to one another, "Look! Here he comes now with his little pushcart full of volumes of the Dogmatics!" And they laugh about the men who write so much about Karl Barth instead of writing about the things he is trying to write about. Truly, the angels laugh.[4]

Thus no Protestant theologian has a right to be too impressed by his own theologizing.[5] There is something comic, if not downright absurd, about the claim that a human creature can penetrate the veil of holiness surrounding the transcendent God, or describe with accuracy the events that took place when God penetrated that veil himself in the incarnation of his Son.

Rule One for every theologian ought therefore to be, "Don't take yourself too seriously." This is a very different thing from saying, "Don't take your faith seriously." It means that all our attempts to express our faith must include an echo of laughter. In this case it will not merely be the heavenly laughter of Barth's angels, but our own very human laughter as well. It will sometimes be the laughter of self-mockery at the notion that our fleshly words can encompass the Word made flesh. But it can also be the laughter of delight and pure joy that through the disclosure of his Word in Jesus Christ, God has seen fit to allow his creatures the audacity of forming words about him.

Authentic religious language is finally not the language of the classroom or the lecture hall, but the language of liturgy and prayer. Singing one of Luther's hymns is usually a deeper act of gratitude than reading *The Bondage of the Will.* Praying one of Calvin's prayers is usually a deeper act of gratitude than reading his *Letter to Cardinal Sadolet.* And Protestants, when all is said and done, express their gratitude more adequately in their hymns and prayers than in their theologizing. But if theology can help us to be grateful by teaching us to sing and pray, it will not have been in vain.

NOTES

1. Karl Barth, *Church Dogmatics,* Vol. IV, Part 1, ed. by G. W. Bromiley and T. F. Torrance (Charles Scribner's Sons, 1956), p. 41.

2. Friedrich Schleiermacher, *The Christian Faith* (Edinburgh: T. & T. Clark, 1928), Ch. 1, para. 2, p. 3.

3. John Calvin, *Institutes of the Christian Religion* (The Westminster Press, n.d.) II, ii, xv; cf. further on this point, "Assyrians in Modern Dress."

4. *Antwort, Karl Barth sum siebzigsten Geburtstag* (Zollikon-Zurich: Evangelischer Verlag AG, 1956), p. 895, my translation.

5. In what follows I have slightly adapted material from the Foreword to R. M. Brown, *The Spirit of Protestantism* (Oxford University Press, 1961).

A Campaign on Many Fronts:
A Report on "How I Am
Making Up My Mind"

How one makes up his mind is partly conditioned by *where* he makes it up, and my locale has recently shifted. Geographically, the move has been a move from Union Theological Seminary to Stanford University. Theologically, the move has been from Jerusalem to Athens. But the move was undertaken out of a conviction that if the theological venture is really justified, it must be able to sustain itself not only in the supportive atmosphere of a seminary community but in the indifferent atmosphere of a secular university. This does not mean that there are not devoted Christians among the Stanford faculty and student body, but it does mean that they—and we—constitute a small minority indeed, and that my contacts from day to day and even hour to hour are chiefly with those who simply aren't involved in many of the things about which I care deeply.

Theologically, I have come to terms with the fact that I nevertheless share many things with these people. Their passion and devotion to politics and civil rights puts mine to shame. We can make common cause on many fronts. We are upset at injustice. We want peace. We believe in the right of dissent. Sometimes we occupy different sides of the hyphen that sepa-

Originally published in *The Christian Century*, May 5, 1965, in the series "How I Am Making Up My Mind," and subsequently reprinted in Dean Peerman (ed.), *Frontline Theology* (John Knox Press, 1967). Copyright 1965 by The Christian Century Foundation. Reprinted by permission.

rates "Judeo-Christian." More frequently we simply share a common humanity.

How does the Christian faith fit into this sort of situation? Plenty of people are obviously living good, decent, even compassionate lives without it. Many are, of course, filled with a sense of emptiness (no contradiction, that) but I have gotten past the point of trying to convince happy and committed persons how unhappy they *really* are if they would only take the time and trouble to find out. If this is a description of Bonhoeffer's elusive "world come of age," then I know what he was writing about. To be sure, some of this contentment is veneer, and the veneer wears thin when a President is assassinated or a student commits suicide. But to a great number of these people, friends of mine, it would never remotely cross their consciousness that Christianity had something important to say to them, either in the crises or in the day-to-day routines. What more can we say than Camus to them hath said?

This is the background against which I am "making up my mind." The picture isn't complete without those members of the community (both students and faculty) who *do* care, who *are* disturbed, whose skepticism is always tinged with wistfulness, and whose faith has been purged of sentimentality. But they, and I, are a remnant, and I get the increasing feeling that for *our* day, Christianity must be the religion of the remnant, and that the true household of believers will not be distinguished by its numbers or its outward strength. I see no evidence that we are on the threshhold of a new Age of Faith. So I am "making up my mind" as part of a remnant, amid a vast company of colleagues, the great majority of whom couldn't care less.

A HERITAGE TO TRANSMIT—CRITICALLY

My stance in this situation is that of genus Protestant, species Presbyterian. My roots are here, not of my own choosing, but because this is the tradition in which I have been nurtured, and I would find no reason to desert it for other ecclesiastical pastures that might occasionally seem greener, unless and until it should seem to me a sin to remain where I am.

I do not, from this stance, re-create the Christian faith for myself from day to day. I have received an inheritance—a faith with a tradition extending back from myself to the apostles (even though the lines of connection aren't quite as tidy in my tradition as they are claimed to be in some others). I am reluctant to jettison this heritage with the ease that some of my Protestant contemporaries appear to be in process of jettisoning theirs. The tradition is not so much called upon to commend itself to me, as I am called upon to be receptive to it. I must first learn before I presume to judge. This does not make me particularly "orthodox," and I would find myself in trouble with a good many presbyteries. But it does give me a responsibility to be faithful to that heritage. Fidelity may involve reinterpretation. Indeed, I am sure it does. But I must always be sure that what gives me difficulty is not simply the result of my own faulty vision. If I turn my back on "Scripture and the Fathers," I am not sure that my resultant message can be commended to others for any reason save the fact that it is *my* message, and since I find it exceedingly difficult to take myself that seriously, I must acknowledge that others would find it even more so. I preach not myself.

I stand, then, in a relationship to a heritage. It may be a critical relationship, but it is a relationship nonetheless to which I must be faithful. I am not about to sue for a divorce, even though I occasionally need the help of a marriage counselor.

Two Directions of Concern

As I try to communicate what I hear in that tradition, I find myself now doing so in relation to two other and very different factors. Let one of them be described simply as that bent, doubting, questioning entity, *the world.* I cannot theologize in a vacuum, or in exclusively ecclesiastical surroundings (the vacuous content of which I leave for the moment unexplored). I must theologize in terms of the world of modern man. If I could sometimes forget that world in the seminary community, I can never forget it in the university community. It is where I live, work, eat, lecture, argue, hang my hat, and marvel. It is not simply "over there" somewhere, confronting me— it is in me, and I am in it. Its doubts are my doubts. Its sins are my sins. If I ever communicate to this world, it is because I know its accents. Students are sometimes surprised that I speak as highly as I do of Albert Camus. What I have to tell them is that there is a part of me to which Camus speaks, a part of me that utters a hearty "Amen" to what I hear from him, a part of me that is not concerned to "refute" him, but rather wants to take up arms with him against the foes we both despise, even though we get our orders to do so through different chains of command. So I will neither scorn nor condemn this world, nor act condescendingly toward it, even though I cannot find my final peace within it.

The other factor that guides my attempt to rearticulate the Protestant faith is *Roman Catholicism.* And I am thus in something of a bind. For it is quite a trick to look upon the unbelieving world and relate to it, and simultaneously to look upon the believing Catholic Church and relate to it. If my common cause with the world is my doubt, my common cause with the Catholic is my faith. The things I can most easily assert to either one are the things most difficult to assert to the other.

It takes a certain dexterity to move from the realm where all things must be doubted to the realm where most things can be presupposed. [It should be obvious that these lines were written before the recent radical self-questioning within Roman Catholicism had surfaced.] But I have no option apart from trying to develop that dexterity, for if I cannot make up my mind oblivious to the world, no more can I make up my mind oblivious to Roman Catholicism. I have learned much about the Christian faith from my associations with Roman Catholics in

the last five years, and there are few things I would less will-
ingly forgo for the next five, than that ongoing relationship. I
am quite as ready now to read Karl Rahner as John Calvin,
and to learn from Hans Küng as from Martin Luther. In doing
so, I feel a sense not of betrayal, but rather of enrichment.
Withal, I do not secretly wish I were a Roman Catholic, nor do
I nurse a deep desire to become one, whatever doubt some of
my militant party-line Protestant friends may have on that
score. If I am to see the Christian faith afresh today I cannot
make up my mind without trying to see—nay, feel—its Catholic as well as it Protestant nuances.

The Catalyst of Doubt

As if a simultaneous concern for the unbelieving world and
the believing Catholic Church were not complication enough,
a dialectic of faith and doubt also informs the way I am making up my mind. I am aware that Calvin has some remarkable
passages on doubt, but I am also aware that this problem did
not ruffle his theological beard unduly. But for many of us
today, however, doubt has become an important ingredient of
faith. I would not have chosen this to be the way, and I do not
cherish doubt or love it, but I would be surprised, and even
disturbed, I think, if it were suddenly whisked away. For it is
not merely a descriptive fact about my life, but even one of
the tools of my trade, in the sense that the presence of doubt
keeps theology from being stagnant. I, at least, am never at
the place where thinking can cease because the problems have
all been solved. I am always at the place where thinking must
continue because old problems have a pesky way of reappear-
ing, and old answers have a disconcerting way of losing
power. This place, I would like to believe, is the location of
any live theology. So I must acknowledge the reality of doubt,
not simply to make common cause with modern man, but be-

cause doubt is the price that must be paid for theological growth. Faith without doubt is dead.

But I must also confess (and thereby risk some of that cherished rapport with modern man) that, save in the low moments, doubt does not have for me quite the terror it once did. I would naturally prefer less of it rather than more, but even when the "more" is oppressively upon me, I find myself able to draw increasing comfort from a fact so obvious that I do not know why its obviousness was hidden from me for so many years: to say that I doubt the reality of God is to say something about *myself*, but not necessarily to say anything about God. That his reality should depend on how I happen to feel about him, strikes me as ludicrous in the extreme, and I can usually gain a restoration of perspective by reflecting on that fact. There are long periods of time when I am existentially unaware of God's presence, and at such times I find no particular reason, in my own "feelings" or convictions or theological reflections, to continue believing in him. But I am willing to believe that this is a manifestation of the dimness of my own sight rather than a manifestation of his unreality. The fact that I do not, at a given moment, "see" the sun, does not mean that the sun is not there. My eyes may be closed. There may be a heavy layer of clouds. I may be looking in the wrong direction. It may be nighttime. *Mutatis mutandis* . . .

This is one of my difficulties in trying to relate to the "God is dead" theology. Its adherents seem to me finally to be saying, "We are no longer aware of the reality of God, nor are most of our fellowmen. Therefore, God is dead." That these are accurate autobiographical statements I do not doubt. That they describe the temper of modern man is beyond dispute. But that they say very much about the reality or unreality of God seems to me more dubious. Autobiographical statements and descriptions of modern unbelief are not necessarily *theological* statements. And here lies my other difficulty with the "God is dead" approach. For the assertion that God is dead

has been with us for a long time in Western history. The new
factor is simply that many who make the statement now make
it from within the Christian conviction about the meaning of
life and death and God and man.

Is it so very perverse and old-fashioned to identify these
statements as bits of information about the state of mind of
the speakers but not bits of information about the object of
the speaker's speech? The temptation in this "new" theological
approach seems to me the temptation that faces every theological generation. It was put with clarity by Msgr. Ronald Knox,
when he said of the book *Foundations* that it seemed to be
framed as an answer to the question: How much can Jones be
persuaded to swallow? How little, in other words, can one believe, and still be a Christian? Which is a bit like asking, How
little is it permissible to love one's wife?

That the gospel should be a scandal and a stumbling block
is nothing new. We had better not glory—or rather, wallow—
in the scandal as though that exempted us from the task of
communication, but we had also better not take for granted
that the task of communication is simply to remove the scandal, to settle for whatever Jones will, in fact, swallow. When I
try to explain some area of Christian faith to one of the *pagani*
and he finally responds with, "Oh well, if *that's* all it means, of
course I can accept that," I am left with the uneasy feeling
that I have been an unfaithful transmitter. Christian faith is
not just sanctified despair nor ethics tinged with concern. Nor,
when we shout *"man!"* in italics with an exclamation point or
two, have we necessarily whispered "God."

As I continue to make up my mind, then, I feel a particular
responsibility not to transform the faith into something no
longer discernible from a noble humanism. If it is indeed no
more than that, let us have the courage to say so directly, and
stop clothing it with trappings from the past. If it is, however,
more than that, then the price for saying so must be paid, even
if this means losing some of the precious identification we

have so amply succeeded in establishing with our contemporaries, and appearing the fool. But as Reinhold Niebuhr, my dearest theological mentor, once remarked, there is a considerable difference between being a fool for Christ and being a damn fool.

THROUGH THE VALLEY—AND BEYOND

But I must not end with too cavalier a dismissal. If doubt is truly real for our generation—and it is—we must not side too easily away from its disturbing implications, or dispose of it by what may look like a trick. For there is a real sense in which I, as modern man *and* theologian, must not shrink from bearing myself the weight of unbelief I see about me. I too must know what it is like to enter into the valley of the shadow of death, if I am to know, let alone communicate, the resurrection that lies beyond the shadow of death. If our theological generation is to speak to godless modern man, it will indeed be in part because we too are godless modern men, or have at one time been so. Our hosannas, like Dostoevsky's, will have been forged out of the crucible of doubt. Our affirmations will have been wrested out of the reality of our negations, and only as the negations have been threateningly real will the affirmations we make beyond them bear the stamp of authenticity. Only if we have borne the weight of unbelief can we also bear the weight of glory.

I continue to believe that only the one who can affirm as well as deny has claim on the title "theologian." To have walked through the valley of the shadow of death is one thing, and no man can evade that route. Indeed, he will traverse it frequently in a single lifetime. But to have walked through the valley of the shadow of death *fearing no evil,* is another and more important thing. We can do so, finally, only as we realize that we do not walk alone and are therefore able to affirm, "I will fear no evil, for thou art with me." The strength to do this and to affirm this is not finally ours. For the rod and the staff belong to another, and the table at which we receive our sustenance has not been set by us.

To affirm these latter things in the Age of Unbelief is not easy. But, then, it never was.

A Decade of Discoveries and Dangers: How My Mind Has Changed, 1960-1970

Once upon a time there was a theologian who, after his mind had changed a number of times, said on the eve of his fiftieth birthday, "Go to, now, my mind has changed long enough. Henceforth my mind shall change no more." Thereafter what he wrote and spoke only confirmed and underlined what he had previously written and spoken. At age eighty he departed this life in wondrous fashion, suddenly disintegrating into dust. A physician, after microscopic examination of the remains, reported, "This was to be expected. The man had already been dead for thirty years."

An accounting of past change must not imply the attainment of a vantage point that precludes future change, and all that is contained below must be embraced by the more precise rubric, "How My Mind Keeps Changing." On the one hand, "Jesus Christ *is* the same yesterday, today, and forever" (italics added), but on the other hand "we always have this treasure in frail, earthen vessels ("always" added). I see theology as a venture doomed to perpetual but creative frustration, since the test of theology's integrity must be its stubborn unwillingness to confuse its own utterances with the one about whom it

A contribution to the series "How My Mind Has Changed," in *The Christian Century,* Jan. 14, 1970, and reprinted in Geyer and Peerman (eds.), *Theological Crossings* (Wm. B. Eerdmans Publishing Company, 1971). Copyright 1970 by The Christian Century Foundation. Reprinted by permission.

is speaking. Here I neither seek nor expect a continuing city. (My most important theological contribution is surely *The Collect'd Writings of St. Hereticus*, an attempt to lampoon the whole venture from within—a book long since remaindered as if in gentle vindication of the fact that attempts to show the transitory nature of theology are themselves transitory.)

I write this essay in France where, in addition to teaching, I am trying to get some perspective on both the past decade and the next. And I can most easily conceptualize the shifts in my thinking by recalling what I was doing exactly ten years ago on a sabbatical leave in Scotland, although this involves the pretentious gesture of referring to my own books—a type of self-advertisement I feel one generally resorts to only in moments of extreme self-doubt, when in need of the psychic shoring up others have denied one. But the books can provide useful shorthand devices for describing the changes. The sabbatical in St. Andrews was devoted to three tasks: (1) writing a book on ecumenism with Fr. Gustave Weigel, S.J., entitled *An American Dialogue*, (2) finishing a book on *The Spirit of Protestantism*, and (3) reading all the then extant volumes of Barth's *Church Dogmatics*. These exercises illustrate two of the three areas with which I was largely involved in the subsequent decade—e.g., ecumenism and theological methodology. (A third area, theology and politics, will be touched on later, and was symbolized during the sabbatical by an unexpected trip to East Berlin.) In each of these areas "my mind has changed," and the end is not yet.

METHODOLOGICAL CHANGES—THE DISCOVERY OF A TWO-WAY STREET

My decision to expose myself in detail to Karl Barth represented a certain decision at that time about theological methodology. While I had not become a "Barthian," I was powerfully attracted by Barth's rediscovery of a gospel that was really "gospel"—i.e., the good news that "God is for us" and has demonstrated this affirmation by coming to us in Jesus Christ. I learned from Barth how easy it is for us to cut God down to our size, to fit him into our systems, to take the cost and sting out of believing in him, and that therefore God supplies his own criteria for the appropriation of his reality, rather than fitting into ours. We start with his self-definition in the incarnation, and everything else follows from that.

Barth I found wonderful in clarifying the faith of the believing community. But the fact that two years later I moved from a theological seminary to a secular university meant that I had to do more than give an accounting of the faith of the believing community; I had to operate largely outside its walls, dealing with religion's cultured despisers. Basically I learned that while I might have something to say to them, they also had important things to say to me. Ten years ago I had pretty well worked out my own understanding of the gospel, and I saw my task as one of finding ways to communicate that gospel to those around me. Now I see much more clearly that the traffic between the gospel and the world travels on a two-way street. The gospel helps to inform and define the world, but *the world helps to inform and define the gospel.* I need more than the resources of Bible, theological tradition, and my own commitments if I am to understand my faith and the world in which it is set; I also need the ethical insights of my secular colleagues, the political and psychological analyses of my friends and foes, and the prophetic jab of nonchurchmen whose degree of commitment so often puts my own to shame.

In other words, I have come to believe very much in "the pseudonyms of God," the strange names he uses in the world to accomplish his purposes when his self-proclaimed servants let him down—an insight, incidentally, that I got not from a theologian but from a novelist, Ignazio Silone. To some, this will seem like a return to the natural theology or general revelation that so upset Barth. I prefer to understand it as a recognition that God is at work in an infinitely wider arena of

activities than I had earlier believed—which might not be a
bad way to start defining a doctrine of grace. To others it may
seem as though this shift is the beginning of the gradual but
inevitable erosion of a once-firm faith. I don't think so, and
one reason I don't is that I was not in the least attracted by
the "death of God" movement and its assertion that the hall-
mark of the modern theologian is his denial of the *theos* that
had heretofore been the whole point of his discipline. I remain
unconvinced that *my* difficulty in believing in God says very
much about God. It may say a great deal about me, but I cannot seriously entertain the notion that the reality of any God
worthy of the name depends on how vividly I am able to conceive of him at a given moment. Charles Williams, in *Descent
Into Hell*, puts my question: "Shall our tremors measure the
Omnipotence?" The question is rhetorical, and Williams' implied answer is also mine: "Of course not."

None of this means that we can build from man to God, or
destroy the infinitely qualitative distinction between the two,
so dear to Koheleth, Kierkegaard, and Karl of Basel. But it
does mean that it is out of the stuff of human life and experience that we get the pointers and hints to suggest, however
faintly, something of the reality of the divine. It means that if
I ever write a systematic theology, I will start with man and
not God. The order of knowing, as the medievalists had discovered, need not be the same as the order of being.

In my teaching, as a result of all this, I am less and less
comfortable beginning with traditional theological vocabulary.
Words such as salvation, repentance, revelation, eternal life,
are so devoid of power for contemporary man that I continually seek for analogies out of human experience that may
hint, however imperfectly and haltingly, at what those words
are trying to describe—namely, realities that are far from
being devoid of power. Example: Students today know a great
deal about the immensely healing and binding quality of a
common meal, particularly when shared under duress (ongoing hunger, a sit-in, jail), and this provides a starting point for

talking about the Eucharist. Example: A girl who has been
wronged by a boy, has suffered, has been able to absorb the
suffering creatively and heal the alienation by her outgoing
love, is not far from being able to appropriate something of
the mystery of the atonement. Example: Last spring, teaching
theology during a campus sit-in, I discovered that the experiences students were having were replete with analogies relevant to our scheduled discussion of revelation. They understood that a particular moment in time could become
revelatory for the meaning of their past as preparation for the
event, and could also inform what they would do with their
future as a result of the event—a *kairos*-moment if there ever
was one, analogous, however faintly, to what Exodus-Sinai
means to Judaism, and Golgotha-Garden to Christianity. They
also understood some of the perils of attaching themselves to
an event that might turn out to be a pseudo-*kairos*, and the
disillusionment that could follow.

"We must hear the voice of God in the voice of the times,"
said the fathers at Vatican II. *Nihil obstat.*

ECUMENICAL CHANGES—THE DISCOVERY
OF SHARED COMMITMENTS

Nihil obstat, indeed. My theological antennae are increasingly sensitive to the whole range of Roman Catholic experience, and a happy by-product of my involvement in the 1952
campaign of a young Roman Catholic congressman from Min-
nesota named Eugene McCarthy was that it initiated contacts
with Roman Catholics during a time when the ecumenical climate was frigid if not destructive. These concerns led to the
publication of the above-mentioned book with Father Weigel,
in which each of us examined the faith of the other. Now, a
scant ten years later, the book has no more than historical interest, so rapidly has the climate changed. (Indeed, when I
decided to "update" my half of it in 1967 I had to give up and
write a new book, *The Ecumenical Revolution*; and when it in

turn had to be updated two years later for a paperback edition, so much had happened even in that short interval that
the fundamental thesis of the book had to be shifted.)

During the first half of 1960-1970 I gave my major time to
the Protestant-Catholic dialogue, making friends across formerly impenetrable barriers, and discovering that to do so was
to be accused by some in my own backyard of being "soft on
Catholicism." I have no regrets. Those years enabled me to
learn that we share infinitely more than divides us, and that
the primary attention must be devoted to shoring up bridges
of understanding, so that from those vantage points we may
build new bridges across the misunderstandings. This conviction was reinforced during my presence at the Second Vatican
Council, reported on informally in *Observer in Rome*. The
friendships made there, both in coffee bars in the mornings at
St. Peter's and in other bars in other parts of Rome in the
evenings, transformed me, to my great surprise, from official
"observer" to unofficial "participant." I became convinced that
all Christians had a tremendous stake in the council, and that
a disaster for Roman Catholicism, rather than something over
which Protestants could derive ex post facto satisfaction,
would be a disaster for all of us. I became a diligent lobbyist.

And this, I think, measures my ecumenical shift of mind
during the rest of the decade. *An American Dialogue* had represented an "outsider" looking at Catholicism, sometimes ap-
provingly, sometimes disapprovingly, but always in terms of
"we" vs. "they." But through increasing ecumenical experiences I came to feel a wonderful kinship with priests
and nuns, a realization that underneath all differences we
were embarked on a common venture. I remember the precise
moment this awareness surfaced in my consciousness. I had
lectured to a Catholic audience in Kansas City, and after the
lecture a group of priests and I talked informally until about
two A.M. As I went to bed it suddenly came over me that we
had not once talked about "Catholic-Protestant differences,"
the staple of dialogue in those years. We had been talking

simply *as fellow Christians* about the problem of communicating our commonly held faith to an unbelieving world. Since then I have ceased to engage in ecumenical head-counting. I feel closer to many Jesuits and Benedictines than to many Protestant ministers. I do not say that to exalt the former and demean the latter, but to describe the increasing irrelevance of such distinctions.

I think that in 1960 there was need for a book on *The Spirit of Protestantism.* If there is such a need in 1970, I must now define it differently. For I no longer see Protestantism as something opposed to Catholicism; I see Protestantism as a stance necessary within the whole church catholic, a stance I find wonderfully portrayed in many Roman Catholic friends and lacking in some Protestant friends. I think I could now comfortably write a book on the spirit of Protestantism called *The Spirit of Catholicism,* and still be faithful to the spirit of that grand old Augustinian monk, Blessed Martin of Wittenberg.

I am disturbed that the revolution going on within Roman Catholicism has ground down many friends, both priests and sisters, many of whom have had to leave the church in order to preserve their integrity. It is a desperate situation when integrity has to be sought outside rather than inside what we call the church. But the ferment, one hopes, may force us to redefine what we call "the church." I can no longer define it institutionally, for I experience it too often with priests and nuns (within or without "church," or wavering) where some of our past differences are overcome and some of our future hopes realized—around a dining room table whereon are bread and wine, and whereat the presence first known in the upper room is once again a real presence.

The ecumenical dialogue has moved me in yet another direction. Through my reading of Martin Buber and my friendship with Abraham Heschel, I have come to an appreciation of Judaism that I did not begin to approach a decade ago. This awareness has been further enhanced by relationships with large numbers of Jewish students in my classes, even classes on Christian theology. I am amazed at how much of Christian faith can be expressed in Jewish terms, and I am wounded daily by the kinds of barriers to understanding and real sharing that have been (almost ineradicably) impressed upon Jewish and Christian psyches by two thousand years of Christian intolerance. And if for me "the hallowing of the every day" is now best focused in a christological framework, I will not try to deny that Hasidism gave me the impetus to begin exploring the question.

POLITICAL CHANGES—THE DISCOVERY OF NEW COMPLEXITIES

Originally I learned about the relation of theology and ethics from Reinhold Niebuhr, and the lesson has been reconfirmed by a recent interest in Teilhard de Chardin: "By virtue of the Creation, and still more of the Incarnation, nothing here below is profane for those who know how to see" (*The Divine Milieu*, p. 35).

The thesis of the revised edition of *The Ecumenical Revolution* is that the "revolution" is the shift from internal ecclesiastical concerns (intercommunion, apostolic succession, etc.) to extramural worldly concerns (economic development, war, racism, etc.). In the latter areas there is simply nothing that divides me from most of my Catholic friends nor—in the further extension of the dialogue referred to above—from most of my Jewish friends. We make common cause together. (Abraham Heschel, Michael Novak, and I tried to symbolize this fact by jointly writing a book, *Vietnam: Crisis of Conscience*, which was jointly published by Protestant, Catholic, and Jewish publishing houses.) I have already indicated my indebtedness in this area to my secular friends.

A kaleidoscope of memories whirls when I recall the past decade in relation to the body politic—the fearful yet liberating "Freedom Ride" through the South in early summer, 1961, leading to two stretches in a Florida jail, a three-year legal hassle in the courts, and a permanent criminal record; the initial encouragement of the March on Washington and the later shifts made necessary by the rise of Black Power; the fears and hopes of being at Selma and other towns in the Deep South; the struggles against the real estate interests in the "Proposition 14" battle over fair housing in California; the ongoing strike of the farm workers at Delano and my increasing realization that in César Chavez we have been given the closest thing to a modern saint we are likely to see; the increasingly difficult experience of being in the midst of student controversy at a time when one is clearly "over thirty"; and, of course, Vietnam.

I tried to avoid Vietnam, but since the military escalation in early 1965 and my conviction that Johnson and Humphrey had betrayed the nation, it has become the dominant reality of my life. Vietnam has forced me slowly along a path that might be called "reluctant radicalization," though the term is relative since in the eyes of "radicals" I am no more than a (adjective deleted) "liberal." True, in 1961 I had engaged in selective law-breaking, defying a local Florida ordinance on segregation on the ground of its unconstitutionality, but I saw this as a very exceptional activity, to be indulged in only when all other strategies were clearly proved bankrupt. Consequently, when Vietnam became a burning issue, I kept trying, along with other liberals, to apply the working-through-the-law-to-bring-about-change tactic.

We had no effect whatever on national policy, which steadily deteriorated, and I found myself pushed inch by inch, and then yard by yard, along the road to civil disobedience, simply by the patent ineffectiveness of other alternatives. I crossed the line in the summer of 1967, and since then have engaged in illegally "counseling, aiding and abetting" those who feel they cannot serve in the army or cooperate with Selective Service, both in private and in many public events involving the receiving of draft cards for transmission to General Hershey in Washington. The mood of the country being what it was up to a few months ago, I expected to be indicted, tried, and convicted. I had done the jail bit earlier and it had no romantic or martyr-complex allure, but along with many others I was prepared if necessary to go to jail, both to indicate my unwillingness to obey an immoral law and to show my solidarity with draft resisters. That likelihood seems now to have diminished to the vanishing point, but the entire experience has left me with an as yet unresolved dilemma.

The dilemma is this: If the "system" remains as resistant to change in other areas as it has proved to be on Vietnam, if genteel protest fails to produce change, and if one believes (as I think one must) that Vietnam is a symptom of a much deeper malaise in our American way of life, is one not called upon to escalate the number and intensity of his political acts, including civil disobedience—to move, in other words, from the liberal toward the radical camp, recognizing that what is at fault is not just little inadequacies in the system that can be eliminated by tinkering, but the system itself?

The dilemma is compounded by the new dimension of violence in social protest. I have been in what radicals call, scornfully, "the Martin Luther King bag," and I expect to remain there, for I have seen too many students slide down the slippery slope from nonviolence to violence-against-property-but-not-against-people, to violence-against-whatever-is-necessary-to-produce-the-desired-end; and they illustrate, quite tragically, Silone's thesis that the persecuted end up becoming the persecutors. However, on the other hand, as I have met Christians from the Third World (particularly at the Uppsala assembly), or as I talk to American blacks, I am forced to acknowledge that in *some* situations nonviolence seems a luxury the destitute cannot afford. How can minimal justice come to some Latin American countries without violent overthrow of a dictatorship? How indeed? But I am not yet ready to extrapolate from that situation and argue that the situation in the United States is so similar as to call for a similar tactic here. If I were a black, however, I might legitimately feel that the two situations are indeed commensurate, and that covert violence here is just as destructive of human potential as overt violence elsewhere. Perhaps there must be different answers and different strategies for different groups. Martin Luther King told blacks in the '60s to respond nonviolently to angry whites. Perhaps his message in the '70s is to tell whites to respond nonviolently to angry blacks.

This, then, is the area of my greatest theological difficulty. I can no longer rest with the easier, simpler view I had in 1960, that an occasional extraordinary pressure will move our Government in the right direction. Lyndon Johnson contributed mightily to curing me of that beautiful but illusory hope, and Richard Nixon has completed the process.

THE DANGERS IN THE CHANGES

And now to turn to the dangers in the changes. I sometimes wonder if my *methodological changes* have transformed my theology into a kind of will-o'-the-wisp, tossed to and fro by every wind of doctrine. Where are the long-range goals, the lifetime projects, slowly being completed? I have given up any hope, or even desire, to live that kind of theological life. I do not think it is given to many in my generation to have the luxury of long-range theological planning, and a recent event in my own experience has confirmed this thought. In the winter and spring of 1967 I received a grant that allowed me to fulfill the long-cherished dream of trying to relate a Christian doctrine of man to the revolution in cybernetics and biology. I had kept my calendar completely free for those six months of research. But when the time came, our nation was in the throes of the Vietnam war. The pressures for Vietnam protest were so strong, and the need for people with mobility was so great, that I felt I had no choice but to devote the six months to speaking, writing, and otherwise helping to mobilize protest against the war.

I cite the example not to try to score points, either pro or con, but to illustrate that for me the theological task is now defined by readiness to respond to needs that arise in areas we have not anticipated. The pressure of future world events will define the directions of my theological endeavor quite as much as, and probably more than, any built-in set of professional expectations I bring to the next decade. I cannot conceive of doing theology in a vacuum, and doing it in the context of contemporary history means responding to the unexpected rather than seeking detachment. This means, inevitably, a measure of theological dilettantism. I think I have made my peace with this. Some men must do the long-range reflective thinking that will mold the theological future. Others will be something like theological journalists, trying to bring theological analysis to bear on contemporary events, and vice versa. A few (perhaps only those named Martin Marty) can do both. But it seems clear to me, in a way it didn't ten years ago, that I have chosen the second path, or that it has been chosen for me. So be it.

The danger in my *ecumenical changes* is the blurring of distinctions that are still real. I agree. But I also find that the distinctions really *do* begin to blur. Who would seriously entertain the notion any more that Protestantism and Roman Catholicism are divided over justification by faith vs. justification by works, or over the theme of *ecclesia semper reformanda?* Who would seriously charge any more that Judaism lacks a concept of grace or that Christianity is automatically purged of legalism? I shall not surrender my convictions, but I shall insist that they may be found in different lexicons of experience, in many more areas than I used to believe possible, and that insights not granted to me through my own tradition may become available to me through others.

The danger in my *political changes* is, of course, always the danger of reducing the faith to a humanistic ethic. But I don't think that will be my temptation. My temptation, which besets ethicists as well, will be to forget the dimensions of life not covered by ethics. Camus has written: "There is beauty and there are the humiliated. Whatever difficulties the enterprise may present, I would like never to be unfaithful either to the one or the other" (*Lyrical and Critical Essays,* pp. 169-170). Yes, there is beauty, there is mystery, there is love, and no political sophistication can create them or maintain them in the hearts of men. There is the recognition that "whether we live or whether we die we are the Lord's"—a conviction I really believe and one that has carried me through a number of tense moments in the past decade. There is the community that is the church, and I really believe in that too. Having had my own share of disillusionment with the church, I find myself believing in it more than ever now; and with whatever radical restructuring is in store, and with whatever accompanying pain, I am sure that the gates of hell will not prevail against it, even if it sometimes looks as though the indifference of man or the obtuseness of the curia will.

In other words, I feel as though my own attempts to justify Christian involvement in the secular movements of the time are getting nailed down, and that from that base we must explore again the whole dimension of the gospel that centers on mystery, grace, transcendence, and "a rumor of angels," for I need continual warning that the minute we Christians begin to sound just like everybody else, we've lost the ball game.

The "death of God" theologians said that faith and hope were gone, and all that was left was a theology of love. Then the Germans told us that the big task was to recover a theology of hope. Maybe tomorrow's job will be to recover a theology of faith, and indeed the more I think about it, the more it seems to me that this line of investigation . . .

But that will have to be another book.

Ecumenism and the Secular Order

Ecumenism is moving in a new direction in our day, the direction of increasing involvement in the secular order. Unless it continues to do this, it will become increasingly precious and ingrown; if it does continue to do this, it can become increasingly creative and forward-looking.

Until recently, discussions of ecumenism have concentrated on the problem of unity, a noble theme in the light of the tragic disunity that has so blunted the witness of the church as a healing and redemptive force in the lives of men. Quite rightly, the conciliar decree *De Oecumenismo* highlights this concern:

> The "ecumenical movement" means those activities and enterprises which, according to various needs of the Church and opportune occasions, are started and organized for the fostering of unity among Christians.[1]

Concern for unity has also been a major thrust in Protestant and Orthodox ecumenical activity, particularly through the stream called "Faith and Order," one of the tributaries leading to the formation of the World Council of Churches. Here also the goal was the restoration of the unity of the body of Christ

Originally given as the Robert Cardinal Bellarmine Lecture at St. Louis University in Oct., 1967, subsequently printed in *Theology Digest*, Winter, 1967, and in J. O'Connor (ed.), *American Catholic Exodus* (Corpus Publications, 1968). Used by permission.

throughout the whole of the *oikoumene,* or "inhabited world."

But there is another meaning attached to the various words derived from *oikoumene,* so that when we speak of "ecumenism" today we ought also to be speaking of mission, of the task of the church to reach out to the entire *oikoumene.* It is not unimportant that the original impetus toward the unity of divided Christians, symbolized by the Edinburgh Missionary Conference of 1910, received its propelling force from the mission field, and from the missionary societies even more than from the denominations. This second meaning of ecumenism, the task of mission to the world, is one on which increasing attention should be focused. Very early in its history, the World Council of Churches discovered that concern for unity seemed to be absorbing much of the attention that likewise needed to be directed toward concern for mission. The minutes of the Central Committee in 1951 point to the need for retaining an emphasis on both concerns:

> We would especially draw attention to the recent confusion in the use of the word "ecumenical." It is important to insist that this word, which comes from the Greek word for the whole inhabited earth, is properly used to describe everything that relates to the whole task of the whole Church to bring the Gospel to the whole world. *It therefore covers equally the missionary movement and the movement toward unity,* and must not be used to describe the latter in contradistinction to the former . . . Every attempt to separate these two tasks violates the wholeness of Christ's ministry to the world.[2]

I believe we can presuppose widespread concern about ecumenism as unity, and need to highlight concern about *ecumenism as mission.* To those who are wary even of a temporary disjunction, I would point out that not only do these two understandings of ecumenism need each other if we are to do full justice to ecumenical concern, but that either one, carried through in any kind of significant way, sooner or later embraces the other.

This point is important enough to illustrate by an interesting example out of ecumenical history. After the 1910 Edinburgh Missionary Conference, two subsequent conferences were held on the theme of "Life and Work," i.e., the ways in which Christians could register the impact of the gospel in their daily activities both individual and corporate. These conferences (at Stockholm in 1925 and Oxford in 1937) pursued themes dealing with the economic order, political responsibility of the churches, education, the state, and so on. At the beginning of Life and Work, doctrinal concerns were rigorously eschewed, for, as the slogan went, "Doctrine divides, service unites." But it soon became apparent that the slogan was a half truth at best, and that theological considerations inevitably intruded; to raise a question about the nature of the church's responsibility in the political order, for example, was to raise the previous question about the nature of the church itself, and to be led into the theological arena of questions about unity, ministry, and sacraments.

During the same period, and also growing out of the Edinburgh Missionary Conference, two further conferences were held, focusing precisely on the theological issues of the church, unity, ministry, and sacraments. These conferences on "Faith and Order" (at Lausanne in 1925 and Edinburgh in 1937) dealt with ecumenism in terms of the search for unity. But those in Faith and Order made the obverse discovery of those in Life and Work; they discovered that they could not do their theological task properly if they were not also concerned about the outreach and mission of the church. To raise a question about the nature of the church itself was also, from their perspective, to raise a question about the nature of the church's responsibility in the political order. Thus Life and Work (concerned with mission) discovered that it needed Faith and Order (concerned with unity), while Faith and Order (concerned with unity) discovered that it needed Life and Work (concerned with mission). Each presupposed the other; neither could adequately define itself without the other. And it was the marriage of these two partners, each unfulfilled without the other, that produced the World Council of Churches.

Subsequent assemblies of the World Council of Churches have therefore addressed themselves to the themes of both unity and mission. Amsterdam (1948) dealt not only with "The Universal Church in God's Design" but also with "The Church and International Disorder"; Evanston (1954) dealt not only with "Our Oneness in Christ and Our Disunity as Churches" but also with "The Responsible Society in a World Perspective" and "The Church Amid Racial and Ethnic Tensions"; New Delhi (1961) dealt not only with "Unity" but also with "Service," and Uppsala (1968), in addition to dealing with themes related to unity, also discussed the mission of the church to the world, the church in economic and social change, international affairs, worship in a secular age, and the nature of a Christian "style of life."

It is my own belief that this theme of concern for the secular order is the direction in which the next ecumenical steps are going to be most creatively taken, and that the watershed in this development was the Geneva Conference of 1966 on the theme, "Christians in the Social and Technical Revolutions of Our Time," which concentrated its attention almost exclusively in this direction, dealing with "Economic Development in a World Perspective," "The Nature and Function of the State in a Revolutionary Age," "Structures of International Cooperation—Living Together in Peace in a Pluralistic World Society," and "Man and Community in Changing Societies."

It is important to notice another aspect of the ecumenical development here. At the Geneva conference, Roman Catholic theologians were not only present, but participated actively in the discussions, and two of the major papers were given by Roman Catholics, Canon Charles Moeller and Lady Jackson (Barbara Ward). It is also important to realize that at Uppsala fifteen Catholic observers were present, not merely to observe, but to have the privilege of the floor, if not yet the privilege of the ballot.

Let us briefly examine what has been happening from the Roman Catholic side in this area of ecumenism. One need only recall the earlier "social encyclicals" from Leo XIII on, to realize that concern for the secular order has been a part of Catholic teaching to Catholics for many decades. *Rerum Novarum* and *Quadragesimo Anno* are landmarks on this road, as is the more recent *Mater et Magistra*, which consciously attempts to stand in their succession. But with the ecumenically-minded Pope John, something new emerged. *Pacem in Terris,* while still a papal encyclical, was addressed not only to Catholics but also to "all men of good will," indicating that a decision had been made to deal ecumenically with the most pressing problem of the saeculum, world peace.[3]

This tradition was continued at Vatican II. The pastoral constitution on *The Church and the World Today,* dealing specifically with issues such as marriage, economics, politics, war, and world peace, was one of the two Council documents likewise addressed not only to Roman Catholics and other Christians but to the whole of humanity. In like fashion, the encyclical of Pope Paul, *Populorum Progressio,* dealing once again with matters of concern to all men, particularly in the economic order, was addressed not only to Catholics but likewise to all men of good will.

What this brief history suggests is that from both sides, our concerns about the *world* have led us closer to *one another,* and we have discovered in the process that we cannot properly concern ourselves about the secular order save ecumenically, save in close concert, working together. When talking about such issues, pope and council no longer address a Catholic constituency exclusively; they address all their fellow Christians and, indeed, all men. Similarly, Protestants and Orthodox in the World Council of Churches do not only consult among themselves when dealing with such issues; they reach out to an ever-deepening Roman Catholic involvement in their own concerns. Ecumenism as concern for the world has gained a substantial foothold.

To concentrate on ecumenism as outreach to, concern for, and involvement in, the secular order is not to eschew the importance of ecumenism as a quest for unity. I believe, indeed, that it may be only through the concern for ecumenism as mission that we will break some of the theological binds that constrict us in our present concern for ecumenism as unity, and that a pursuit today of what were, in an earlier day, the concerns of "Life and Work," will help us see more incisively the ongoing concerns of "Faith and Order."

1. THE DIASPORA SITUATION—AND SOME CONSEQUENCES

Fr. Avery Dulles, S.J., sets the context for where we must go from here:

> Ecumenism has become too exclusively taken up with religious questions—with matters of doctrine and worship. . . . From many quarters therefore one hears the call for a new ecumenism—one less committed to historical theological controversies and more in touch with contemporary secular man; one less turned in upon itself, more open to the world and its concerns. The greatest decisions affecting man's future are being made in the sphere of the secular, and Christianity does not seem to be there.[4]

This is both a description and an indictment, and I have an increasing feeling that unless we are truly found in the saeculum, the things we do elsewhere are going to amount to no more than trivial irrelevancies. I therefore accept *both* the description and the indictment. We have not sufficiently concerned ourselves with this arena of the secular in the past, and we must do so in the future. We no longer confront a "Catholic" problem or a "Protestant" problem, we confront a "human" problem. Men are in desperate need. Time is running out. How shall we respond?

The most seductive response, and the most fatal, is the one to which we almost instinctively turn: Let us shore up the crumbling walls of the church, regroup our scattered forces, and assault the enemy as we have done in the past; let us, in other words, recapture our lost territory, let us restore Christendom.

Now I shall not take long to respond to this (as I regard it) highly mistaken plea. There can be no simple return to the past; we cannot restore Christendom, whether of the thirteenth-century variety or the sixteenth-century varieties. The church is not going to dominate our society, and even if it could, to attempt to do so would be to misconceive its role. After centuries of both Catholic and Protestant triumphalism, we have begun to see that the proper stance for the church is not as lord but as servant, since its own Lord was a servant. It would be hard to overstress the importance of the fact that the servant imagery was prominent in Vatican II, even if a lot of the old triumphalist language still lingers on. The church's task is not to assume power from the state, but to offer itself so that the state can use its own power more responsibly. In our time the church will represent at best a tiny minority that might, by the grace of God, become what Toynbee describes as a "creative minority."

The Biblical image for this stance is an image that Karl Rahner, Stephen Neill, Thomas Merton, Richard Schall, Hans Reudi-Weber, and others have recently been expounding—the image of diaspora. The church is scattered, dispersed, to the ends of the earth. It no longer has terrestrial power, nor should it seek it once again. It is that band of people, here and there, united along the conduits of power mysteriously supplied by the Holy Spirit, who, wherever they are, offer themselves and the resources of their institution in the service of all men, and not just in the service of those who happen to belong to the institution. Richard Schall describes the situation:

Christendom is rapidly dissolving around us. . . . Without our going into exile, the non-Christian world has engulfed us as modern means of communication create one world in which we are a small minority, and as the population explosion indicates that each year the percentage of Christians decreases. We are thus in a situation similar to that of the Jews of the diaspora, scattered among people whose culture, mores and thought patterns are not like ours nor will they become so; our cathedrals and temples are no longer in the center of life nor do they bring the whole community together under God. If we hope to reach modern man, it will not be so much in terms of gathering him into the church as of going to him in the midst of our dispersion.[5]

In such a situation Karl Rahner reminds us not to yearn wistfully for an earlier era but to accept the present era joyfully. The diaspora situation is no cause for despair. It is the situation in which God has placed us today, and we must live the diaspora-life affirmatively, rather than seeking to restore the Christendom-life frantically. The church need not, as Thomas Merton and Hans Küng have pointed out, speak in the language of victory communiqués.

I am not sure how much we have really understood what a radically new set of outlooks and postures would be required if we took this description seriously. And I am not sure how many of us, if we did come to such a realization, would be willing to cope with it. For such a discovery would be very threatening and very risky, even at the level of our accustomed ways of doing things and our ordinary day-to-day structures.

The geographically isolated seminary, for example, is a structure reflecting the old Christendom mentality. Earlier prescription: Isolate your shock troops for sufficient years to insulate them thoroughly against contamination from the world, and then set them loose to regain all that lost territory for the Queen of Heaven. The new prescription would read:

Educate your shock troops right along with the enlisted men
(for which read "in the context of an urban university") so
that they are completely at home in secular culture and can
share in its best while offering a fresh alternative to replace its
worst.

Seminary education, however, is hardly the key to secular
man's redemption. We are going to find that many of the other
things we have taken most for granted, most associated with
the "fullness" of the faith, are going to have to be put up for
grabs. The religious orders furnish a further example. Is it
right, in the diaspora situation, that whole communities should
live together in isolation, even on a university campus? Should
not members of such communities be dispersed through the
dormitories, through the surrounding area, in the apartments
and the slums, sharing fully in what it means to be a modern
man, rather than being protected from the political, social,
and economic problems that beset ordinary mortals?

The plight of many Protestant ministers extends the problem. Selective Service exempts from military duty the physi-
cally unfit, the mentally incompetent, and the clergy. Why
should ministers have exemption? Why should they not be full
men, either fighting if they so choose, or declaring their conscientious objection if they so choose, like other men? Why, to
press another point, should they be professional holy men, exempted from the task their parishioners face of earning a living day by day? Why not, after the manner of Paul, earn their
living at a "secular job," and thereby be freed from being be-
holden to those who ante up the salary check? If the criterion
is *diakonia*, service, involvement in the affairs of men in
today's world, is the structure of a "kept clergy" really defensible any more?

What about the very physical structures in which we worship? Are they not also a reflection of the Christendom mentality. The medieval cathedral *dominated* the town. The New
England meetinghouse *dominated* the village green. We like

our church spires to be higher than surrounding structures—though the fate of St. Patrick's Cathedral, dwarfed for decades by Radio City, symbolizes the fate of such ecclesiastical *hubris*. The rank and file still insist that a church must "look like a church," by which they mean, I discover, what John Betjeman calls the "ghastly good taste" of nineteenth-century Christians who decided that pseudo Gothic was ordained by God at the moment of creation in an irreformable ex cathedra decree. Does not all this still create the impression that God is somewhere else than where people normally are, and that if we want to find him we must go apart to find him, withdrawing from the saeculum into the holy?

I am always baffled by the high degree of initial Catholic resistance to having the Mass elsewhere than in a church, since on historical grounds alone the precedent of having Mass on the second floor of somebody's house would seem most Scripturally fitting. I suggest that if we take the diaspora situation seriously, we are going to be far less concerned about church buildings in the future (save for concern that we probably have too many of them), and will find that in our scattered existence, wherever we happen to find ourselves may be the ideal spot in which to worship the Lord of all creation, since it will be precisely in the midst of his creation. Jesus did not choose a very religious spot on which to be crucified—in fact, it was chosen for him by the secular authorities and it turned out to be the city dump heap. Perhaps today a sanitation project would be a more appropriate place to celebrate Good Friday than before a high altar.

But we must not linger overmuch with such matters, which are merely illustrations of the fact that if we take seriously our new situation in the saeculum, as the scattered and dispersed people of God, many things are going to be up for grabs, and everything will have to be rethought in the light of our new situation. The posture in that new situation must be one of *diakonia,* and it must not be *self*-regarding, i.e., for the sake of the church, but *other*-regarding, i.e., for the sake of the neighbor in need, whether in the church or not.

2. Involvement in Power Structures

Now such a possibility, unfortunately, can become hopelessly romantic and unrealistic. If we really want to minister to the neighbor in need, it will not be enough to do so merely on a personal, individualistic scale, important or rewarding as such an action may be to all concerned. Nine Jesuits, let us say, moving to the slums of St. Louis and living among the people, sharing their hardships, being there as humane individuals, can engage in genuine ministries of healing and compassion, but they are still likely to remain "Band-Aid ministries," i.e., effective only in repairing damage that has already been done. But nine Jesuits, in concert with some ministers and rabbis and informed lay people, moving in on city hall to demand new rent control commissions, or helping people organize to fight corrupt landlords, or setting up precinct caucus groups to force politicians to do something about ambulance service or price gouging—such groups could begin to have an impact on the whole structure of the city, and on the basic structure of human lives. Apart from such action, both structures will remain pretty much the same, for there is a clear axiom of modern life (which the doctrine of original sin corroborates), that those with power do not voluntarily surrender it. What I am saying is that the Christian, living in diaspora, who does want to serve his fellowmen must, whatever else he may do, act politically. He must gather others together, form groups that can exercise power, and work from some kind of power base, with all the temptations and abuses to which he thereby becomes liable.

There are those who become very nervous in the face of such suggestions, and who feel that overnight the church will reduce itself merely to the level of another secular social-service agency. I concede that we would be in difficulty if the church in fact were nothing but a kind of equivalent of the AFL-CIO sprinkled with holy water, or if the church became no more than one pressure group among other pressure groups. But I passionately insist that this is not our problem, that it is not likely to be our problem for at least half a century, and that in the interval we can count on the inertia of good Christian folk to keep us from rushing pell-mell into the secular arena leaving everything else behind us. Surely the thing we need to fear is not overinvolvement in the world of contemporary politics; if there is to be an indictment of the church today it will not come from our overinvolvement but because we are so pathetically underinvolved.

What have we been doing, we church people, for the last few decades, that the painfully obvious conditions in our cities, with their inevitable (I repeat, inevitable) outbreak into riots and violence, simply were not acknowledged by us until too late? What have we been doing, that our nation can become involved in the wrong war at the wrong time in the wrong place, and we church people engage in only pitifully feeble protests of a foreign policy that is killing thousands of Americans and hundreds of thousands of Asians in an exercise of demonic futility? Do not let anyone say that racism and Vietnam are political rather than theological issues—they are both, but they are fundamentally human issues, which means that they are also fundamentally theological issues, for any issue that involves the life and death of the children of God is a theological issue, whether the proper theological formulations are pronounced or not.

3. A Sampling of Problems

What I am saying is that if modern ecumenical history demonstrates that Christians are now beginning to attack contemporary problems together, modern world history demonstrates that the kinds of problems we must now attack together are problems like racism and Vietnam. This raises baffling predicaments for many churchmen.

The period of recent church history by which I am most instructed in facing the task of the church in the early '70s in America, is the period of the early '30s in Germany. The German church, Catholic and Protestant, faced the rise of a monstrous evil, Nazism, and was unable to speak an effective word against it, or do an effective deed to counter it. Either because it felt that politics was not its business (part of the legacy of a Lutheran "two-realms" doctrine of church and state) or because it kept waiting for the "right" moment to speak and act (part of the legacy of a Catholic heritage that overemphasized the virtue of prudence), the time passed when the church could speak and act. There was left to it nothing but the individual voice from the' prison cell. The voice from the prison cell counts—perhaps it speaks to us across three decades more powerfully than it did contemporaneously—but it comes too late to affect the immediate situation, which in this case was the build-up of Hitler's demonic power, the systematic slaughter of six million Jews, and the death in warfare of many more millions.

And my great fear today is that those looking back at the churches in the late '60s and early '70s will pronounce upon them the same indictment pronounced upon the church in the early '30s—"too little and too late." Let me therefore single out four kinds of problems that usually inhibit us from acting ecumenically in the secular arena and attempt to speak to them, using Vietnam as a way of making the discussion concrete.

1. There are those who say that the issues are too complex for the church to be able to speak. Some issues are morally clear-cut, we are told, but other issues, such as Vietnam, are perplexing and ambiguous, demanding a degree of political, historical, and military expertise the church cannot claim to have.

But recognizing the complexity and ambiguity of a problem

will simply not get us off the hook. Every social issue is complex, full of implications we may not have grasped. To favor a minimum wage for migrant farm workers may be a matter of simple justice, but it does indeed jeopardize the profits of the owners of the farms on which the migrants work. To vote for any candidate for public office is to support policies of the candidate of which one does not approve, as well as supporting the policies of which one does approve.

But there is nevertheless a point to the complaint, and the point is that churchmen must never let piety go bail for expertise. In this much advertised "age of the laity," we must call upon our laity who are experts in Southeast Asia, or Sino-Russian relations, or international diplomacy, and learn from them. We must not presume to a political or military expertise we do not possess. But even a decent humility in the face of the immensity of the problem does not permit uninvolvement—silence is merely complicity with existing policy. The church need not say everything, but it can say some things, and say them well. One example: In Vietnam we have been bombing civilian areas without apology as a matter of "military necessity." Hanoi aside, we bomb, strafe, napalm, and bulldoze whole towns and villages, utterly destroying them, also as a matter of "military necessity." Can such things go unchallenged by the church? Father John Sheerin has pointed out that our daily military actions are almost perfectly described in the Vatican Council document on *The Church and the World Today*:

> Any act of war aimed indiscriminately at the destruction of entire cities or of extensive areas along with their populations is a crime against God and man himself. It merits unequivocal and unhesitating condemnation (article 80).

Splendid. But where is the "unequivocal and unhesitating condemnation" that should be on the lips of every churchman today? If, in solemn council, we are willing to speak strongly, but then not apply such speech to particular situations, it would be better not to have spoken at all.

As far as the danger of making wrong judgments is concerned, we can be sure in this secular day and age that if churchmen make mistakes they will be so informed by their fellowmen. (I speak from the vantage point of considerable personal experience, that the day when clerical statements had sanctuary from critical dissection has passed.) What is called for, in this situation, is not reserve and timidity, but a certain daring and even brashness. A statement by Karl Barth in the last volume of his *Church Dogmatics* might well be the charter for such a day: "Better something doubtful or overbold, and therefore in need of correction and forgiveness, than nothing at all." [6] So let us do our homework, on Vietnam or whatever, and not let complexity become a device for avoiding involvement at risk.

2. A second problem involves the degree of specificity we should give to our statements or actions. Can we advocate specific programs, specific actions, specific candidates? Doing so involves many risks, not all of them wise. The great danger is in creating the impression that a given policy or candidate is the "Christian" one, and that others are, by the rules of logic, anti-Christian, or at least sub-Christian. There is a great danger in claiming too much for our insights, illustrated by the remark of that great Missouri theologian Harry S Truman, that American foreign policy during his administration was based squarely on the Sermon on the Mount. What I am pleading for is considerably to the right of such a claim, but it is also considerably to the left of those who would permit us only to utter platitudes. Our danger is more from platitudes than from particularities.

Let me illustrate once again in terms of Vietnam. I have felt for several years that we cannot discharge our prophetic duty simply by saying earnestly that we are for peace in Vietnam, or that the love commandment should be implemented in Southeast Asia. I have advocated that the churches, as churches, must at least back such proposals as U Thant's Three Points. In a book recently published with a Catholic lay theologian and a Jewish rabbi (by which format we were trying to demonstrate the need for secular involvement in ecumenical terms), I repeated these and other suggestions, such as greater use of international agencies to initiate negotiations, and made some less than cordial remarks about Mr. Johnson, Mr. Rusk, and Mr. Humphrey. One critic, however, faulted my portion of the book on the ground that I was too specific. While sharing many of my concerns about the war, he did not feel the churches should so unqualifiedly back certain political actions designed to bring the struggle to a conclusion. Similarly, in sharing a platform with another theologian in Washington, I discovered that he agreed that the churches should urge our country to find ways of ending the war, but disagreed that we had any right to recommend a bombing pause as a way to achieve this end.

To propose a specific alternative to present policy, however, is at least to call upon the policy makers to justify their present course of action. Nothing in the public debate thus far has persuaded me that the Government's response is adequate. In such a situation, I would insist that rather than being silent, the churches should become more vocal than ever, forcing the experts to constant scrutiny of our policy. And when we discover, as we have, that the experts themselves do not agree, and that most Asian experts, as a matter of fact, feel our policy is wrong, we have an even greater responsibility to keep such issues alive and on the conscience of our nation.

3. A third problem is tactical as well as theological. To what degree do we make common cause, in the public arena, with those whose presuppositions we do not accept? The old fear was always that to espouse anything to the left meant being manipulated by the Communists. (In California there is a new fear that if you espouse anything at all you will be manipulated by the Birchers.) But let us not surrender too quickly. We need not be embarrassed if some of the convictions of

Christian faith are shared by Marxists. To be for social justice is not wrong just because people with beards are also its champions. Opposition to Vietnam is not evil because others couple their oppositions with disenchantment over the procedures and traditions of Western democratic culture.

Let me illustrate concretely. I was asked (by the editor of *Ramparts*, if truth be told) to speak at the April, 1967, Mobilization Against the War in Vietnam. It was clear that the planning for the mobilization was in the hands of what would be called the far left, that anybody could appear under whatever presuppositions appealed to him provided he was against the war, that Vietcong flags would be flying, and that almost all of the church groups had officially forsworn support. I was engaged at the time in a pretty intensive tour of speaking and writing on Vietnam aimed at the middle class, which is where I figured the votes and the power were. So I declined the invitation, fearing that I would become "tainted" by such an appearance, and would be written off by those I most wanted to reach, as a tool or pawn of the left. But the more I reflected, the more it seemed to me that this was a very superior and condescending attitude to take, so I changed my mind and did appear on the program.[7] And while there were a couple of speeches that made me cringe, by and large the affair was an amazing display of concern, outrage, and moral protest, 62,000 strong—in which the churches were virtually unrepresented. The absence that day of the religious community was a very conspicuous absence since all other segments of the community—doctors, union officials, public entertainers, professors, whatever—were present. But we churchmen had been afraid to sully ourselves by contact with those outside our ranks. We insisted on a privilege one doesn't get—the privilege of fighting on a battleground solely of our own choosing.

I hope the religious bodies of San Francisco learned a lesson from that day. I think I did. It is that we must not be so concerned about our own purity that we forget about human need. If Pope Paul and the Vatican Council address their concerns to "all men of good will," we had better be willing to associate with such people and make common cause with them.

4. A final complaint against church involvement in the secular arena goes: "But if we take a stand, we'll divide our membership." The statement is true. We will. But the question is whether this is such a bad thing. I am persuaded that people are going to leave the church in droves in the next decade or two, and that they are going to do so for one of two reasons: either (a) because the church takes too clear a stand on social issues and they disagree with that stand, or (b) because the church doesn't take a stand on anything and they figure it's not worth the bother. I'd much prefer to be caught on the initial horn of that dilemma. The question is not, "Can we avoid offending people?" but rather, "Can we relate the offense of the gospel to the contemporary scene?"

It seems to me inconceivable that in the name of the Christian gospel our churches could condone a public policy stating that we must achieve a military victory in Vietnam at any cost, even if it means risking the involvement of China and thus triggering World War III, the direction in which our present policy seems irretrievably to be taking us. And if we cannot condone such a policy, then we must oppose it, however unhappy that fact makes some churchmen.

And if there is going to be too much institutional lethargy for us to move as far as many would like to move in opposition to Vietnam, then at the very least the church must give massive support to those within its ranks who are constrained to move beyond the present ecclesiastical consensus. There is a witness of conscience that many individuals within our fellowship feel constrained to make about racism or Vietnam, based on the attitude of that old ex-Augustinian monk who said, "Here I stand, I can do no other, God help me." The witness is not only for the sake of conscience, but also for the sake of the church, offered in an effort to move it from timidity to venturesomeness. A time comes when one must oppose evil even if he cannot prevent it.

That time always comes sooner for individuals within the church than for the church itself, and yet it seems to me quite conceivable that Vietnam is forcing such a choice even upon the institution. And we always run a danger of being institutionally insensitive to those prophetic spirits within our midst who summon us to a higher degree of commitment and risk than we might otherwise be prepared collectively to take.

4. CONCLUSION: THE NEED FOR RISK

What I plead for, therefore, in conclusion, is the willingness of the church in our day to take immense risks in the arena of involvement in the secular order. Let us be prepared to fail a few times, if only that we may learn by those failures how not to fail the next time, if only that we may persuade the suffering race of men that we desire to stand at their side, sharing their burdens, working on their behalf, bearing their cross.

If the church is to err in our day, let it err on the side of overinvolvement rather than underinvolvement. Let it be specific rather than general, making mistakes of commission rather than of omission. Let it be too far to the left rather than too far to the right, or (as is its usual posture) comfortably and complacently in the middle. Let it be too radical rather than too conservative. Let it spend itself now for a bleeding and bent world, rather than conserving itself for a future it may never have. Let it, finally, trust not in its own wisdom, much as it must employ its own wisdom, but let it trust rather in the resource of the divine wisdom that can overrule human folly, even ecclesiastical folly, for its own ends. Let it trust not in its own power, but in the grace of God, who can turn our weakness into his strength, and out of our faltering footsteps erect a clearer highway for the pilgrims who follow us.

NOTES

1. W. M. Abbott (ed.), *Documents of Vatican II* (Association Press, 1966), p. 347.

2. Cited in Lukas Vischer (ed.), *A Documentary History of the Faith and Order Movement, 1927-1963* (The Bethany Press, 1963), pp. 177-179. Italics added.

3. The only earlier encyclical I recall that was similarly directed to non-Catholics as well as Catholics was Pius XI's *Mit brennender Sorge* (1937), addressed to the German nation and dealing, albeit cautiously, with the issue of Nazism. In this case, even the customary Latin form was forgone. Unfortunately, the message did not get through to non-Catholics. Cf. Albert Camus's critique in *Resistance, Rebellion and Death* (Alfred A. Knopf, Inc., 1961).

4. Cited in *Convergence*, The Gustave Weigel Society, Vol. I, No. 1, pp. 4-5.

5. Cited in M. E. Marty and D. G. Peerman (eds.), *New Theology, No. 2* (The Macmillan Company, 1965), p. 271.

6. Karl Barth, *Church Dogmatics*, Vol. IV, Part 2, ed. by G. W. Bromiley and T. F. Torrance (Charles Scribner's Sons, 1958), p. 780.

7. Cf. below, "Protest for the Sake of Persuasion," for the text of the speech.

II
THE PSEUDONYMS OF GOD

The Pseudonyms of God

The language about God these days tends to be a curious combination of modesty and extravagance—modesty at how little some people claim to know about him, extravagance at the degree of assurance with which others claim we can know little or nothing.

To some, of course, God is still totally and triumphantly *present*, and a noted evangelist can rebut the charge that God is dead by countering, "I know that God is alive, because I talked with him this morning," a response that effectively stops further discussion.

But the mood generally is more chastened. Ever since the time of Isaiah, and probably before him, men have spoken of God as *hidden*, and Pascal was not the only one to echo Isaiah's plaintive cry, "Truly, thou art a God who hidest thyself." [1]

Martin Buber has spoken of the *eclipse* of God, another dramatic image, and has insisted that in spite of this eclipse, brought about in part at least by man's sin, we must seek to redeem the word that has fallen into such disrepute. "We cannot cleanse the word 'God' and we cannot make it whole," he writes, "but, defiled and mutilated as it is, we can raise it from the ground and set it over an hour of great care." [2]

Originally published in C. F. Mooney (ed.), *The Presence and Absence of God* (Fordham University Press, 1969), Ch. 7, with a final section that is now incorporated in the next essay. Used by permission.

In our day, the notion of the *absence* of God has gained much currency: there may be a God, but if so the evidence of his presence is so agonizingly slim that we must discount the possibility that he will reappear in our time. Until he does, we must, in Gabriel Vahanian's words, "Wait without idols." [3] This theme seems new and rather daring, but it may in fact be little more than a refinement of the deistic notion, not of the absent God, but of the absentee God, the one who was once around but has now retired to the sidelines, leaving the universe to run its own course, virtually independent of him.

Even more extravagant than these images, of course, is the contemporary theme of the *death* of God, although it is not always clear what the proponents of this theme mean. Sometimes they mean that the idea of God, as a theme of human contemplation and commitment, has died, and that the term is thus a description of our cultural situation rather than a metaphysical or ontological statement.[4] Many of them find the news curiously liberating and seem unimpressed with Rabbi Richard Rubenstein's disavowal of such optimism: "The death of God as a cultural phenomenon is undeniable," he comments, "but this is no reason to dance at the funeral." Others, however, press beyond this phenomenological statement to the assertion that God really and truly has died, that this death is a historical event, and that it took a so-called Christian civilization about nineteen centuries to catch up with the truth. But even those who most buoyantly proclaim God's death go on to insist that there has been a kind of resurrection of God in a new form, as the epiphany of new possibilities for a humanity now liberated from false and outworn beliefs.[5]

In connection with this last position, I happen to be among those who believe that reports of God's death, like the initial reports of Mark Twain's, have been somewhat exaggerated, and I agree with the editors of *New Theology, No. 4* that the so-called "death of God theology" was a phenomenon already passing from the theological scene when it was belatedly dis-

covered by *Time, Newsweek, Playboy,* and other representa-
tives of the mass media.[6] I do not therefore intend in what follows to flail a dead horse, let alone a dead God.

These modes of speech in our day which speak of God as
present, hidden, eclipsed, absent, or dead, are, I suggest, extravagant modes of speech. I do not use the term pejoratively
but descriptively, and partly as a means of setting off by contrast the more modest and less extravagant task with which
this essay is concerned. For I want to deal with the more circumscribed theme of the *pseudonyms* of God, the "strange
names" I believe him to be using in our time, the unexpected
ways in which he is at work.

This theme suggests that to the degree that God is *present,*
he is present in strange ways, and that the usual criteria for
measuring his presence have to be revised. To the degree that
God is *hidden,* he has chosen to hide himself (as Isaiah sus-
pected) so that we are forced to search him out in unlikely
places. To the degree that he is in *eclipse,* the shadows bringing about that eclipse can force us to survey the once-familiar
terrain from new perspectives, and finally see that terrain with
greater clarity than was possible when it was fully bathed in
the sunshine of an undisturbed faith. To the degree that God
is *absent,* such absence is his self-imposed catalyst to force us
into acknowledging fresh modes for his apprehension. And to
the degree that he is *dead*—but here, of course, the compara-
tive mode of speech breaks down, for it is not possible to
speak of degrees of "deadness." The death of God as a description of a cultural phenomenon, however, can be so described, and to the degree that our notion of God has suffered
mortal blows, this may in fact be precisely the prerequisite for
a genuine resurrection in our experience of the true God,
purged of some of the confining and distorting notions we
have tried to attach to him.

And it is for this task of trying to make ourselves open once
again to the reality of one whose dimensions we cannot meas-

ure, and whom eye cannot see nor ear hear, that the imagery of the *pseudonym* may be of some use.

SILONE'S USE OF PSEUDONYMS

The theme was first suggested to me in the very moving novel of Ignazio Silone, *Bread and Wine*.[7] The novel tells the story of Pietro Spina, a communist revolutionary in Italy in the 1930's, during the rise of Italian fascism, and the period in which Mussolini waged his savage war against Ethiopia. Spina is concerned to discern the signs of the times, and an elderly priest, Don Benedetto, who had been his teacher, makes the rather startling remark to him:

> In times of conspiratorial and secret struggle, the Lord is obliged to hide Himself and assume pseudonyms. Besides, and you know it, He does not attach very much importance to His name. . . . Might not the ideal of social justice that animates the masses today be one of the pseudonyms the Lord is using to free Himself from the control of the churches and the banks?[8]

To get the full force of this statement, it must be realized that "the ideal of social justice that animates the masses" in Italy in the 1930's, to which the priest was referring, was Italian Communism. Don Benedetto was saying, in other words, that the hand of God might be more clearly discerned among the Italian Communists than among the Italian priests or bankers.

Initially this seems a strange idea, perhaps even a demonic idea. It seems strange that a God who presumably wants to enter into fellowship with his children should show himself not directly but indirectly, and it seems demonic that the vehicle through which he should indirectly show himself— the pseudonym or false name he should use—would be something so apparently antithetical to his purposes as Communism. But Don Benedetto, as he pursues his theme, makes clear that there is nothing new in this idea. It has, in fact, a long history.

This would not be the first time that the Eternal Father felt obligated to hide Himself and take a pseudonym. As you know, He has never taken the first name and the last name men have fastened on Him very seriously; quite to the contrary, He has warned men not to name Him in vain as His first commandment. And then, the Scriptures are full of clandestine life. Have you ever considered the real meaning of the flight into Egypt? And later, when he was an adult, was not Jesus forced several times to hide himself and flee from the Judaeans? [9]

Silone is so caught up with this theme that in his stage version of *Bread and Wine* he renames the story, *And He Did Hide Himself*,[10] developing even more prominently the notion that Jesus himself had to assume pseudonyms.

We may push the matter a bit farther, therefore, not only in terms of Silone's use of the theme but also in terms of his insistence that this is not a new theme but an old one, and that it is indeed a consistent Biblical theme as well.

BIBLICAL EXAMPLES OF THE PSEUDONYMOUS GOD

Three Old Testament examples of the theme of God's use of pseudonyms may be suggested as the foundation for a further consideration of its possible contemporary usefulness.

The *first* of these occurs in Gen. 28:10-17. Jacob is en route from Beersheba to Haran. Night comes, and so he camps along the road, stopping at what is described as "a certain place." There is nothing special about this place at all. It is not a shrine, it is not a holy place, it is not the goal of the day's journey. It is simply where Jacob happens to be when the sun goes down. During the night he has a dream about a ladder set from earth to heaven, upon which angels are ascending and descending. What is important for our present purposes is neither the dream nor the content of the dream, but the comment that Jacob makes when he awakes, since it becomes almost a paradigm of the experience of the pseudonymity of

God. The next morning Jacob makes two statements, both of which are very true: first, "Surely the Lord is in this place," as indeed he was; second, "I did not know it," as indeed he did not (cf. Gen. 28:16). God's presence was not dependent upon Jacob's perception of that presence—a fact from which we can derive some comfort when we today too readily identify the reality or existence of God with our own degree of perception of his reality or existence.

But even more important was the fact that the reality of that presence came home to Jacob in a quite unexpected place and set of circumstances. Jacob did not discover God in a shrine or place of worship, but far from any such place. He did not discover him in the midst of any cultic exercise or act of mercy. He did not suddenly in the midst of prayer experience the healing reality of God's presence. No, it was in the totally unexpected event of setting up camp in the desert, in the midst of a tedious journey, that God manifested himself in a strange way. How strange and irregular it was to Jacob's experience is rather perversely attested to by the fact that Jacob's reaction was precisely to build a shrine on that spot, to try to regularize the unexpected experience, to divest the experience of its pseudonymity and make it predictable, calculable, and manageable.

A *second* Biblical example of God's use of pseudonyms is one to which Don Benedetto himself makes oblique reference in his conversation with Spina, and one that is recounted in I Kings 19:1-12. A little later in Israel's history Elijah is also leaving Beersheba, only this time the journey is not a calculated one; Elijah is fleeing to the wilderness to escape from that very domineering queen named Jezebel, who is after his neck. Yahweh pursues him and orders him to stand upon the mount before the Lord. "Before the Lord": but how will Elijah know of the presence of the Lord? The account continues:

> And behold, the LORD passed by, and a great and strong wind rent the mountains, and broke in pieces the rocks before the LORD, but the LORD was not in the wind; and

after the wind an earthquake, but the LORD was not in the earthquake; and after the earthquake a fire, but the LORD was not in the fire; and after the fire a still small voice.[11]

The Lord strong and mighty was not in the wind. The Lord of heaven and earth was not in the earthquake. The Lord of all power was not in the fire. Recall that these means—earthquake, wind, and fire—were the normal ways through which a man in Elijah's time would have expected a theophany of the divine presence. But no, after these usual manifestations of the divine comes "a still small voice," or as one translator has put it, "the sound of a soft stillness." [12] And it was in "the sound of a soft stillness" that the God of earthquake, wind, and fire was present—the last place on earth in which Elijah would have expected to find him. Once again, God is working through the unexpected, and confronting man not in the normal way but in a strange way, through pseudonymous activity.

A *third* example of this strange activity of God occurs still later in Israel's history, recounted in that curious and disturbing passage in Isa. 10:5-19.[13] Isaiah is rightly worried because Israel is paying no attention to Yahweh's demands. He feels that Yahweh is about to engage in a mighty manifestation of his sovereign power. And he links this with the fact that Assyria, a great "secular" world power, is poised on the northern borders about to invade the land of God's people, the Jews. Isaiah feels that the power of Yahweh will be manifested in the ensuing battle.

Now the customary thing to assume in such situations was that God would, of course, work through his chosen people. They who were to be "a light unto the Gentiles" would surely be the vehicle through which the strong right arm of Yahweh would be manifest to the Gentiles. But Isaiah did not say that at all. Instead, he said the scandalous and shocking thing that God's instrument would be the pagan Assyria, and that it would be through Assyria's power that God would show forth his will. Assyria, of course, did not know that it was being used by God, and did not even acknowledge the existence of God. Indeed, Assyria would later claim that it had won the victory by the power of its own strong arm, and would scoff at the notion that it was the instrument of Yahweh. But nevertheless, so Isaiah asserts, it will be by means of Assyria that God will declare his will to his people Israel.

Once again, God uses a strange name. He does not use the name of his people Israel, he uses the name of a pagan people, Assyria. Assyria, not Israel, becomes "the rod of his anger, the staff of his fury," and the "godless people" against whom Assyria is sent is, paradoxically, the very people of God.

These are three instances, taken almost at random, of a theme that could be reproduced many times over from the Old Testament. They illustrate that God can use whatever means he chooses, whatever means are to hand—a rest stop on a trip, the calm after a storm, the hosts of the pagans—in order to communicate his will to his people. His ways of working are not limited to the ways people expect him to work, and he clearly refuses to be bound by man's ideas of how he ought to behave.

There is a further interesting thing about these examples. They illustrate three classic ways in which men have claimed to "find God"—through *personal experience* (in the case of Jacob), through *nature* (in the case of Elijah), and through *history* (in the case of Isaiah). In each case, indeed, a confrontation takes place between man and God, but in each case it takes place in an unexpected way. The personal experience is not the personal experience of worship or some other conventional means of encountering God. The confrontation in nature is through the vehicle of nature least expected to produce such a confrontation. The lesson read from history is the lesson least expected and the hardest to accept. In each case, God uses a pseudonym, a strange name, and upsets all human calculations.

GOD'S PSEUDONYMS TODAY

Let us accept, then, Don Benedetto's theme that God is sometimes obliged to hide himself and assume pseudonyms, and that he does not attach very much importance to his name. The name men conventionally attach to him may now be an empty name, the place men look for him may now be the place he is not, and the places men fail to look may be precisely the locations in which his hidden activity is most apparent to those who look with eyes of faith.

Where, then, do we find signs of his pseudonymous activity today? Are we to look for him *only* in strange places? I do not believe so. To say that he acts pseudonymously does not mean he can never be found in his church, but it surely means that he is not confined to his church. To say that he acts pseudonymously does not mean that his light no longer shines through the saints, but it surely means that his saints are more numerous, and are found in more unlikely places than we are usually inclined to acknowledge. To say that he acts pseudonymously does not mean that Scripture is no longer useful in discerning his hidden ways, but it surely means that other literature as well is a vehicle for discerning his veiled presence, not only in Silone, who knows the lineaments of a Christian faith he cannot directly profess himself, but in a host of other writers who plumb the depths of the human predicament with a sensitivity not found in most contemporary pulpits.[14]

To try to discern the signs of the presence of the pseudonymous God in the world today is surely a risky business, but the risk must be taken, if we are not to leave the thesis of this essay irrelevantly suspended in midair. I therefore offer two examples of places where I see signs of his activity more compelling to me than the conventional modes of his expression theologians normally delight to trace.

The *first* example of this pseudonymous activity of God in

our present age is in the agitation and demonstration in which
our country has been engaged in the field of civil rights for
minority groups, whether through cries for "Freedom Now" or
for "Black Power." The white church, to its shame, has not
been very active in this struggle. One does not look to those
who call themselves "God's own people" for leadership in this
matter. There has been little significant indication that many
white Christians have really been concerned about the indig-
nities that they and other white people have visited upon the
black people of this country for the last three hundred years.
If we are to be honest, we must acknowledge that the real battle has been carried on by the secular groups, or by the black
church groups, but not by the white church groups. Whatever
advances have been won in the cause of social justice have
been won either in the face of white Christian apathy or white
Christian opposition. As Martin Luther King has forcefully and
correctly put it, "What is disturbing is not the appalling actions of the bad people, but the appalling silence of the good
people."

We do not usually expect to see the hand of the Lord in secular groups, in public demonstrations, in picket lines, in sit-ins,
in civil disobedience, in people being herded off to jail, in
court rooms, and all the rest. But can we escape the fact that
those are the places and activities through which concern for
the fact that *all* men are God's children is being expressed today? And that the same fact is not expressed, but denied, in the
white communities with written or unwritten covenants of
closed occupancy, or the white churches with the token black
tenor prominently displayed in the choir? No, the Lord is in
those strange places, and like Jacob, we have not known it.

The tragedy has been that we have not learned it soon
enough, and that because of our blindness and callousness and
indifference, the incredible patience of nonviolent black discipline has turned to violence. The white community, holding
all the power, has done too little, too late, and forced the de-
spairing outcry that finally has exhausted any hope of working

through the white-dominated political process, and turns in total frustration to all that is left—the brick, the stick, the fire, the bullet.[15]

To me the most haunting line in contemporary literature occurs in the exchange between Msimangu and Kumalo, the two black priests in Alan Paton's book *Cry the Beloved Country.* They are talking about the white man. And Msimangu says to Kumalo, "I have one great fear in my heart, that one day when they are turned to loving they will find we are turned to hating." [16] So insistent is the theme that Paton has Kumalo recall it a second time at the very end of the book: "When they turn to loving they will find we are turned to hating." [17] It is already possible that this could become the epitaph of our nation. And the question is: Can we hear that as the insistent clamor of the pseudonymous God in our day, addressed to us, warning us, "Do not look for me just in the sanctuaries, or in the precise words of theologians, or in the calm of the countryside; look for me in the place where men are struggling for their very survival as human beings, where they are heaving off the load of centuries of degradation, where they are insisting that the rights of the children of God are the rights of all my children and not just some; and if you will not find me there, expect to find me acting in more heavy-handed fashion elsewhere."

There is a *second* place where I see the pseudonymous God at work in our nation today. I believe that he is using his "strange name" in trying to tell us something desperately important through the rising voice of protest about American involvement in Vietnam.[18]

That there is something wrong about the most powerful nation on earth systematically destroying a tiny nation ought long ago to have been crystal clear to everyone—but it has not been. Dropping napalm on women and children and the aged so that peoples' chins melt into their chests, ought long ago to have aroused in us the height of moral indignation—but it has not. That we justify our presence in Vietnam in the name of opposing a monolithic "world communism" that began to crumble over a decade ago, ought long ago to have made us demand a stern accounting of our leaders—but it has not. That we are entitled to impose our will wherever we wish in the world, supporting military dictatorships that do not represent their people, ought long ago to have made us cry out in protest—but it has not. "Destroying a city in order to save it," as an American officer recently described our destruction of Ben Tre, ought to impress us as a hideous example of Orwellian doublethink—but it does not.

Where did the prophetic denunciation of this sort of thing begin? Not in the churches, not in the business world, not in the labor unions. No, it began with the students, who on this issue have displayed considerably greater moral sensitivity than their elders. They have helped to remind the rest of us that national pride and arrogance are things in which they take no pride, and for which their generation is not willing to kill dark-skinned peoples thousands of miles away. The gradual escalation of moral protest in response to the escalation of military power came as students across the land began to tell the older generation that the war we are fighting is both futile and immoral. Many from both generations may not like some of the stridency of voice and action that accompanies the protest, but it has been our deafness that has made the stridency necessary, and woe to those of any generation who do not hear in this anguished protest a strong note of moral urgency.[19]

That the manner of contemporary protest against the war— or anything else—is disquieting, is no sign that God is absent. Indeed, we can expect that God's presence in whatever form will be disquieting. We will find him not just where there is peace, but where there is turmoil; not just where things are calm, but where things are stirred up; not just where things are satisfactory, but where dross and gold are being separated. For, as the prophet told us long ago, "He is like a refiner's fire."

NOTES

1. Isa. 45:15. Pascal picks up the theme in *Pensées*, 194, 242.

2. Martin Buber, *Eclipse of God* (Harper & Brothers, 1952), p. 18. Cf. also the very perceptive pursuit of this theme in Emil L. Fackenheim, *Quest for Past and Future: Essays in Jewish Theology* (Indiana University Press, 1968), esp. pp. 229-243.

3. Gabriel Vahanian, *Wait Without Idols* (George Braziller, Inc., 1964).

4. Cf. Gabriel Vahanian, *The Death of God* (George Braziller, Inc., 1961), and writings from William Hamilton's "middle period," such as *The New Essence of Christianity* (Association Press, 1961).

5. The literature is endless. Cf. *inter alia*, T. J. J. Altizer and W. Hamilton, *Radical Theology and the Death of God* (Bobbs-Merrill Company, Inc., 1966), and T. J. J. Altizer, *The Gospel of Christian Atheism* (The Westminster Press, 1966), for firsthand expositions.

6. Cf. M. E. Marty and D. G. Peerman (eds.), *New Theology, No. 4* (The Macmillan Company, 1967), esp. pp. 9-15.

7. Ignazio Silone, *Bread and Wine* (Atheneum Publishers, 1962), a revision of an earlier form of the novel published in America by Penguin Books, Inc., 1946. I have pursued this theme further in "Ignazio Silone and the Pseudonyms of God," in H. J. Mooney, Jr., and T. F. Staley (eds.), *The Shapeless God* (University of Pittsburgh Press, 1968).

8. Silone, *op. cit.* (Penguin), pp. 247-248. Silone's later revision does not contain the quotation in this precise form.

9. Silone, *op. cit.* (Atheneum), p. 274.

10. Ignazio Silone, *And He Did Hide Himself* (London: Jonathan Cape, 1946).

11. I Kings 19:11-12.

12. J. A. Bewer, *The Literature of the Old Testament* (Columbia University Press, 1938), p. 48.

13. Cf. further below, "Assyrians in Modern Dress."

14. On this theme, cf. *inter alia* such recent writings from diverse viewpoints as N. A. Scott, *The Broken Center* (Yale University Press, 1965); S. M. TeSelle, *Literature and the Christian Life* (Yale University Press, 1966); and Peter M. Axthelm, *The Modern Confessional Novel* (Yale University Press, 1967).

15. The above words were initially written before the release of the Presidential Advisory Commission's Report on Civil Disorders. This "secular" document insists, in hard-hitting terms, that the

reason for the riots is not black conspiracy but "white racism." Cf. *Report of the National Advisory Commission on Civil Disorders,* with an introduction by Tom Wicker (Bantam Books, Inc., 1968). The document is a splendid example of the voice of the pseudonymous God speaking in our time.

16. Alan Paton, *Cry the Beloved Country* (Charles Scribner's Sons, 1948), pp. 39-40.

17. *Ibid,* p. 272.

18. Cf. further below, the section on "Vietnam and the Exercise of Dissent."

19. Cf. further below, " 'Those Revolting Students.' "

The Supreme Pseudonym

The previous examination of the pseudonyms of God has brought us to a point at which it might be argued that the case has been made: God can work in unexpected ways, employing pseudonyms, and we have illustrated the theme with examples drawn from both Biblical and contemporary history. Q.E.D. It is a temptation to stop right there.

But one must not succumb to the temptation to stop right there. For out of a number of further questions that could be raised, there is one at least that must be faced, whatever others are omitted. This is the question: How can one be so sure that it is *God* who is working in these various ways, and not someone or something else? Isn't this whole approach likely to make God simply capricious, not really trustworthy or knowable, to be looked for merely in the bizarre or curious circumstance? Or, to focus the question even more bluntly: Don't we simply pick our own pet social hobbies and try to invest them with ultimate moral worth by saying that they are the activities through which God is working? Aren't we simply trying to enlist God on our side?

The first section of this essay was originally included in the preceding one. The latter portion has been written expressly for the present volume.

THE CRITERION FOR PSEUDONYMOUS ACTIVITY

That is a fair question. The guidelines for an answer involve, for me at any rate, a shift from the Old Testament to the New, though I think an answer congruent to the one I shall suggest is possible on Old Testament terms as well.

If we want a criterion by means of which to discern where God is employing pseudonyms today, I think we find it in relation to the time and place where God did show us most clearly who he is and how he makes himself known to us. Other attempts to trace his activity must be tested against how adequately they reflect what we know of him from that central event. The time, of course, is the first thirty years of what we now call the Christian era, though it presupposes the many generations of Jewish history preceding it. The place is that tiny little strip of land known as Palestine, tucked off in a corner of the Roman Empire. And the important thing for our present concern is that this event likewise underlines the unexpectedness of the divine activity, the sense in which *here too God used a pseudonym,* the sense in which here too his activity was just as strange and unexpected as in the case of Jacob, Elijah, or Isaiah, the sense in which all that came to fulfillment in the life of Jeshua bar Josef is simply contrary to the way any of us would have written the script.

Let us seek to drive the point home by the following device: Suppose we were waiting now for some tremendous manifestation of God's activity. Suppose that it had been promised that God would intervene in our human situation, and that it was now clear that the time was at hand. Where would we look for him?

Surely, the answer would be, in one of the great nations, where as many people as possible would be exposed to this important fact; surely in a well-established family with much influence; surely in such a way that all the resources of public opinion and mass media could be used to acquaint people with what had happened; surely it would be the most public and open and widely accessible event possible.

But in terms of the way the New Testament reports it happening back then, if it were to happen today, it would be more like this: A child would be born into a backward South African tribe, the child of poor parents with almost no education. He would grow up under a government that would not acknowledge his right to citizenship. During his entire lifetime he would travel no more than about fifty miles from the village of his birth, and would spend most of that lifetime simply following his father's trade—a hunter, perhaps, or a primitive farmer. Toward the end he would begin to gather a few followers together, talking about things that sounded so dangerous to the authorities that the police would finally move in and arrest him, at which point his following would collapse and his friends would fade back into their former jobs and situations. After a short time in prison and a rigged trial he would be shot by the prison guards as an enemy of the state.

Most of us would find it hard to take seriously the claim that such an event was God's supreme manifestation of himself. The whole episode would indeed appear to be a pseudonymous act, with the emphasis on the "pseudo," inflected this time as "false." And yet that is precisely what the attitude of almost any first-century person must have been to the assertion that the Son of God had been born in a cowstall in tiny Bethlehem and that he was, of all things, a lower class Jew, whose parents became refugees, and who himself had to go into hiding on several occasions. If on some occasions "the common people heard him gladly," when it came to the showdown and there was a public "demonstration" in the streets of Jerusalem, they quickly shifted their "hosannas" to cries of "Crucify him." [1]

And yet those episodes and others like them are the very stuff out of which the Christian claim has come. Jesus of Nazareth becomes God's unexpected way of acting, God's pseudonym, and he becomes the norm or pattern in terms of which we are to believe that God will continue to act. So if it strikes us as strange today that God should be working through blacks in cities, or through students who for reasons of conscience defy a law, or through groups that are not part of the religious establishment, such assertions are at least consistent with the strange way God acted back then through one who was looked upon as a criminal, spat upon and despised, and finally strung up on the city dump heap.

Since he was an outcast, we must not be surprised to find contemporary reflections of his presence among the outcast. Since he was a servant, we must look for signs of his presence today among those who serve. Since he was part of an oppressed minority, we must expect to hear the echo of his voice today among those who are oppressed. Since two thirds of the world goes to bed hungry each night, we must recall that he made available not only spiritual comfort but solid and tangible loaves and fishes. Since he became man, we must acknowledge that in every man there is one who can be served in his name, just as he served all men in his Father's name. Since he lived very much in the world, we will look for him not only in holy places or by means of holy words, but we will look for him also in the very common, ordinary things of life for which he gave himself: bread (whether broken around a kitchen table or at an altar), carpentry, men in need, even tax collectors.

In a time when men suffer, we will not be surprised to discover that he suffered also, nor will we flinch when Bonhoeffer pronounces the initially disturbing words, "Only the suffering God can help," [2] even though it is probably the ultimate in the pseudonymous activity of God that he could be acquainted with grief. And yet in this grief-stricken world that appears to be one of the chief places where we must look for him today. In his parable of the king and the maiden, Kierkegaard responds to the claim that in Jesus the incarnate God is present:

> The servant-form is no mere outer garment, and therefore God must suffer all things, endure all things, make

experience of all things. He must suffer hunger in the desert, he must thirst in the time of his agony, he must be forsaken in death, absolutely like the humblest—behold the man! His suffering is not that of his death, but his entire life is a story of suffering; and it is love that suffers, the love which gives all is itself in want.[3]

So the point of greatest clarity is the point of greatest incongruity and surprise. Jesus himself is the grand pseudonym, the supreme instance of God acting in ways contrary to our expectation, the point at which we are offered the criterion in terms of which the action of God elsewhere can be measured. And if we miss his presence in the world, it will not be because he is not there, but simply because we have been looking for him in the wrong places.

IMAGES FOR THE SUPREME PSEUDONYM

It is not only an interesting cultural fact, but a matter of theological importance, that the person of Jesus has been rediscovered by the youth of our era. Whether one is listening to *Jesus Christ Superstar* on the radio, encountering Jesus Freaks in a public park, or reading the latest popular rewriting of the New Testament story, one cannot help being struck by the widespread acceptance of at least certain parts of the message that originally transformed a bunch of case-hardened skeptics in Palestine into devoted followers who were willing both to live and to die for their leader.

Such people today still seem to have a good deal of difficulty with the notion of the church, and if there is a single recurring indictment on their lips it focuses in the question to churchmen, "Why don't you follow your leader?" There is a feeling that Jesus put a great deal of himself on the line, and that the trouble with his followers is that they're unwilling to do the same. So there is a new mood of openness to asking the question about the ongoing importance and significance of this Jesus of Nazareth.

If we are to deal with this question in a meaningful way today, we must begin by seeing Jesus first of all as a man, as someone who entered into and fully shared our human creaturehood. He is not a kind of "reverse astronaut," of whom it could be said, "We men have sent an earthly creature into the heavens and brought him back down, so why should not God be able to send a heavenly creature down to earth and take him back up?" The trouble with such a position (long implicit in certain kinds of orthodoxy) is that it makes virtually impossible an appreciation of Jesus as a flesh and blood creature like ourselves. No—the Jesus with whom we must start is a Jesus who really walked along dusty roads, was hungry, tired, and disillusioned; who on one occasion is reported to have wept, and on another was described as "a wine-bibber and a glutton." When he spoke in a synagogue he was thrown out; when he went to a wedding it was not to officiate at the ceremony but to provide the wine for the last round of drinks; when he appeared to his followers on a lakeside after his resurrection it was to invite them to a fish fry. If we can start with this fact of the humanness firmly established, then we can go on to employ a variety of images that will illustrate the point and also carry us beyond it. Here is a sampling of images, ranging from clown to fish, with a few more in between for good measure.[4]

1. *Christ the clown.*[5] A number of the paintings of Rouault depict the face of a clown, and a number of his other paintings depict the face of Christ. It is often hard to distinguish between the two. There is an instructive point in that fact. If we think about the face of the clown, we discover that he is not only comic, he is also tragic. He not only makes us laugh, he makes us want to cry. The laughter he evokes from us is not far from tears. When he takes a broom and tries to brush away the spot of light that is focused on the circus floor, we know very well that the light will always elude him and move beyond his reach just as he gets to it. We are amused at his efforts to catch up with the spot of light, but we are also

troubled because we know that he never will. He shows us the gap between how he looks at the world, and the way the world really is, and he enables us to enter vicariously into his own experience and discover that the way *we* see things is not the way things really are. He calls into question our perception of things.

This is likewise one of the functions that Jesus has fulfilled in the history of man. He too calls into question our perception of things. No matter how we look at the world, he challenges our viewpoint. If we believe that the world is an evil place, we are confronted by the fact that he embodied love within it in such a way as to suggest that love is at the very heart of things. If we believe that the world is a beautiful place, we are confronted by the fact that when Jesus gave expression to that beauty the world could not fit him in, and very quickly did away with him. There is no stance we can take about ourselves or our world that is not challenged when we confront Christ the clown.

2. *Jesus the revolutionary.*[6] In this age of revolution it is not surprising that revolutionaries have been claiming Jesus as a revolutionary. At the very least, this is an important counterbalance to a traditional Sunday school picture of "gentle Jesus, meek and mild." But it is much more than that, for if one reads the Gospels with any kind of openness, it is clear that Jesus was a constant challenger and disturber of the established order. The religious establishment took its lumps from him, and so did the political establishment, from Herod ("that fox") on down. We forget too easily that he came to bring not peace but a sword (a disturbing thought even if no more than a metaphor), or that when he took on the establishment directly it turned massively against him, so that the Roman Empire found a convenient way to get rid of him within a couple of years of the beginning of his public ministry. When we look at the nature of his teaching and the quality of his actions it is not at all surprising that the authorities should have been upset, or that as men look at him today they should continue

to be upset, for this man was a "convicted criminal" who was put to death by the state and we do not usually look to convicted criminals for insights into the meaning of life.

When religious people decide that it is centrally important to observe the Sabbath, he issues the rude rejoinder that the Sabbath was made for man, not man for the Sabbath. When we decide that piety and proper belief and membership in the church are the criteria of Christianity, he reminds us, in a disturbing story about sheep and goats, that it is not piety or proper belief or church attendance that count, but whether or not we have been concerned with the neighbor in need. This is indeed revolutionary stuff, and many a *status quo* has foundered on less severe challenges. And when we temporize with indecision or inaction, he confronts us with his assessment of the church at Laodicea: "How I wish you were either hot or cold! But because you are lukewarm, neither hot nor cold, I will spit you out of my mouth." (Rev. 3:16, NEB.)

3. *Jeshua bar Josef,* the teacher. Much of Jesus' revolutionary challenge comes through his teaching, for although he is a first-century man, the son of a carpenter, he spoke words that we cannot avoid or evade. Many people go so far as to say, "I can't take seriously the claim that Jesus was divine, but I'm willing to admit that his teachings were sublime."

Kierkegaard had an appropriate response to the point. He applauded his reader for having made this acknowledgment and suggested that the reader illustrate his commitment by the simple act of living out Jesus' teachings. He predicted, however, that the reader would find himself with a difficult task on his hands, since the teachings are not easy and comfortable, but make extraordinary demands upon us, culminating in the imperative, "Be ye therefore perfect, as your Father in heaven is perfect."

Furthermore, if one tries to build a case for the uniqueness of Jesus on the basis of his teachings, one is in for trouble, since there is nothing in Jesus' teachings that is not found somewhere in the Hebrew Scriptures or in Jewish commentaries on them. To be sure, he sifted out the best in the tradition that was his, but on the level of teacher alone the most we can finally say is that he provided a useful verbal anthology of rabbinic insights.

4. *"The man for others."* The real value of Jesus' teaching, then, is that he embodied what he said. And the message he spoke—and lived—had to do with a love that put others before self. Dietrich Bonhoeffer described Jesus as "the man for others," the one who is the model of a love that is available for all men.[7] This love, as expressed in Jesus' life, and not just in his words, has at least two significant qualities. First, it is *love for the unlovable,* not merely love that is offered to those who appear worthy of it. It is love that reaches out across all boundaries, whether of class, creed, race, or nation. It is an all-inclusive love. Second, it is *suffering love,* a love that is willing to take on the burden of the other, willing to stand in the place of the other—what Bonhoeffer described as "deputyship."

There is a corollary to this contention: if Jesus is "the man for others," then the church that describes itself as his body must carry on that function today by being "the church for others." [8]

5. *Christ the offense.* All these demands begin to get to us. Instead of soothing us, they make us uncomfortable. If we are honest, our response is liable to be like that of Peter, who, when first confronted by Jesus, did not respond positively at all. Instead, he said, "Get away from me, leave me alone!" (A modern version of "Lord, depart from me for I am a sinful man.") And on a number of occasions Jesus himself suggested that no one could really understand him unless he had gone through the possibility of being offended by him. Kierkegaard says there are at least three ways in which Christ becomes an offense to us.[9] First of all we are offended that a mere man should make such demands on us—the demand that we sell all that we have and give to the poor, that we pray for our enemies, and so on. Who is this man that he should ask so much

of us? Secondly, we are offended that this man should claim to be the Son of God. Kierkegaard feels that it is not the nature of the claim, but the nature of the claimant, that is so offensive, for this particular man is from the lower working class; he is a Jew, a member of a minority group; he is not educated, cosmopolitan, or sophisticated. That *this* man should claim to be the Son of God is simply not entertainable. Thirdly, we are offended by the fact that the one who claims to be the Son of God should come to the end that he did, that the one who is God in the flesh should end up hanging on a cross in a dump heap, with flies buzzing about his putrefying body. That is not the way we expect God to be at work on the human scene. And Kierkegaard concludes that we must at least go through the *possibility* of being offended by Christ on all these scores, if we are ever to be able to take him seriously.

6. *Healer and feeder.* There is obviously more to the New Testament picture of Jesus. He is not only the one who offends, challenges, and tears down. He is a positive reinforcing presence as well as a threatening and challenging one. It is clearly recorded that "the common people heard him gladly," even if they did fail him in the pinch. Many people were in fact drawn to him. Many of those who encountered him received salvation, which is simply our word for "health" or wholeness. People in his presence not only felt condemned, they also felt accepted. People who were sick became well. If Peter's initial reaction to Jesus was to want to get away from him, at the end of his life he realized that only Jesus' healing forgiveness could make life tolerable once more. Those who were hungry when he was in their midst were fed, whether they were nourished by the bread of the earth or the spiritual bread of his nourishing presence. Indeed, it was in the sharing of an evening meal at Emmaus that some of Jesus' followers recognized that it was he who had been with them all afternoon. We can never say that he was unconcerned with the body or the things of this earth. His healing and sustaining

power was not only spiritual but also physical—thereby showing that the two cannot be separated.

7. *The clue to the cosmos, or, the picture in the empty
picture frame.* Most people when confronted by the word
"God" are unable to give much content to the term. It is as
though they had a picture frame with the title "God" beneath
it, but had no idea what kind of picture ought to go within the
frame.

The only materials we have to work with are those drawn
from our own human experience, and if we want to picture
what is ultimate for us, then we must point to that which is
closest, in our human experience, to ultimacy. And here is
where the images we have thus far invoked begin to coalesce
into an image we might put into the picture frame. For when
we point to the one who challenges all our perceptions, who
lives a life of suffering love as "the man for others," and whose
presence is not only disturbing but also healing, then we are
moving toward a human description of what ultimate reality
might be like.

This is what the early Christian community was talking
about when it developed the first and shortest of all Christian
confessional statements, *Kurios Christos*, Christ is Lord, since
the word *kurios*, or "lord," was the word for the highest allegiance to which one could be committed. Those early Christians were saying by such a declaration, "The highest loyalty
which we can pledge is given by us to this man, who represents for us in human terms who God is." In him they found
God defined, but they also found themselves defined, which is
why—much later—their descendants could write a much
longer creedal statement that included a definition of Jesus as
"true God and true man."

8. *Christ the fish.* The whole thing is brought together in
one of the early Christian symbols. In those first decades, during a time of repression and persecution, Christians needed secret code words and symbols by means of which to communi-

cate with one another. One of the symbols that was early
adopted was the fish, since the Greek word for fish, *ichthus*,
was an acronym for the Greek words *Iesus Christos Theos
Uius Soter*, meaning, "Jesus Christ, Son of God, Savior."

"Savior" is a word that first-century people used more easily
than most twentieth-century people do. "Liberator" would be
our closest equivalent. When we talk about being "liberated"
from self-preoccupation or white power structures, we are
talking about being "saved" from them, released from them, no
longer dependent on them. Similarly, when we talk about
being "liberated" for new opportunities or a new society, we
are talking about being "saved" for something. And it was just
this experience of being liberated or freed that the early Christians associated with Jesus. Just how free they were is indicated by the fact that they were not only willing to live, but
also to die, on his behalf.

Eight images do not exhaust the meaning of Jesus as the supreme pseudonym for God's activity in the world. But they
may in their turn suggest others, which in their turn may
cause us to see God working in even stranger ways, and to
say, first in perplexity, "There too?" and then, with more
assurance, "Why not?"

NOTES

1. Cf. the shift between Matt. 21:9 and Matt. 27:22-23.
2. Dietrich Bonhoeffer, *Letters and Papers from Prison* (The
Macmillan Company, 1967), p. 197.
3. Søren Kierkegaard, *Philosophical Fragments* (Princeton University Press, 1962), p. 40.
4. For a fuller treatment of the theme of contemporary images
of Jesus, cf. Geoffrey Ainger, *Jesus Our Contemporary* (Seabury
Press, 1967) and *Which Jesus?* by John Wick Bowman (The
Westminster Press, 1970).
5. A fuller, though somewhat different, treatment of this theme is
contained in Harvey Cox, *The Feast of Fools* (Harvard University
Press, 1969), Ch. 10, "Christ the Harlequin."

6. On this theme, cf. the two contradictory estimates in S. G. Brandon, *Jesus and the Zealots* (Charles Scribner's Sons, 1968), and Oscar Cullmann, *Jesus and the Revolutionaries* (Harper & Row, Publishers, Inc., 1970).

7. Cf. Bonhoeffer, *op. cit.*, esp. pp. 209-210, foreshadowed in his earlier lectures, *Christ the Center* (Harper & Row, Publishers, Inc., 1966).

8. For some of the implications of this contention, see below, Part III, "Discovering God's Pseudonyms Today."

9. Cf. Kierkegaard, *Training in Christianity* (Princeton University Press, 1941), esp. Part II, pp. 79-144.

Assyrians in Modern Dress

The annual catalog of a religious publishing house recently contained several pages of book titles under the heading "Christian Fiction." This was followed by a shorter section of book titles under the heading "Interesting Fiction."

Some religious-minded people seem content to keep the divorce permanent, for they feel that somehow a book that is not a work of "Christian fiction" is suspect, even if it is interesting. Unfortunately there is no necessary connection between a writer's being a Christian and being a good writer. Some good writers *are* Christians (people like T. S. Eliot, W. H. Auden, Alan Paton, and Graham Greene come immediately to mind), but there are many more good writers who are not, and any Christian who proposes to live responsibly in the twentieth-century world must take the latter into account as well as the former.

To what degree, then, is it possible for the Christian to see the hand of God at work in non-Christian writers? What is there to be learned from the Salingers and the Steinbecks, who cannot be dismissed as unimportant, since they tell us important things about ourselves and the world in which we live? Indeed, the claim for the Salingers and the Steinbecks can be put more strongly: They do not merely tell us "interesting" things, they tell us true things; and they do so with greater

Originally published in *Presbyterian Life,* May 1, 1962. Used by permission.

sensitivity and accuracy than many so-called "Christian writers." How, then, are we to understand the way in which non-Christians can operate as God's pseudonyms?

1. CHRISTIANITY'S CULTURAL IMPACT

An initial answer to this question (and a very inviting gambit it is) is to assert that such writers are simply the unconscious inheritors of the Christian faith and culture within which they were nurtured. They reflect and transmit much more of the Christian perspective than they are themselves aware of doing.

To say this is to say that our culture has been nourished by Christian roots. The affirmation that man has particular significance, for example, is an affirmation that was originally made because of an underlying affirmation that man is a child of God and therefore of eternal worth. But for the last several hundred years the affirmation of man's significance has increasingly been made without reference to the underlying affirmation of his dependence on God. The fruit of the Christian perspective is still with us, but it is a blossom that has been severed from the roots that originally gave it life. And Salinger, Steinbeck, and Company still regard man with tenderness and even reverence. Salinger, in fact, has been accused by John Updike of loving his characters more than God loves them. And Steinbeck, for all the demonry he sees at work in human beings, obviously has a deep and abiding love for what one of his characters calls "that glittering creature, man." In other words, these writers covertly confirm much of the Christian perspective that they overtly disavow.

But we must not claim too much for this contention. It can be a cheap and easy victory, with the Christian sitting on the sidelines and claiming that the Christian faith gets credit for everything good that a modern writer says, while it bears no responsibility for the places where the writer doesn't quite ring true. Furthermore, one can legitimately ask whether the

Christian faith is really as pervasive as this view suggests. It is quite possible that the glimpses of truth these writers have are not nurtured by Christian faith at all, but simply by honest examination and reflection of the world they see about them— which is a far cry from a Christian world. Any claims, therefore, that Christians make about the cultural or social impact of the faith must be modest claims.

2. THE GENERAL AVAILABILITY OF TRUTH

There is a second way of relating the theological insights of contemporary writers to the Christian faith. This attitude can be found clear back in the second century. The early Christian apologists had to come to terms with the fact that the pagans had said a lot of true things without benefit of Christian revelation. So Justin Martyr said, "Whatever has been well said anywhere or by anyone belongs to us Christians" (*Apology*, II, 13). Presumably he meant that since all truth was one, and all truth came from God, therefore any manifestation of the truth was a manifestation of God at work. This means that truth is to be welcomed wherever it is found, whether in Christian or non-Christian garb.

The late Archbishop Temple came to much the same conclusion after an examination of the Prologue to John's Gospel. The Prologue deals with the Word of God, the logos, the creative power of God, the Word that has become flesh and dwelt among us, so that God's creative activity is now manifest in the life of men. That Christ is the agent of all creativity made it possible for Archbishop Temple to put a high value, therefore, on every expression of creativity: "By the Word of God— that is to say, by Jesus Christ—Isaiah, and Plato, and Zoroaster, and Buddha, and Confucius conceived and uttered such truths as they declared. There is only one divine light; and every man is in his measure enlightened by it." (William Temple, *Readings in St. John's Gospel*, p. 10.)

The implication of such a statement for the realm of creative literature is obvious. It can be indicated by revising the sentences quoted above so that they read: "By the Word of God . . . Salinger, and Steinbeck, and Faulkner, and Kafka, and Carson McCullers conceived and uttered such truths as they declared. There is only one divine light; and every author in his measure is enlightened by it." (William Temple, revised.)

The conclusion to be drawn is not that the existence of Salinger, Steinbeck, and Company proves that Christianity is really on the ball after all, but rather that Christians must listen to Salinger, Steinbeck, and Company more sympathetically than they sometimes do. God does not limit himself solely to "Christian thinkers" or people within the church, and there must be proper humility on the part of Christians in the face of this fact. Non-Christians can be vehicles of God's truth too.

But the solution has a difficulty. The danger is that the Christian appropriation of non-Christian literature will be no more than a patchwork affair. Rather than hearing the author on his own terms, the Christian lifts from a given author only those things that are congenial to a Christian view, and thus mutilates the author's message. In this way a kind of man-made gospel is created: a slice of life from Nathanael West, a dash of despair from Franz Kafka, a note of compassion from J. D. Salinger, a bit of realism from Robert Penn Warren, some bright battlements of hope from John Steinbeck, possibly even a bit of raucous mysticism from Jack Kerouac—the Christian mixes all these together, tops them over with a thin Christian icing, and then says, "See? This is what I have been talking about all along!"

That these various voices may all, in their various ways, be witnessing to a part of the truth, or even a part of the Christian gospel, need not be doubted. But to pick and choose this way is to end with a synthetic product and to fail to do justice to the integrity of the author's own point of view.

3. Assyrians in Modern Dress

Is there a way to avoid these difficulties? If there is, it would seem to come by recognizing more than the cultural impact that Christianity may make on writers, or even the general availability of truthful insights to all men, who try to write honestly. It would come by affirming that God can use *all* things for his purposes—the forces of truth, to be sure, but also the forces of untruth. Modern writers can, in other words, be understood as "Assyrians in modern dress."

The figure of the Assyrian is meant to conjure up a remarkable passage in the Old Testament, Isa. 10:5-11. Israel, understood by Isaiah to be God's people, is being besieged by the pagan Assyrians, who are definitely *not* God's people. The usual pattern in such situations is for the prophet to call down God's judgment upon the pagans and to gird Israel for the task of being the agent through whom God's power and might can be displayed to the pagans. But in Isa., ch. 10, precisely the opposite conclusion is drawn: God uses the Assyrians to make his way known to Israel. It is an astonishing notion—"pagan" Assyria is God's vehicle of revelation to "believing" Israel.

Such a perspective is a useful one for understanding a Christian approach to "pagan" writers. The Christian need not claim that the non-Christian writers are covert Christians, nor need he appropriate from their writings only those things that are congruent with a Christian witness. For the thing that makes Assyria so forceful a witness against Israel is precisely its unbelief. Isaiah never says that Assyria is to be taken seriously only at those points where Israel and Assyria agree. Assyria must be listened to and reckoned with as Assyria, as nonbeliever. Assyria must be seen on Assyria's terms.

And this is the stance from which the Christian can most profitably look upon Salinger, Steinbeck, and Company as "Assyrians in modern dress." They must first of all be allowed to speak as themselves, with their own full voices, to be heard first of all and basically *on their own terms.* That they should be vehicles of God's revelation to Christians may sound surprising to the Christian, but it is no more surprising than the original notion that Assyria was a vehicle of God's revelation to the Israelites. The Assyrians in modern dress can likewise speak their word to us.

But it will not only be their word. It will also be God's word. To some, perhaps not least to the writers themselves, this will sound preposterous. To clarify it, another look must be taken at the Isaiah passage. After asserting that God makes use of pagan Assyria to effect his will in Israel, Isaiah goes on realistically to assert that it never enters Assyria's mind that it is being so used by God, and that the Assyrian king would probably have been either amused at, or contemptuous of, such a suggestion. For, as Isaiah says, "he does not so intend, and his mind does not so think" (Isa. 10:7).

But to whatever degree it is proper to assert that the Assyrian is the unconscious, or even unwilling, instrument of a God in whom he does not believe, to just that degree it is proper to assert that the modern Assyrians can be the unconscious, or even unwilling, instruments of a God in whom they do not believe either. It may be true of Arthur Miller, as it was of the Assyrian king, that "Arthur Miller does not so intend, and his mind does not so think" (Isa. 10:7, revised).

The modern writer, then, can be used by God without his willingness to be so used, or even his consciousness of being so used. He too may find himself amused at, or contemptuous of, such a description of himself. But this does not lessen the effectiveness of what he is and says. It may even heighten it. His very disbelief may be the one thing needful to disturb the contemporary complacent Israelite from his shallow and inadequate belief. All of which may mean that the writer will be speaking more significantly and effectively and challengingly today than many of the theologians who overtly and too glibly pronounce the name of God.

There are at least two other ways in which the modern Assyrians can speak to the modern Israelites who are ourselves. *First* of all, they can show us what a world without God is really like, and set forth in all its starkness the world as seen through eyes of disbelief. Tennessee Williams starts out to talk about pity and love, but before he is through he has to talk about fear and evasion:

> Men pity and love each other more deeply than they permit themselves to know. The moment after the phone has been hung up, the hand reaches for a scratch pad and scrawls a notation: "Funeral Tuesday at five, Church of the Holy Redeemer, don't forget flowers." And the same hand is only a little shakier than usual as it reaches, some minutes later, for a high-ball glass that will pour a stupefaction over the kindled nerves. Fear and evasion are the two little beasts that chase each other's tail in the revolving wirecage of our nervous world. They distract us from feeling too much about things. Time rushes toward us with its hospital tray of infinitely varied narcotics, even while it is preparing us for its inevitably fatal operation. (Preface to *The Rose Tattoo*.)

This is the world apart from grace, a world in which the promises of the gospel, the good news, have not been heard. And it may be part of the purpose of God that men be reminded, by his unknowing servants, just what his world is really like if men exclude him from it.

But it is not enough to describe the modern Assyrian as depicting a world that the Christian need not inhabit. For their *second* contribution can be that of forcing Christians to recast their complacent forms of faith. It may be that modern men cannot really come to mature faith today until they have gone through the depths of disbelief with Tennessee Williams or Albert Camus or (for all their overtones of gentleness) John Steinbeck and J. D. Salinger.

It may be that such men must be our guides in the contemporary *descensus ad infernos,* the descent into hell, which, in the hell the modern world has become, must be gone through if there is ever to be a resurrection. We are called upon to entertain their vision, to run the risk of standing with them, so that we may see everything they see (the bad along with the good) and receive no prior assurances that there is more to see than they describe for us. We can be sure that faith will not emerge unscathed from such a venture. But a faith fearful of attack is hardly a faith worth having, and better that it be demolished than that it fortify a world of illusion. Commenting on the artistic achievement of T. S. Eliot, Amos Wilder writes:

> Dante traverses all the circles of Hell to know what Paradise means, and this Hell was not a private one alone, but the inferno of a whole age and of many cities and courts. T. S. Eliot's great achievement rests on the fact that he has himself been initiated into the furies and stagnations of our age and its cities. (*Otherworldiness and the New Testament*, p. 31.)

An initiation into the "furies and stagnations of our age and its cities" is what is promised us by the modern Assyrians. Some, indeed, offer us much more, but if they do, it is only because they too have accepted that bitter initiation. Faith undergoes attack at the hand of the modern Assyrians, but the faith that enters the fray with openness and courage has the possibility of emerging a stronger faith, dignifying rather than debasing the name of faith. The Assyrian who forces us to this extremity can be God's instrument, and is God's instrument, whether he wills it or not. He must not be expected to carry us over the great gulf that separates belief from nonbelief. But he can take us to the brink of that gulf and show it to us. He may not be the bearer of grace, but he may at least be the preparer for it.

And who knows but what the one who prepares the way may also, in the mysterious providence of God, participate himself in that which is to come?

III
DISCOVERING
GOD'S PSEUDONYMS TODAY

1. EDUCATION

No Promise Without Agony: An Address to Educators

In the old days, the preacher spent most of his time telling good, decent people what a terrible state the world was in, and how they'd better hop to it before Satan got a stranglehold on the future. Both preacher and analyst could afford the luxury of announcing doom. But that's not news anymore. We do not need to be reminded that next year might be worse than last. Our most extravagant hope is simply that it will not be too much worse. Furthermore, no educator has to feel guilty any more that he has fled from the "real world" to the "ivory towers of the university." Everybody knows about the agony. We do not need a description of that. The real question is: Is there any promise? Can we believe in more than the agony?

I am going to suggest that if there is any promise for America, it will be only as we go through, and not try to circumvent, the agony. President Nixon, in a curiously contradictory metaphor in his inaugural address, said, "The American dream will not come to those who sleep." Somewhat intoxicated by that figure of speech, I respond that the American nightmare will be creatively appropriated only by those who are wide

Originally given as an address to the Twenty-fourth Annual Conference of the American Association for Higher Education, and published in G. Kerry Smith (ed.), *Agony and Promise: Current Issues in Higher Education* (Jossey-Bass, Inc., Publishers, 1969). Used by permission.

awake, and who can see from within it some pointers to hope. No promise, then, without agony.

Let me suggest some shifts of perspective through which we must go if we are to discover signs of promise in the midst of the agony, centering on the words *violence, power, materialism,* and *compassion,* and keeping two further prescriptive words up my sleeve for the conclusion.

1. From the Fear of Overt Violence to the Acknowledgment of Covert Violence

The first shift involves a deeper analysis than we usually make of the quality of contemporary life that scares us most. Our fear of overt violence must be countered by our acknowledgment of covert violence.

When I refer to "the fear of overt violence" I am pointing to something all too real to the middle-class white American. If he has not yet been the victim of violence, he fears that he soon will be. If he is on a campus, he fears a sit-in, maybe in his office, during which his files will be destroyed. If he is in a computer center, he fears what might be called a smash-in. If he is in a classroom, he fears a disruptive teach-in. If he is white, he is scared silly when he sees as many as three blacks with Afro hair styles, black jackets, and dark glasses, moving in his direction. When he hears angry rhetoric by members of any minority group, he is sure that the verbal overkill is just about to escalate into the unveiling of hitherto hidden knives, clubs, and guns.

And this is not just a white middle-class hang-up. The protesting student cannot but fear the stock-in-trade of his opposition—mace, billy clubs, and tear gas, used to put down what the student thinks are the legitimate concerns for which he is protesting—fearing the kind of treatment his fellow students got in Chicago, in August, 1968, or in Berkeley, in May, 1969. The black or the Puerto Rican or the Mexican-American has every reason to fear the violence that may be perpetrated against him if a cop or a white gang happens to catch him in a secluded spot.

But I suggest that we will not advance from agony to promise, until we recognize that such an analysis of violence is superficial. Our fear of overt violence must be countered by our acknowledgment of covert violence. By *covert violence* I mean something more subtle and destructive than physical violence, terrible as that is, and the common threat that links together the two kinds of violence I am describing is the denial of personhood. The violence manifested when Sirhan Sirhan squeezes the trigger, and the violence manifested when a white man denies a job to a black man, are finally cut from the same cloth. In each case, the perpetrator of the violence is saying, "You don't count. I will get you out of the way." When a city rezones its school districts to make sure the black students will not get into the good schools and thus "lower standards," that is covert violence. When landlords pile up tremendous profits from rat-infested slums, that is covert violence. When society gives a dole to minority members but will not restructure itself to provide jobs for them, that is covert violence. When we send an eighteen-year-old to jail for five years because he says, "I refuse to kill Vietnamese peasants," that is covert violence.

The report of the World Council of Churches Geneva Conference commented, "Violence is very much a reality in our world, both the overt use of force to suppress and the invisible violence (*violencia blanca*) perpetrated on people who by the millions have been or still are the victims of repression and unjust social systems . . . the violence which, though bloodless, condemns whole populations to perennial despair." That unfortunately describes America. We are not only committing overt violence in Vietnam, but we are committing covert violence in Oakland, Chicago, Memphis, Detroit, Seattle, Jackson, and Boston.

What has come to be called "institutional racism" is a particularly telling example of covert violence, illustrating that even though as individuals we may be very open and understanding and unbigoted, we participate in institutions whose very structures guarantee that they will perpetuate the things we think we are opposing. Individually as educators, we believe in a fair shake for all students, regardless of race, color, or creed, but our entrance examinations have tended to cater to middle-class, white, suburban Americans, so that *de facto* it has been exceedingly difficult for members of minority groups to gain admission by our "normal" standards. That is covert violence. In principle, we believe that military service should not exempt certain classes of people, and yet we condone a selective service system that *de facto* discriminates in favor of white middle-class kids who lived in good enough parts of town to get good enough high school educations to get into colleges, and whose parents can pay the tariff to keep them there, so that those who actually get drafted are more likely to be the disadvantaged who do not have enough education to get a II-S deferment that will enable them to dodge the draft for four years. That is covert violence.

Until we see the agony in such terms as these, we will be in no position even to begin to look toward any promise.

2. FROM THE ABUSE OF POWER TO THE CREATIVE USE OF POWER

Let nobody in this day and age try to argue that power per se is evil—or good. Power is what we make of it, and the choice is in our hands. And it is the abuse of power that has led not only to the overt, but also to the covert, violence we have been examining.

Why are students so turned off by the older generation? Surely a major reason is their feeling that we of the older generation have engaged in a monstrous abuse of power. Without turning this talk into a panegyric against the American presence in Vietnam, let me use that simply as the most glaring example of the point, since it is the event most responsible, I

believe, for the great disaffection the young presently feel for
the old (and for "old" read "anyone over twenty-six," which is
when you become nondraftable). How does the student view
our presence in Vietnam? He sees the most powerful nation on
earth using overwhelming force to pummel one of the tiniest
nations on earth. He sees incredible technological resources
being used almost solely for destruction—pellet bombs timed
to go off sporadically and destroy civilians, napalm melting
the flesh indiscriminately of young and old alike, biological in-
genuity being used to defoliate tens of thousands of acres of
verdant jungle, half a million men being deployed eleven
thousand miles (40 percent of whom have been injured),
more explosives being used in a single day than were used in
the entire North African campaign of World War II, political
and economic and military resources being used to shore up
an oppressive dictatorial regime in Saigon, the verbal overkill
of the President and Vice-President being used to justify it all
in the name of "moral commitments"—the student sees all this
and he cannot help thinking, "Here is power, all right, and it is
power that is being terribly abused."

And then he looks back over the last half decade and asks,
"Who was opposing all this? Were the Catholic bishops? Or
the Protestant preachers? Or the businessmen? Or the congressmen? Or the trade unions? Or the educators?" And after
citing the few brilliant exceptions—the Bishop Shannons, the
William Sloane Coffins, the Eugene McCarthys, and the William Fulbrights—he has to say that the older generation has
not been opposing all this. And the student verdict, justifiably,
has become: America has abused its power, and become so intoxicated by the exercise of it that America has lost all sense of
proportion and moral value.

The answer is not to disavow power, though some, students
included, tend at least temporarily to think so. But "flower
power" will not feed starving peoples. No, the answer is to
move from the abuse of power to the creative use of power.
To some, such talk may sound utopian, but wearing both of

my hats—that of educator and that of clergyman—I respond
that if between them the universities and the churches and
synagogues cannot begin to work toward the creative use of
power, we might as well throw in the sponge.

What would this involve? It would involve setting some
new priorities, saying in effect: Very well, we *do* have the
most power in the world. How are we going to use it? It
would involve recognizing that the most important use of
power in which we could engage would be the sharing of it.
Suppose that instead of using our foreign aid to shore up corrupt dictators in Southeast Asia and South America and the
Caribbean, we were to use our resources to help the economies of younger nations get on their feet? Suppose we took seriously the very minimal goal that the Pontifical Commission
for Justice and Peace, and the World Council of Churches,
have recommended—the contribution of 1 percent of our
gross national product to an international monetary fund, the
resultant pool to be available to developing nations for use in
making their own economies more self-sufficient? Suppose we
did that? We would at least be making the first beginning
steps toward using power responsibly and creatively. Suppose
that instead of spending eighty-seven billion dollars a year on
the military budget, and thirty billion dollars a year on Vietnam alone, we rethought our sense of priorities and realized
how grotesque it sounds to the black man when in the face of
those expenditures we tell him that we cannot find six billion
dollars a year to implement the Kerner Commission Report?
When our own increase in gross national product in one year
is more in dollars than the total budgets of all the countries of
South America combined, do we have any right to expect the
South Americans to look at us in any but the most distrustful
terms? Is it a creative use of power to be spending billions of
dollars on moon shots and space exploration of other planets—
exciting though those may be—when on this particular planet
two thirds of the peoples of the world will go to bed hungry
this very night?

And I submit to you that if educators and churchmen are not willing to dedicate the finest hours of their lives to emphasizing the incredible reallocation of priorities that is called for by our present abuse of power, we have no reason to believe that anything less than holocaust and revolution will result. We either shift from the abuse of power to the creative use of power, or we face Armageddon—and possibly in our own lifetimes.

3. From Misplaced Materialism to Transformed Materialism

It is a cliché both political and clerical that we have lost our sense of "eternal values" and that we must "recover the spiritual." I have nothing against eternal values, but my point just now is that they are expressed in and through the material. Thus if somebody talks about "the eternal value of the human soul," I want to remind him that in both Judaism and Christianity, persons are not viewed as having eternal souls and transitory bodies, but as possessing a kind of psychosomatic unity of body and soul, indivisible. This means that if you talk about a human being as having eternal or infinite worth, you are cheating on the evidence unless you are just as concerned with whether he has enough to eat as you are with whether he has experienced a presence that disturbs him with the joy of elevated thoughts. We have no right to be more concerned with a person's soul than we are with whether or not he has soles on his shoes. Our neighbors' material concerns, if we may so put it, are our religious obligation.

And for reasons hard to fathom, an incredible proportion of the material goods of this world has been entrusted to the United States of America. For the first time in the history of the world, we now have the technological know-how to see to it that nobody in the world needs to starve or be cold. For the first time in history! And if you want a job as an educator, if you want a challenge, look for ways to put all that information and

technique to work. Let us train scientists who will increase our
technological expertise to grow food and thus get greater pro-
ductivity per acre; let us train economists who will find better
ways to make capital available to underdeveloped nations; let
us train political scientists who will help to develop regional
economic and political alliances to increase trade within the
Third World and between the Third World and us; let us
train teachers who will instill the vision of the one family of
man in our young; let us train politicians who will lead us
rather than simply follow where the latest poll suggests the
rank and file want to go. Let us do these things so that, as the
richest nation on earth, we can shift from a misplaced materialism, dedicated to providing luxury items we do not need
(complete with built-in obsolescence), into a transformed materialism dedicated to the task of sharing the goods of this
earth with the two thirds of the world that is ill-fed,
ill-housed, ill-clothed, so that such clichés remain clichés no
longer, but merely epitaphs of a world we refused to accept
and were determined to transform.

4. FROM ACADEMIC DETACHMENT
TO MORAL COMPASSION

In the light of such needs, it is high time that, self-
consciously and determinedly, we address ourselves to the
question, "Education for what?" and indeed "Education for
whom?" and that we take careful stock of the ends to which
our knowledge is being put. I take my cue for the moment not
from the humanists and theologians but from the scientists.
On Tuesday, March 4, 1969, scientists participated in a Day of
Concern. By the hundreds, they left their classrooms, laborato-
ries, and field assignments to ask the question, "For what and
for whom are we doing this work?" They were rightly disturbed that biologists are being paid by the Government to do
research in germ warfare, that physicists are hired to provide
us with more efficient antiballistic missile systems, that money

that could be going into cancer research is being diverted into poison gas research, that medical expertise that could be ministering to a ghetto is being hired to research more hideous forms of napalm. They were saying, "It is time we took a long, hard look at what society is telling us to do with our knowledge."

I hope their example will force the rest of us to take a similar look at what we are doing with our knowledge. There is a moral question to be asked of political scientists who devote their energies to devising new methods of counterinsurgency, when those methods will be used to stifle peoples' revolutions against tyrannical regimes. There is a moral question to be asked of educators who promote a school system in which students come to believe that the right of dissent must be stifled when it goes against the *status quo.*

Do not misunderstand me. I am not making the specious plea for "instant relevance," which says that I need not complete a book if it does not immediately turn me on, or says that history is a waste of time because only the twentieth century is important, or claims that every experiment, every discussion, every lecture, must equip me instantly to go outside the classroom or the laboratory and cope. Rather, I am pleading for the breadth of vision that can enable us to see that any study of any significant body of material will make us more usefully equipped citizens to cope with a world that continues to multiply problems even as we study. It is particularly true in our day that those who ignore history are doomed to repeat it. I am pleading for study that is infused with moral compassion—and I remind you that that word *compassion* means "to suffer with," to be alongside the other, in his misery as well as in his joy, in his terror as well as in his triumphs, in his agony as well as in his promise. Let us not be embarrassed by this concern; let us rather see the nobility of it, and realize that it is the sense of compassion that makes us human, that makes us brothers, that separates us from the animals and from the machines.

All well and good, but how do we get from here to there? Let me suggest two qualities that could help us in that transition.

The *first* of these qualities is conveyed by the Greek word *metanoia*. This means an about-face, a turning in an opposite direction, or, as theology has translated the word, a conversion. Do not be turned off by the word, I beg you. For nothing less drastic will suffice. It will simply not do to say to rich, contented, and unconcerned Americans, "Just go on being more of the same." No, what is called for is a change of direction, a fresh start. It means, "Take a fresh look at *violence*. You are so afraid somebody will beat you up that you don't realize that you are beating people up all the time." It means, "Take a fresh look at *power*. If you continue using it so destructively it will destroy you as well." It means, "Take a fresh look at *materialism*. As long as you keep goods only for yourself you build up a head of steam that will soon explode and destroy us all." It means, "Take a fresh look at *education*. You are so busy describing life that you are stifling peoples' power to live." And at this point at least, we could afford to take a leaf from Karl Marx, appropriate his final thesis on Feuerbach, and see it as an indictment of ourselves: "Philosophers [for which now let us read 'educators'] have interpreted the world in various ways; the point, however, is to change it."

To all of this, the plea for *metanoia* means, "You are on the wrong track, or at least you are going the wrong way, a way that leads only to mounting agony. You may be fooling yourself, America, but you are fooling nobody else. The rest of the world sees through your rhetoric, your self-justifying talk, your cloaking of your own vested interests in the name of pious double-talk."

Can education demand conversion or force it? Of course not. But what education *can* do is to force people to confront choices, to point out the consequences of given courses of action, so that a decision can be made to turn about, to begin again, to make a fresh start, to undergo (and I do not apolo-

gize for the phrase) a conversion experience. Will we learn
from Vietnam that backing a dictator is no way to liberate a
people, and that destroying a city is no way to save it, so that
we do not make the same mistakes in Latin America? Only as
we become wiser than we were before Vietnam. Will we learn
from the escalating race riots in this country that white people
cannot indefinitely coerce and maim and destroy black people
without a day of reckoning finally coming? Only as the lessons
of Watts, Detroit, Newark, and a dozen other brutal realities
are learned more quickly than we have learned our lessons in
the past. Can we move from agony to promise? Only by measuring the agony full scale, with no illusions and no sentimentalities, and then committing ourselves to a new direction,
again with no illusions and no sentimentalities, recognizing
that we undertake great risks, but that they are risks infinitely
worth taking, for they commit us not to narrow nationalism,
but turn us about to the whole family of man.

And where do we find the vision and power to do that?
Here I suggest a *second* quality. Let me sneak up on it by
suggesting that perhaps the opposite of agony is not promise,
but (as the title of Irving Stone's biography of Michelangelo
suggests) ecstasy. Ecstasy is a situation in which one is in *ex-
stasis,* or "standing outside oneself." That is to say, it is the situation of having perspective on oneself, of seeing oneself in
relation to whatever is beyond oneself. It is the quality—to
employ another theological word—of transcendence. By this I
am not insisting upon the image of a Great Big Being off
somewhere in the sky, and I immediately remind you that
Herbert Marcuse, whom nobody is about to accuse of being a
theologian, can use the word to describe engaging in what he
calls "the great refusal," the unwillingness to accept things
simply as they are, the repudiation of one-dimensionality, the
recognition that we make a judgment about the present in
terms of something that is not in and of the present.

Perhaps this could be described simply by saying that we
are called upon to have a sense of humor about ourselves, to

apply to ourselves the reminder Kierkegaard wished he could
have suggested to Hegel, namely the comic fact that he who
thought himself the infinite surveyor of all that is, had occasionally to turn aside from his manuscript to sneeze. The thing
that most frightens me about the New Left, or the radical
right, is not that they threaten middle-class values. Middle-
class values need to be threatened. What frightens me about
them is the absolute humorlessness of their crusade. There is
something terrifying about the crusader who is never for a
moment aware of his own shortcomings, the partiality of his
insights, the finitudes of his being, the actual narrowness of his
angle of vision—for he has no resources to guard him against
the fanaticism of taking himself with such utmost seriousness
that it would be beyond his capacity to admit that in any particular instance he had been wrong. This ability to laugh at
ourselves, to see something slightly comic in our pretensions,
is a blessed gift, for it is an acknowledgment of some standard
of judgment or value, beyond ourselves, in the light of which
we can cut ourselves down to size.

And when we can do that, then we can experience *metanoia*, turning about, conversion. People describe this over-
againstness, this "other" that judges them, in many ways. I am
not saying you have to be a Christian or a Jew to experience
it, though I have found that in my case it helps. But I am
saying that this sense is what makes one a human being—a
person—and that only because of it, only because we feel confronted by it, can we know either agony or promise—or
ecstasy.

"Those Revolting Students"

The way a reader inflects the word "revolting students" will indicate his underlying attitude toward present-day undergraduates. If his instinctive reflex is verbal ("Today's students are revolting against society"), he may or may not have a high regard for them; but at least he recognizes that they are doing something. If the reflex is adjectival ("How revolting those students are!"), then he has clearly made a value judgment, and a negative one at that.

Many people share a sense of revulsion at what is happening on the campuses. The words "Berkeley" and "sit-in" are likely to render the middle-aged apoplectic. It is not hard to find four-square Americans who feel that the solution to such campus unrest is simple: "Kick out the commies, kooks, and perverts." Dr. Max Rafferty, formerly the highest official in the California educational system, describes an education at Berkeley as "a four year course in sex, drugs and treason."

As one who teaches on a campus that has its fair share of "revolting students" (and I opt for the verbal rather than the adjectival reflex), and who has talked to some, listened to more, and read a fair number of pages both by and about them, I cannot help feeling that the new breed has hardly

Originally published in *Presbyterian Life*, Nov. 15, 1966, and subsequently printed in *Church and Home, The Episcopalian, The Lutheran, Presbyterian Survey, Together,* and *United Church Herald.* Used by permission.

gotten a fair hearing in the mass media. These students are saying some things to which the rest of us need to listen; and we are not entitled to cover our ears simply because we object to the stridency of an occasional voice or the length of an occasional beard.

What, then, is their word to us? Why is there such a widespread attitude of revolt on the part of today's students? Let us examine the dissatisfactions, the remedies, the motivations, and the problems.

THE DISSATISFACTIONS

1. One big gripe surely centers around the theme of *depersonalization*. The IBM card is a symbol of what disturbs students in our culture. "I am a person," a placard at a student rally will often read, "do not fold, spindle, or mutilate me." And they feel that the university fosters rather than diminishes depersonalization. Part of this is because of the sheer size of so many institutions of higher learning. Clark Kerr, president of the University of California, coined the term "multiversity" long before the outbursts began. Classes today are too large and the term "mass education" is just that—education of masses rather than persons. The university is an assembly-line factory in which a student (reduced to a number) is processed through a diploma mill, seldom meeting faculty, and all too frequently knowing the top professors only by hearing their lectures over closed-circuit television.

If it isn't that bad everywhere (and it isn't), that is nevertheless the direction in which the revolting student sees the university moving. It can only get bigger and more impersonal, and nobody seems to be doing anything about it. So he protests. Let it be added that he protests rightly. It is wrong for education to move in this direction, and if nobody else is crying "Stop!" more power to the student when he does so.

The new concern could be symbolized by asking the question, "Where is the center of the university?" In the medieval university, the answer was clear: the center was the chapel, a fact emphasized both in the architecture and the curriculum. Somewhere along the way, the center shifted to the classroom, in which the professor imparted (paternalistically) the insights of his research. A case could be made for saying that the center of the university is now the library, for the invention of movable type has rendered the lecture method outmoded, even if the lecturers have not yet caught up with the ugly truth.

But it would not be accurate to say that for the revolting student the center of the university is any of these things. The new center might be symbolized by the student's place of residence—not necessarily a campus dormitory, since these tend to be rejected as impersonal and confining. The new center is a place for talk, discussion, informality, and exchange of ideas; where hypocrisy can be disavowed, and in which a connection can be made between thought and action, from which the student might go to a lecture but might also go to tutor a ghetto child, and from which either activity would be equally appropriate.

2. The protest is lodged against the university, because that is where the student is. But the protest is more deeply lodged than that. The protest is actually against the *whole of contemporary society*. The Byrne Report to the Regents of the University of California grasped this fact succinctly: "We conclude that the basic cause of unrest on the Berkeley campus was the dissatisfaction of a large number of students with many features of the society they were about to enter." The university is seen as a microcosm of the whole culture, a culture characterized by impersonality in business, in living arrangements, even in social life, a culture in which nobody dares to be himself and everybody wears a mask for fear he may be found deviating at some point from timid conformity.

The revolting student rejects this whole conception of life as phony. Part, indeed, of the adult restiveness in the face of student revolt is surely based on the disturbing accuracy with

which the younger generation has unmasked the pretentious-
ness and insecurity of the older. The indictment against the
older generation goes: "You set off the atomic bomb. You were
complacent until Dachau. Your Depression wasn't so great.
You got trapped in Korea. Now, you want to threaten my life
in some place like Vietnam. You assassinated Kennedy and
gave me in his place a professional politician from Texas. Your
generation has failed us and yourselves utterly" (in Katope
and Zollrod, eds., *Beyond Berkeley*, p. 233). Here is part of
the reason for the campus slogan, "Never trust anyone over
thirty."

This disillusionment cannot be understood apart from a
word often on the lips of undergraduates: Vietnam. Virtually
all the revolting students place Vietnam high on the list of
what is wrong with the Great Society. They are unimpressed
by White House propaganda, disenchanted with the President, shocked by napalm, and unwilling, many of them, to
serve in a war that seems to them morally indefensible. In
1964, most of them worked for Johnson's election (or at least
against Goldwater's election), and they then found the President doing in Vietnam precisely what he promised them
during the campaign he would not do. Next time around they
wanted a peace candidate and got Nixon, whom they see as a
rerun of the Johnson duplicity. So they doubt the sincerity
and even the integrity of the decision makers. The "Pentagon
Papers" do not surprise them, but merely confirm their suspi-
cions. They are therefore the more upset when they discover
how much of a university budget is supplied by Government
funds that support research related to the military, and how
silently the university establishment appears to acquiesce in
being "used" by what they feel is an immoral national policy.

So the wheel comes full circle. The university is a part of
the Establishment the student rejects. He sees too many
trustees and administrators and faculty members working
hand in glove with a society dedicated to human destruction
and the denial of the meaning of personhood. Or, at the other

end of the spectrum, the student sees the university training him to be an uncomplaining middle-class person, adjusted to all the proper middle-class mores, doing nothing to jar the well-oiled machinery called the Great Society. He sees his father caught in society's rat race, and he wants no part of it: "So you win the rat race. You're still a rat."

3. The student also feels that the university has adopted *an ambivalent and inconsistent attitude* toward him. On the one hand, the university tells him that he is mature enough to discuss all ideas in the classroom; on the other hand, the university tells him he is not mature enough to order his own social life, and fights a rearguard battle for "social regulations." On the one hand, the university urges him to think for himself and arrive at his own conclusions; on the other hand, if the student thinks his way through to a negative assessment of our Vietnam policy, or opposes some generally accepted pattern of moral behavior, he is likely to find himself in trouble with the trustees. On the one hand, the university tells him that he is bright, and that he must make a responsible contribution to society; on the other hand, when he tries to improve the society of which he is presently a part, namely the university, he finds himself reproved for his audacity. To press the latter point: on the one hand, the university tells him that the decision-making process is a precious part of the democratic heritage; on the other hand, it excludes him from any significant role in the decision-making process of the university, save for a relatively powerless student government system or token membership on committees.

So goes the complaint. Overstated? Perhaps. But not so overstated that it can be ignored. For there is an uncomfortably large dose of truth behind each item on the complaint sheet, focusing on the last point. The revolting student feels that as a part of the university, he should have some share in the decisions the university makes, particularly since the decisions are bound to affect him. He wants to share in making the decisions that determine his future.

4. This suggests another note to the protest, the note of *impatience*. A given student has only four years. He is not willing to wait five years for gradual change in the direction of curriculum reform—a pace that would strike most administration officials or faculty committees as breathtakingly rapid. Just as the black does not want his dignity to be a reality only in the next century, and cries "Freedom *now!*"—so the student does not want the university to become what it ought to be only when his grandchildren matriculate. He wants a true community of learning, and he wants it now. He wants curriculum reform that will liberate him from dull courses and foolish requirements. He wants to become acquainted with his professors before his twenty-fifth reunion. He wants to be treated as a person rather than a number during the current semester, and not only when he has acquired the means to endow a new physics building.

THE REMEDIES

So what does the revolting student propose, and how does he expect to achieve his ends? As Martin Meyerson said, in reviewing the events at Berkeley, "The protesting students are more sophisticated in their condemnations than in their proposals." To indicate that this is not merely the jaundiced view of one over thirty, a letter from a group of undergraduates, seeking radical change in the university, can be cited: "What kind of activities do we envisage? To be frank, at this point our intentions outstrip a clear understanding of how best to achieve them. One of the greatest problems we have with planning is that we do not believe there should be too much of it—at least, not beforehand."

This refreshing candor illustrates the mentality of much of the revolt. The students feel that they have been the victims of overplanning. They want education to be a little more *ad hoc,* to play it by ear, to let a structure evolve from new relationships that will develop when impersonality has been rooted out, rather than to impose a structure in advance that will depersonalize those who submit to it.

Certainly the dominant concern is with the importance— one could even say the sanctity—of the person. If present structures don't enhance that, so much the worse for the structures. Some students live in open disdain of the present structures, but have a resigned willingness to try to bend them a bit. A few, the ones who get the headlines, have given up on the structures as archaic beyond hope of redemption, and are ready, in the words of Mario Savio during the earliest Berkeley difficulties, to do whatever is necessary "to bring the university to a grinding halt." Others have decided to experiment with parallel structures. Staying within the university, they are trying to create experimental courses, in which the goals they desire—small classes, give-and-take, informality, less rigidity, relevant subject matter—can create an atmosphere in which true learning will proceed, and provide the type of education they feel the university is not now providing for them.

Although some revolting students have given up, a great many really do believe that things can be changed. What gives them the feeling that change can be brought about, even in so recalcitrant a body as a university community? The reason for the early optimism, at least, is clear. It was founded in the remarkable success in the middle 1960's of the civil rights movement, however much that movement may now have lost its initial momentum. Many of the early revolting students had had active involvement in the civil rights movement and were determined to apply that experience back on the campus. As the movement developed, the early emphasis on nonviolence gave way to a willingness to engage in violence for certain ends and this has widely divided the ranks of student leaders.

When the elders protest such pressures, the students reply that if injustice exists (as they are sure it does in their case), they have the right, indeed the moral right, for a redress of grievances, and if they are not listened to, to move to stronger measures. The university is entitled to expel students who break its rules, and it sometimes does. But it must be said that the results of student pressure—however much some may deplore it—have in fact often brought confrontations between students and administration that have sometimes led to change. A great deal depends on whether an administration can see through angry rhetoric to justified demands for change, or whether it remains defensively "up tight" at the least sign of trouble. Most administrators would rather solve problems around a conference table than have to request local police to remove students forcibly from the university administration building.

THE MOTIVATIONS

Why do the revolting students occasionally go to such extremes? What are their motivations? It is not sufficient to write them off as "commies, kooks, and perverts." The Rafferty analysis is doomed from the start. Indeed, I cannot discern any clear ideological center to the movement, Marxist, anarchist, or otherwise. Many of the students are confused and not all are involved from similar motivations. There are surely some for whom marching in protest against Vietnam has been a convenient way of kicking the old man in the teeth. But for others, the motivation has been a high commitment and idealism, an almost desperate assertion that society need not remain the way it always has been. It is these same students, it must be remembered, who initially responded in droves to the idealism of the Peace Corps.

Pervading the whole, it seems to me, is a high degree of idealism mixed with impatience at the lethargic rate of society's adjustment to the revolution of our time.

To see the point, one must compare the students of the late '60s with the students of the early '50s. The latter were the "silent generation," the students who wanted to play it safe. They lived in the era when "speaking out," or espousing causes, meant trouble with Congressman Velde or Senator Joseph McCarthy. It meant getting one's name on the wrong list in Washington, or being labeled "too controversial" to be a good employment risk. By contrast, the emancipation of university students from that kind of cowering conformity is to be understood not as a sign of moral degeneration, but of moral health.

Education, after all, has left its mark. A truly educated person must be a dissatisfied person. If he has been exposed to enough of the greatness of the past and the possibilities of the future, he must remain permanently dissatisfied with the present. His vision may have come from the Old Testament prophets, or from the moral passion of Albert Camus, or from that social critic least honored in America, Karl Marx. He may have learned of the true, the good, and the beautiful from Greek philosophy, or of sin and grace from Paul and Augustine. But wherever he has gotten it, such exposure cannot help but give the student a perspective in terms of which he must endure a state of permanent dissatisfaction. And the task of the university is not to keep such a student separated from the world, but to enable him to involve himself more responsibly in it. The real cause for worry is not student action but student apathy.

THE PROBLEMS

But new problems ride into history on the back of every advance. What are the problems the revolting student faces?

One criticism has already been implied. It is clear that students oppose depersonalization, and it is clear that they want a new respect for the person as person. But it is not nearly as clear how they propose to get it. They disdain structures without realizing that, particularly when large numbers of people are involved, structures can enhance personal freedom as well as destroy it. The alternative to bad structures is not lack of structure but better structures, structures that are designed to maximize the creative interplay of freedom and order.

In coping with this problem, there is a danger that the idealism of the revolting student may turn sour. By next spring some of the dreams of last fall will have turned out to be impractical, if not impossible. Leaders in experimental courses will have found that objectives must be more clearly defined, that in the process of such definition clashes of opinion will emerge, that factions and cliques will develop, that programs will have to be scaled down to fit existing financial resources, that not every student will be highly motivated to work without being graded. In short, most of the traditional problems of the traditional university, having been shoved out the front door, will unhappily and inevitably reenter from the rear. And while some will be impelled to work harder to resist the old patterns, others will become disillusioned. A precursor of such disillusionment is the ease with which revolting students cry "sellout" when someone in the midst of a crisis suggests a modification of tactics or a scaling down of immediate demands.

Another problem centers on the students' vision of the university. Their cry goes, "The university belongs to the students." However true this may be, it is only part of the truth. The students are not the whole of the university. One can imagine the uproar on the part of the students if any other segment within the university made such a sweeping claim, viz.: "The university belongs to the faculty." The university is not only a place students inhabit, but a place where research is conducted, where writing is done, where scholarly resources are collected, even when undergraduates are not on the scene. The university, furthermore, is responsible to future students as well as present ones, and it is not self-evident that those who inhabit the university for a four-year period should write all the ground rules that may have as much as a twenty-year series of implications.

Coupled with this less-than-total vision of a university is a tendency to downgrade those dimensions of education that are not strictly in the realm of interpersonal relations. The university is more than one vast experience in sensitivity training, and education is more than human exchange of points of view "in depth." There is a content, a subject matter, to master, and some of it has to be gotten from methods as old-fashioned as reading books and engaging from time to time in writing down, on pieces of paper, in sequential fashion, and by a certain date, one's thoughts about a subject, either in the form of a blue book or a term paper. If one wrote a paper only when he felt like it, it is a safe guess that not many papers would get written. This does not mean that writing papers is the goal of the educated man, but it does mean that certain disciplines (of which writing papers is one) are essential to some kinds of ordering of one's mind, however passionately the revolting student may demean them.

In recent times student revolt has come up against the ancient problem of the relationship of ends and means. In search of ends that enhance personhood, students have sometimes been willing to use means that violate personhood. The escalation of violence on campus is the best example. There is a certain inconsistency in claiming to be against violence abroad while engaging in violence at home. And there is no clear line between violence-against-property and violence-against-persons. In a recent case of arson at Stanford, a fire was started at two A.M. so that no persons would be harmed. But the fire destroyed twenty years of research of a visiting professor from India, thus doing irreparable violence to the personhood of that professor. The widespread "trashing" on campuses after the United States invasion of Cambodia in the spring of 1970 made the nation aware of student revulsion at Mr. Nixon's action. But it also turned off many other students, who did not find throwing rocks through the nearest available window a very creative way either to mobilize support or to counter what they considered a grossly immoral action by the Administration in Washington. Thus there have been significant attempts to find new means of lodging protests. But the means will remain creative only if those with power listen and respond creatively.

There is another side to student revolt that has received insufficient attention above, although it has gotten inordinate attention in the public press. This is the revolution in personal mores and ethical choices. The concern of the student not to conform to a middle-class image of what society expects him to be leads to the beards, the long hair, or the sandals—which, after all, are extraordinarily harmless ways of revolting. But in the search for self, and in revolt against the moral codes of the society they reject, some students go much farther. In the name of freedom, they experiment with drugs, particularly marijuana and LSD, and insist that their sexual activities are their own business and nobody else's.

There is a danger here. It is the danger, not to be scorned by those who express devotion to personhood, that people will be badly hurt. LSD can enslave and destroy as well as occasionally liberate. Promiscuous sex can do immense psychic harm, and the presumably casual liaison may have far-reaching and damaging effects beyond what can be anticipated at the time. There is, in other words, an unrecognized inconsistency in the attitude of many revolting students. They risk irreparable harm, not just to themselves but their friends, in areas of experimentation that are too dangerous to be treated lightly and cavalierly. Furthermore, the increasing preoccupation among a segment of the revolting students with drugs and sex can actually be an expression of a withdrawal from the problems and pressures of society by retreat into a private and presumably more easily managed world that turns out, in fact, to be very public and not so easily managed after all.

These are all areas, then, in which the revolting students will need to do more thinking. But the conclusions they reach will have to be their own rather than those of their elders. After all, we're over thirty.

2. POLITICS

The Faces of Patriotism

A Los Angeles businessman protests the use of a certain textbook in a high school American history course, because it contains "controversial" opinions. He concludes his plea with the words, "It just confuses our young people today to be exposed to both sides of a question."

A prominent theologian warns that we must not assume that God is automatically on our side in the cold war, and reminds us that much of the appeal of Communism has sprung from the indifference of Western nations to those in need. A South Carolina newspaper calls this a "coward's religion," and replies that of course God is on our side, while a columnist for a national weekly attacks "downgrading ourselves" and asserts that we must "upgrade" ourselves instead.

School children find themselves being exposed to the famous oath of Stephen Decatur, "Our country! . . . may she always be in the right; but our country, right or wrong!" and urged to emulate the attitude.

A pastor in a western city says that we are too concerned about ourselves, and that we should be sending more money, materials, and personnel to underdeveloped areas of the world. The local paper accuses him of being "communist-inspired"; his children are hooted off the school yards as "un-American"; and his wife receives abusive phone calls whenever he is out of the house. It is still an open question whether his church board will support him or ask for his resignation.

Incidents like these are not hard to come by. They could be multiplied a hundred times over. The papers are full of them. And there is a common thread running through such incidents and holding them together despite their apparent diversity. The common thread is an attitude that goes something like this: America is right. America is God's nation. To criticize America is unpatriotic and un-Christian. The good citizen doesn't criticize his country. Rather, he defends it against all attacks, whether military or verbal.

A group of displaced persons, still catching their breath after their flight from a totalitarian and despotic government, huddle near a mountain in a desert. The word comes to them from the one they are called to serve, "You shall have no other gods before me."

Another group of people, living under a regime of far-reaching power and state control, a tiny minority in the midst of those who do not share its beliefs, gathers once a week and utters a simple and apparently innocuous affirmation, a two-word creed that goes, "Kurios Christos," meaning "Christ is Lord."

A third group, living in a country just taken over by a new political party whose members wear swastika armbands, meets in a church synod at Barmen, and in the face of the new political threats, declares to the world, "Jesus Christ, as He is attested to us in Holy Scripture, is

*the one Word of God, whom we have to hear and whom
we have to trust and obey in life and in death."*

Incidents like these—of the Hebrews returning to Israel,
and Christians living under the Roman Empire and the Nazis
—are a little harder to come by. But with diligent searching
they too could be multiplied a hundred times over, even
though the papers are not full of them.

What do the two sets of incidents have in common? At first
sight, apparently nothing. The first incidents seem to have all
sorts of political overtones, while the second seem to be devoid of any political consequences at all. The first incidents
occurred in a democracy, the second in areas under totalitarian rule.

But perhaps all these incidents speak to a common problem
more clearly than seems apparent on the surface. Are the latter incidents really as "nonpolitical" as they appear to be?
They deserve more careful scrutiny.

The people huddled in the shadow of Mt. Sinai were not
being given lofty and irrelevant advice. For the commandment "You shall have no other gods before me" is at least as
down-to-earth and relevant as the commandment "You shall
not steal," or "You shall not commit adultery." It exposes what
was the constant temptation of Israel, and what has been the
constant temptation of people ever since—the temptation to
worship gods other than the one true God, to worship idols or
deities of their own creation. This means that the alternative
to the worship of the living God is not, as we usually assume,
the temptation to atheism, but rather to idolatry.

And the truth contained in that observation is not limited to
wandering Israelites at the foot of Sinai. Today, for example,
Communism is to be feared not because it is so atheistic, but
precisely because it is so "religious," because it makes such a
total demand upon the individual, because it demands total
commitment from him, a total giving of the self to the cause,
in response to the invitation, "Sell all that thou hast, and give

to the poor, and come, follow the dialectic." If the Gospel according to Mark demands total allegiance to God, the gospel according to Marx likewise demands total allegiance to another god, the god of the party, the god of the system.

So there are gods many and lords many. Our problem is not atheism but polytheism, that is to say, not that there is no God but that there are too many gods. The temptation to "follow the dialectic" may not entice many Americans today, but other temptations do entice us. If we do not serve this god, we are serving some other god. It may be the God of Sinai—or Calvary—but it may also be the god of successful suburban living, or the god known today as The Organization, or the god (at whose demands we must presently look) of Americanism and superpatriotism.

Turn to the group whose creed was *"Kurios Christos."* These people derisively called "Christians," who met in the first-century Roman Empire, were more political than their simple formula of commitment might suggest. For they lived in a world where everyone was required to assert, once a year, *"Kurios Caesar,"* meaning "Caesar, the state, is lord." Ultimate allegiance, in other words, had to be given to the state, and the state could tolerate no higher allegiance given elsewhere. So when the Christians said *"Kurios Christos,"* they were not only saying "Christ is Lord," they were also saying, "The state is *not* lord." They were affirming a higher loyalty than their loyalty to the state. They were saying in the new Christian context what their Jewish forebears had said at Sinai, "We will have no other gods before God." This got them into considerable difficulty, from which difficulty the hungry lions in the Roman arena were the chief beneficiaries.

The German churchmen, meeting together at Barmen in the shadow of Hitler's rise to power, appeared to be ducking the political issue and making an innocuous and irrelevant theological statement. Was that the best they could manage in the face of the Nazi menace?

It was, in fact, the very best thing they could possibly have said. For when they asserted that "Jesus Christ . . . is the one Word of God, whom we have to hear and whom we have to trust and obey in life and in death," they too were saying that no one else, nothing else, could usurp the place of that one Word of God, and claim an allegiance more binding than allegiance to Him.

"We condemn the false doctrine," they went on, "that the church can and must recognize as God's revelation other events and powers." The implication was clear: Since Jesus Christ is the one Word of God, "other events and powers" such as Nazism, anti-semitism, allegiance to Hitler, must be repudiated. This got them into considerable difficulty, too, and many who started talking this way at Barmen stopped talking at Buchenwald, paying with their lives for their refusal to bend the knee to the new idols.

"But even if the second set of incidents *is* more political than appears on the surface," the complaint would run, "What has all this got to do with America? These incidents all took place in totalitarian countries where the proper thing was to oppose the regime in power. That kind of attitude would be unpatriotic and subversive in a democracy like the United States."

Is the complaint a proper one? Is it unpatriotic to be critical of one's country? Does it undermine democracy to raise questions about how adequately it is working in a given place? Surely the answer to these questions must be "No." It is *not* unpatriotic to be critical of one's country; this is rather the true and proper kind of patriotism. It does *not* undermine democracy to call attention to places where it needs to be improved; this is the only true way to strengthen it. The very fact that some people would question the legitimacy of the two previous sentences is a sure indication that they need to be said loudly and with increasing frequency today. For the lifeblood of a true democracy lies in the right of dissent, the privilege of the public forum, the inherent correctness of questions to those holding power. If these things are denied, then in principle the totalitarian mentality has already conquered. For it is the essence of the totalitarian mentality precisely to deny to its members the right of dissent, the privilege of the public forum, the inherent correctness of questions to those holding power.

And it can always "happen here." It is a curious fact about the present American scene that those who must blatantly shout about their "Americanism" are precisely those most determined to deny the right of dissent to those who disagree with them. They believe in the right of dissent for themselves, but not for those who disagree with them. In the name of "patriotism," another word they abuse, they insist that all Americans must think alike, namely the way *they* do, for their point of view is (*a*) American, (*b*) right, and (*c*) Christian. This means that anyone disagreeing with them is (*a*) un-American, (*b*) wrong, and (*c*) un-Christian. Q.E.D.

Now this type of mentality does not just threaten the outermost political processes; it also threatens the innermost souls of men. For it is nothing but the most current form of idolatry, the worship of a false god, the same idolatry that was condemned at Sinai, in the first-century Roman Empire, and at Barmen. It is an attitude that says, against Sinai, "You *shall* have another god before the living God, the god of our ideology." It says, against the first-century Christians, "Our point of view, our way of conceiving what is good for men, is lord, and claims our absolute allegiance. Let no one disagree." It says, against Barmen, that "other events and powers"—namely, *our* reading of events, our program—are the "one Word of God" who must be obeyed in life and in death.

This is not an extreme or melodramatic way of putting it. This is merely the logic of the position when held up for examination. And what it means is that uncritical patriotism is no true patriotism at all. It is no service to one's country to hide its faults as the only way of extolling its virtues. And it is no true service to God, to identify him and his will with one nation, and assert that anyone who has reservations about making the nation an idol is unpatriotic. The true patriot will recognize that to say "This nation under God" is not to say something bland and comforting, but to say something revolutionary and disturbing, for "This nation under God" must mean, "This nation under the *judgment* of God, as well as under his protection." No nation can be worthy of the protection if it is unwilling first to submit to the judgment.

When Americans spend increasing millions each year on luxury items they don't need, while millions of other people go to bed homeless and starving, then the nation stands under the judgment of God. When advertisers deliberately falsify their claims, when churches remain segregated, when businesses put a premium on dishonesty, when tax evasion is a favorite indoor sport, then the nation stands under the judgment of God. And when young people should not be exposed to both sides of a question, when it is a "coward's religion" to assert that God may not be unambiguously pleased with us, when Stephen Decatur's oath is the grade school password, when concern for underdeveloped nations is "un-American," then, too, the nation stands under the judgment of God.

It is not "unpatriotic" to say such things. It is, in fact, an act of patriotism. For the only patriotism worth talking about is the patriotism of the one who loves his country enough to criticize it, who extends the same privilege to all who love their country, and who does not set himself up as the one to decide who may and who may not speak. Another way of putting it is to say that the one who loves God can properly love his country, because he is saved from the danger of making his country into God and can thus avoid the temptation of the new idolatry. It is not "this nation, which is God," or "this nation, alongside of God," but "this nation, *under* God," that expresses the true context for patriotism.

A number of years ago in Britain, G. K. Chesterton wrote some lines that are astonishingly descriptive of our situation in America today:

> The walls of gold entomb us,
> The swords of scorn divide;
> Take not Thy thunder from us,
> But take away our pride.

In a later verse, he proposed a further remedy, in typically Chestertonian terms, appealing to God to "Smite us and save us all." The super-patriots today want to be saved without being smitten. On the other hand, the complete defeatists have decided that we will be smitten and not saved. But the person who takes patriotism seriously, patriotism "under God," will realize that smiting and salvation are always mysteriously intertwined.

An Open Letter to Spiro T. Agnew

Dear Mr. Agnew:

I do not know how many of your letters you read, let alone answer, and since I would like you to read this one I send it as an "open letter."

I write out of deep concern about the divisiveness that both your rhetoric and your ideas are creating in our country—a divisiveness that may well destroy us as McCarthyism threatened to destroy us in the 1950's, unless you are willing to hear the case of those who are disturbed by what you say. I want to try to make that case to you.

I have no right to insist that you change your ideas, though I hope I will persuade you to rethink some of them. But I have every right to insist (the verb is carefully chosen) that you change your method of proclaiming them. You do not escape responsibility simply by accusing your critics of "hot, wild rhetoric," for it is by "hot, wild rhetoric" that you have made your name a household word. You have indeed won instant fame, but at a price—a price higher for the nation than for yourself: the phenomenon of a Vice-President spreading fear and invective across the land reflects a country being urged by its elected leadership to abandon thought and rationality at a

Written in May, 1970, shortly after the invasion of Cambodia and published in *The Christian Century*, Oct. 14, 1970. Copyright 1970 by The Christian Century Foundation. Reprinted by permission.

time when we have special need of the ability to understand one another rather than to hate.

In so addressing you I wear a number of hats, and they are all hats that you have made the object of your scorn. To avoid pretense, I will describe them at the outset. On the most immediately human level, I am the father of draft-age sons—sons who love their country and are not going to tarnish its image further by participating in a war they believe to be immoral; some of your choicest epithets have been reserved for such young men. Second, I am a university professor; I work for one of the institutions of our society against which you have leveled sweeping accusations of social irresponsibility, and I represent a profession you have repeatedly accused of corrupting our young. Third, I am a clergyman, committed to the ecumenical attempt of groups like the National Council of Churches to relate religion to life; and these are groups for which you have expressed contempt. Finally, I am an American; but I am not the kind of American you approve of, since I express disagreement with many of the domestic and international policies of the administration you represent.

On all four counts, then, I am what you have described as one of the rotten apples you would like to clean out of the barrel. Can you listen to a reasoned plea from such a person? Before you throw me out of the barrel, let me try to explain to you what the concerns of these four groups are, and why members of them feel so strongly that you are doing a disservice to our country.

I

First, as *the parent of sons of draft age,* I plead with you to make another attempt to understand that youth can oppose this war for honorable reasons. I shall not speak in the name of my own sons, who are quite capable of representing their own position, but I must try to speak in the name of the hundreds of young men I have talked with over the past four or five years. As I hear your scathing descriptions of American youth who oppose the war, I wonder if you have ever actually listened to a nineteen-year-old pouring out the anguish of his soul as he decides that he cannot obey the command of his Government that he kill. I have listened to many of them. They are not the "effete snobs" or the cowards and moral degenerates you describe at fund-raising banquets. They simply believe (along with increasing numbers of older citizens who are beginning to catch up with their ideas) that the American military presence in Vietnam is *wrong*. They see America backing a corrupt military dictatorship that does not represent the South Vietnamese. They see us inflicting appalling destruction on a country and a people. They know that civilians —women, children, and old people—are slaughtered day after day whether by bombs from 50,000 feet, napalm from 5,000 feet or rifles from 5 feet. They know that the Vietcong are ruthless, but they are unimpressed by the argument that our moral posture should be dictated by the enemy. They reject the rhetoric of "victory" and the theory that the way to end a war is to widen it.

In the face of this, what do they do? They say, "No." They say, "I will not fight in such a war." They say, "I will choose prison or exile before I will do such things." Do you have any idea, Mr. Vice-President, what goes through the mind and heart and soul of a nineteen-year-old who decides, out of the most honorable of motives, that he must follow his conscience, and then discovers that his country offers him only the dishonorable alternatives of five years in jail or a lifetime of exile? I wish that just once you would seriously entertain the possibility that such youths do in fact represent an immense source of moral health for our nation, rather than being rotten apples.

If you did so, you might not be won over to their position. But you might come to realize that young men in this nation can oppose a particular war for reasons other than the cowardice, malice, or stupidity you attribute to them, and that they have a right to expect the Vice-President of a nation such as ours to be the advocate of the rights of conscience rather than the prosecutor.

Consider further what your rhetoric does to these young men once their consciences have been formed. Many of them are still too young to vote. Denied that course of action, they have written letters, they have spoken, they have pleaded, they have marched. To no avail. So finally, last fall, they organized peaceful demonstrations on a national scale, to express their moral convictions. And what happened? They were told beforehand by their President that he would ignore them, and afterward that while they had been expressing their moral concern, he had been watching a televised football game. And these demonstrations became the occasion for your now-famous attack on the "effete snobs" who engaged in such activities and led to your suggestion that such rotten apples be thrown out of the barrel.

Such was the response of our *two highest officials* to the anguished voice of youth. What did you expect them to do after that? Resume "business as usual" and thus betray their consciences? Go back to touch football and junior proms while their nation continued to destroy civilians half a world away? Can you not see that your language, which has only escalated in intensity since that first speech, made students despair of being heard without speaking more bluntly and acting more determinedly? I weigh my words with most sober care when I say that it was not only cartoonists, columnists, and commentators, but also countless American parents who saw in the Kent State massacre the culminating logic of your rhetoric. You have not disposed of a problem that must lie on your conscience simply by accusing such people of "sick invective." For Kent State tragically juxtaposed students totally frustrated by your scorn, and guardsmen confirmed in all their negative views of students by your reiterated contempt for them. Many other things contributed to that senseless slaughter, to be sure. Yet there must be some moment when, deep in the inner recesses of a decency all men share, you have to confront the fact that rhetoric such as yours—the rhetoric not of an ordinary citizen but of the Vice-President of the nation—helped cause those bullets to fly.

II

In referring to students, I am already putting on my second hat, that of a *university professor*. I believe that education is the prerequisite of responsible democracy, and therefore that your attacks on our colleges and universities are destructive not only of education but of democracy as well. It may be that your polemic against universities desiring to admit members of disadvantaged minority groups (read "blacks," "Mexican-Americans," "Puerto Ricans," etc.) is based on a lack of understanding of how higher education is trying to democratize itself and overcome the social elitism of what have heretofore been predominantly white middle-class preserves. Since you are an infrequent visitor to our campuses, you can perhaps be excused for having a less than comprehensive picture of what is happening there—though by the same token you might also be urged not to express such confident assurance that you know how to cure all the ills you claim have invaded those campuses.

But there is one point at which I must try to make you see how your prescriptions, far from curing educational ills, would simply destroy the educational process. You have made it very clear that you would like to impose a kind of political loyalty oath on everybody in the universities, from the president down through the faculty and students. Let me illustrate that charge. At a time when university presidents have been notably tardy in standing up and being counted, you have urged the firing of the president of Yale University, Kingman Brewster. The sins of which you have convicted him are (1) raising questions about the adequacy of our present electoral process and (2) voicing skepticism about how fair a trial black men can get in our courts today. And not only do you want Mr.

Brewster fired; you have urged that a "hard core of faculty
and students" be dismissed from our colleges and universities
—an updated version of the apple-barrel metaphor. Even if
one were to grant you your self-appointed role as ideological
censor of American higher education, what criteria would you
employ to single out the "hard core" you want to purge?
Would you begin by dismissing all who agree with Kingman
Brewster that we should improve our electoral and judicial
processes?

Can you not see why the very suggestion of an ideological
purge such as you advocate—let alone the criteria you could
be expected to employ—denies everything that a university
should be? Let me try to tell you why. In a democracy,
universities must be the places where *all* ideas can get a hearing, whether they are good or bad, dangerous or innocuous.
Universities must be the places where truth can make it
against error without having to cheat; in other words, the
places where we can believe that truth is not so frail that it
can win only when error is refused a hearing. Your speeches
make clear that you want to deny that free exchange. Were
we to follow your advice, we could not build the intellectual
muscle that can be developed only by the exercise of comparing good ideas with bad; we would be turning out flabby
minds unable to cope with challenge. I cannot think of a more
effective way to destroy democracy. But according to your
scenario, it is unthinkable that a student should be allowed to
listen to Kingman Brewster, or that having listened he could
be trusted to make up his mind one way or the other about
what Kingman Brewster had said.

Beyond that, the thing you seem to fear most is that the universities not only will foster an exchange of opinion among
themselves but will become the seedbeds of dissent throughout our society. You do not want either the Kingman
Brewsters or the "hard core of faculty and students" challenging our society. But those of us in the universities look upon
them as among the few institutions left in America where the

right of criticism is built into their very existence. Educated people help society precisely by refusing to let society—any society—become complacent about itself, by raising awkward questions about where foreign policy is leading, by asking why housing is so low on our list of national priorities, by insistently reminding us that those who ignore history are doomed to repeat it. Not only is the right of dissent the condition of the university's staying healthy; it is the university's task to keep insisting that the right of dissent is the condition of the nation's staying healthy.

And you misread the situation very badly when you can assume—as late as May 22, 1970 (three weeks after the Cambodian invasion)—that the advocates of such concerns are no more than the small "hard core" you propose to dismiss. No, the group that is now speaking up in opposition to what America is doing in Southeast Asia is large and widespread; it has united students and professors, squares and dissidents, administrators and sophomores, secretaries and Nobel prize-winners. If you realize your desire to "dismiss" those responsible for the hue and cry, you will have to dismantle and destroy the universities—and if that is your aim, let us have no further pretense. As long as you insist that there is no place in higher education for a Kingman Brewster or for faculty and students with unpopular ideas, then the universities must more than ever be seedbeds of dissent, not only to preserve themselves but to preserve society from such repressive ways of thinking. Demagogues used to burn books; you would fire educators. The difference is imperceptible.

So we are deeply alarmed when we hear you urging the destruction of the things that can protect a free society. In the name of such things—truth, rational inquiry, freedom of expression, willingness to hear other points of view, the right of dissent—we see it as our task to keep the light of reason alive in a land frighteningly bewitched by the unreasoned and emotional rhetoric of which you have become the chief propounder. No longer are we reassured by your occasional lip-service tributes to the right of dissent, for unfailingly, when the chips were down, we have seen you fall back upon the insistence that those who disagree must be removed.

III

And now, of course, I am putting on my third hat, that of *clergyman*, for I am beginning to preach a sermon. But I shall resist the temptation even though there will not be another occasion for you to hear me in the pulpit, since I am not one of those clergymen who will be invited to preach at the White House. You have been very caustic in your comments about preachers who say, for example, that pollution might be a moral problem, and about church organizations that recommend recognizing mainland China so that we can begin talking together before we are reduced to the alternative of bombing each other. You want us to talk about "evil" rather than about contemporary issues.

Can you not understand how false that dichotomy is? Can you not understand that those of us who believe in God as the father of all men are by that very belief forced to concern ourselves precisely with *all* men and not just with white Americans? Can you not understand that when we protest the use of napalm in Vietnam, it is not because we are secret agents of the ghost of Uncle Ho but because we deplore burning the flesh of innocent villagers who are created in God's image? Can you not understand our conviction that help for black people who are destroyed in our cities might be a higher moral priority than sending a man to Mars? Can you not understand our own indignation when you indignantly attack people who want to cut the space program and, as you so graphically put it, pour the money down the drain of the nearest slum?

It is part of a clergyman's appointed task to look at political decisions and ask what they do to *people*. It is part of our task to press the question of whether the whole family of man is helped or hindered by what a single nation does. I thank God that for increasing numbers of clergymen America's pollution of the atmosphere *is* a moral problem, even if for you it is not. If such destruction of this good earth is not a moral problem, I would like to know what is. If the destruction of a small defenseless country is not a moral problem, I would like to know what is. If nominating mediocre men for the highest court in the land is not a moral problem, I would like to know what is. If an excessive use of executive power to enlarge a war (to the almost total disregard of legislative power) is not a moral problem, I would like to know what is.

These are some of the things with which clergymen today are concerning themselves. Such concerns are not a flight from the gospel; they are an attempt to say that the gospel means something here and now in the total life of all men. I hope you can begin to understand that American clergy are not going to follow your advice and tune out on such issues. There is, for example, a group today called Clergy and Laymen Concerned About Vietnam. It includes Catholics, Protestants, and Jews. Its mandate now has widened to include Cambodia. In the future it will turn to Laos or Guatemala or Baltimore slums or whatever next presents itself as a threat to the dignity of dispossessed peoples.

I take heart in the company of such men, for we have a peculiar and wonderful kind of freedom. We have an allegiance to our country, but we also have a more ultimate allegiance, for we have been told on the highest authority that whenever it comes to a showdown, "we must obey God rather than men" (Acts 5:29). And I hope you will begin to understand that in the light of such a commitment increasing numbers of us clergymen will endure not only your verbal wrath (if it continues); we will endure whatever implementations of that wrath the Attorney General may devise, before we succumb to that most dangerous of all creeds, "My country, right or wrong."

IV

Such a statement may sound to you as though I have forfeited the right to wear my fourth and final hat, that of an *American*. But can you not see that I am unhappy with America today not because I hate it but because I love it so much? Can you not see that *for that reason* I fear an America in which you say it is wrong for Congress to object when the President nominates a mediocre judge to the Supreme Court, an America in which you insist that Congress should give an automatic rubber stamp to a unilateral Presidential decision to invade a neutral country, an America in which you state that those with ideas you dislike should be excluded from university life, an America in which you want the churches to stay out of the arena of politics, an America in which you become wrathful when the mass media criticize the decisions that Republican officeholders make?

In contrast to all that, I want an America in which the "checks and balances" the Founding Fathers created between the executive and legislative branches of government are honored rather than impugned; an America in which the best men possible sit on the Supreme Court bench; an America in which there is a stern review of decisions that threaten to widen wars nobody wants; an America that is not afraid that its youth will crumble if exposed to new ideas on a university campus; an America in which churchmen can offer their best to the body politic, like everybody else; an America whose leaders do not simply name-call in the face of criticism but are willing to learn from criticism. And most of all, right now, I want an America whose elected officials will set an example of moral leadership rather than fan sectional hatreds, and who will unite us in the pursuit of justice for minorities rather than divide us by playing upon our fears of one another.

As the second-highest official of our country, you had an unparalleled opportunity to provide some of that badly needed moral leadership. You have rejected the opportunity. After the tragedies of Cambodia and Kent State and Augusta and Jackson, some of us hoped that Mr. Nixon had learned that part of the task of governing is to listen, and that he would communicate that truth to you. Either he did not or you chose not to hear, for you have specifically stated since those tragic events that you will up rather than lower the ante of inflamed rhetoric.

I grieve. In a time when we have the greatest need in our history for elected leaders who will set a responsible style of public discussion, I grieve at your petulant insistence that you will not cool your words until your critics cool theirs, and that you see no responsibility, imposed upon you by your high office, to set a high tone for public discourse. I not only grieve; I come close to despair. For if I take you at your word, I can only anticipate an America in which the Vice-President himself continues to take the lead in dividing, inflaming, wounding, and so destroying our country.

V

But *must* I "take you at your word" in this matter? I wonder if you might still realize how grievously you are dividing America with your recently invented oratorical style. I wonder if you might still understand how the office of Vice-President has lost dignity at home and abroad by the use to which you have put it.

I hope you might. I hope it is not so late in the day that you have become the prisoner of a style from which you cannot shake loose. I want to believe that you could still "cool it," lower your voice, delete your ripest adjectives, try to draw men closer together rather than pushing them farther apart. Then you could still set an example, as Vice-President, that would elevate political discussion rather than continue to degrade it. I am afraid that not even a radical rhetorical change of pace could win you back the trust of the millions you have alienated. But you still could, if you chose, lessen the flow of divisiveness and harm that has followed in the wake of almost every speech you have made. And you could decide even at this late hour not to add further to the harm you have already done. For that we could thank you, and then get back to the task of restoring reason and understanding to political discourse.

But if you do not so choose—if you continue to pierce us with the rhetoric that divides, the hyperbole that inflames, the excesses that challenge the very freedom to challenge you—what then? I know that I myself shall do two things, and I hope my fellow Americans will do them too. First, I shall draw my own conclusions about a President who lets your destructive rhetoric continue to speak for him, and then I shall summon all my willpower to ignore you henceforth, to realize that I have heard a hundred times over all you have to say, to resolve that Spiro T. Agnew is no longer news.

ABC—Assy, Bonhoeffer, Carswell

The twenty-fifth anniversary of the death of Dietrich Bonhoeffer (April 9, 1970) involved a cluster of events that were centrally related to the way I heard about the congressional refusal to ratify Judge Carswell's nomination to the Supreme Court—an action my family and I learned about when we were four thousand miles and six time zones away from Washington, on the border between France and Switzerland.

During the fall and winter quarters of the 1969-1970 academic year I taught theology to a group of eighty Stanford University students at the university's overseas campus in Tours. Toward the end of March we all dispersed—most of the students to return to the California campus, my family and I to go to Geneva where I was to have a spring-quarter sabbatical. As expatriates of six months' standing, we had endured together the rise to instant fame of Spiro T. Agnew, smarting collectively under the strident proclamations of the second-highest official in our native land, though we had held our heads a bit higher when the Senate refused to ratify the nomination of Judge Haynsworth to the Supreme Court. But when Carswell's nomination was announced, we took it as a foregone conclusion that the Senate could never pull off a defeat of a Nixon Supreme Court appointee twice in a row. So we parted, discouraged about our country and wondering how

Originally published in *The Christian Century*, March 24, 1971. Copyright 1971 by The Christian Century Foundation. Reprinted by permission.

it and the rest of the world would survive both Agnew and Carswell. (This was before Cambodia broke and gave us bigger things to worry about.)

I

I settled down in Geneva to continue work on a translation of a book about Dietrich Bonhoeffer, the German theologian who was martyred by the Nazis on April 9, 1945, for his part in the plot against Hitler's life. Since I had been closely studying his life and thought over a number of months, the approach of the twenty-fifth anniversary of his death had special meaning for me. And it was that anniversary that brought together three most unlikely items in my life—items that arranged themselves, I noted in retrospect, as an ABC: Assy, Bonhoeffer, Carswell. In good theological fashion, rather than starting at the beginning I shall begin in the middle.

By a strange—I am even willing to say "providential"—coincidence, the early morning post on the anniversary of Bonhoeffer's martyrdom brought me a copy of the huge book on Bonhoeffer's life by Eberhard Bethge, the friend to whom Bonhoeffer sent most of his famous *Letters and Papers from Prison*. There seemed no more appropriate way to spend that particular morning than with that particular book. So, putting my translation aside, I read the sections in which Bethge describes Bonhoeffer's decision not to remain in the safe refuge he had found in America in the summer of 1939, but to return to Germany, knowing full well that he had, as he said, to work and pray for the defeat of his country, and having a pretty good inkling that it might cost him his life. I followed Bonhoeffer through his increasing activity in the resistance movement, his deeper and deeper involvement in the plot against Hitler, his arrest, his eighteen-month imprisonment, his lengthy interrogation, and finally his hasty trial and quick death, just a week before the Americans liberated the Flossenburg concentration camp where he had been held.

Bonhoeffer's story belongs, as Reinhold Niebuhr said, to "the modern acts of the apostles." For me it has had increasing meaning as I have come to believe (1) that churchmen today must be willing to put a great deal on the line to oppose evil policies of evil governments and (2) that the evil policy of our own Government in Southeast Asia makes it an evil government. I have tried to resist making facile comparisons between Nazi Germany and the United States, but as the Vietnam war has mounted in intensity, the Bonhoeffer experience has seemed more and more relevant to the American experience. We too have undergone the exclusion, one after another, of viable political alternatives to bring about change, and we find ourselves forced to contemplate "resistance" activities as the only means of sensitizing the conscience of the nation.

II

Such uncomfortable thoughts were the net result of my reliving of the Bonhoeffer story, with Bethge's help, on the anniversary of the day when he paid the full price for his convictions. April 9 was a Thursday, and since our children had a half-holiday from the Geneva school on Thursday afternoons, we were taking advantage of this weekly opportunity to see the surrounding country before our ten-week sabbatical ran out. We had decided to drive over to Haute-Savoie in France that Thursday, to visit the church of Notre Dame de Toute Grâce at Plateau d'Assy. This remarkable building is one of the first modern churches to incorporate the work of contemporary "secular" artists: Léger—brilliant mosaics on the exterior; Matisse—a painting of St. Dominic on tile; Chagall—the baptistery; Rouault—two stained-glass windows; and Jean Lurçat—a magnificent woven tapestry hung in the chancel.

It was that tapestry which caught my eye and kept my attention. I was both fascinated and repelled by it, and I found myself returning to it again and again. It is a huge and brilliantly colored depiction of scenes in the Biblical drama, drawn particularly from the twelfth chapter of Revelation, which deals with the struggle between a woman (presumably the church) and a beast (presumably Satan). In harsh tone and line, Lurçat portrays the ongoing battle between good and evil, a battle that, as the book of Revelation indicates, will mount in intensity until the last days—a theological notion whose accuracy I would judge to be among the most empirically evident in today's world.

At first, as I looked at the tapestry, it seemed pretty clear to me that the forces of evil were in the saddle and that the huge beast would make short work of the maiden. However, the printed description of the tapestry that is handed all visitors instructed viewers to hold on to the ultimate truth that the final outcome of the battle, to be decided at some eschatological moment, is already assured: Satan will be defeated and evil overthrown, the virgin will be victorious over the beast, St. Michael will conquer the dragon. But the victory, to say the least, is veiled. Lurçat has not tried to provide a central focal point for his tapestry, since this is given by the crucifix on the altar below—another sign that victories, if they come, are indeed veiled; for to see "victory" in the cross is surely to find it in the face of a fairly obvious kind of historical defeat.

I could not help juxtaposing the scene on the tapestry with the scene at the Flossenburg concentration camp twenty-five years earlier to the day. And although I left the church buoyed up eschatologically by the claim that good would triumph on the last day, I was contemporaneously much depressed by the apparent evidence that good was bound to get it in the neck right up to the last day itself. It occurred to me that we were indeed living in what Bonhoeffer's contemporaries in Germany described as *zwischen den Zeiten,* between the times—between the disclosure of some partial meanings in history and an ultimate fulfillment of history. But I felt that the time between those disclosures was a sorry business in which the Bonhoeffers were sure to lose and the Carswells sure to win.

My mood was temporarily lifted—enough so that for a few moments I forgot all about Carswell, whose confirmation was then being debated in the Senate—by an exchange with a wonderful Dominican priest in a T-shirt whom we met in the presbytery behind the church just as we were leaving Assy. I told him that I was a Protestant theologian, that I had been an observer at Vatican II, that I wanted to buy some of the postcards he had on display to use in my classes at Stanford, and that I would like to know what they cost. "My dear friend," he told me, "this is not a den of robbers, but a house of prayer"; he refused any money and gave us all his blessing.

III

Down the mountain we went, blessed indeed and needing it badly, for we went into a fearful storm, in the midst of which almost with the force of a lightning bolt, my wife uttered the word "Carswell!" She was suggesting that the vote must have been taken by now. We switched on the car radio, resolved to believe that a fairly close vote to confirm would represent some kind of moral victory. After much dial-turning we did get a fragment of a sentence: ". . . phoned him from the White House urging him to remain on the bench." It wasn't enough to satisfy the mind, but it did boggle the mind. For the first time in weeks we were confronted with the possibility, the unbelievable possibility, that the Senate had twice in a row voted its conscience. By the time we got back to Geneva the storm was over, and we could begin to pick up enough consecutive sentences to be sure that the impossible had happened. There was a rainbow in the firmament, even though nobody saw it but us.

Having spent the morning immersed in the Bonhoeffer experience of the futility of trying to transform governments, and the afternoon at Assy being reminded that evil is going to continue winning some pretty impressive triumphs—having, in short, come to a very gloomy conclusion about what could be done on the human scene, I found a modicum of hope restored to me through the action of the United States Senate: hope that there can, after all, be some frail but important victories, and that one is never entitled to give up on the fresh possibilities that even an unpromising day may bring.

Before this becomes a simplistic homily of hope, I should report that virtually everything Mr. Nixon has done since last April 9 has served to make my straw of hope seem an ever more slender reed. But even in the midst of growing despair about the future of our nation and increasing frustration about how its policies can be effectively opposed, I am sustained by that word out of a thunderstorm that all is not always lost, that though there may be new setbacks forcing us to go down with the Bonhoeffers, we can at least go down in the company of good men, supported by the fact that there are just causes which are worth any sacrifice and that even out of apparent defeats new hopes occasionally materialize. And so I remain grateful for the rekindling of faith that was given me in the way those courageous U.S. senators faced their very lonely, and very public, moment of truth.

3. LIGHT IN THICK DARKNESS

Meditation on a Particular Death:
A Fragmentary Adventure in Grace

I believe in . . . the communion of saints.
                              —The Apostles' Creed
Neither shall there be any more pain . . .
                              —Rev. 21:4
Greater love hath no man than this, that a man lay down
his life for his friends.
                              —John 15:13
The peace of God, which passeth all understanding . . .
                              —Phil. 4:7

This is an inadequate labor of love. It is an attempt to set
down, while the experience is still fresh with me, something of
the impact which a particular death, D.'s death, has had upon
me. It is a rather personal testimony, but it somehow seems
terribly important to try to record it, in the faith that it may
be an act of love to share what one has learned, even though,
or perhaps particularly because, the learning has been very
painful. I want to try to capture something of what has been
going through my heart, so that others who have been affected
by D.'s death may perhaps be able to say, "Yes, I felt that
too!" or more important, "There was more to it than that!" and

Written one week after the death of David E. Roberts at Union Theological Seminary in Jan., 1955, and published anonymously in *Religion
in Life*, Vol. XXVI, No. 4 (Autumn, 1957). Copyright 1957 by Abingdon
Press. Reprinted by permission.

then be empowered in the Spirit to continue the process of sharing in the community of faith.

D. taught me many things by living, and these I shall presuppose. It is the things he taught me by dying that I shall describe here. I need say of his life only that I had heard him laugh, I had seen him in pain, I had sought his counsel, I had looked forward to a lifetime of work with him—so that it is clearly the case that it is *who* D. was in his lifetime that makes his death so important for me. It is not death in general, then, or the death of *x*, which has touched me. Something much more intimate, much more precious than that is involved. It is his particular death which has helped me to know that many things, which heretofore were only words, are triumphantly real, and for these things I must give thanks.

I

The most significant thing D. has done for me by dying has been to make real for me the meaning of the affirmation, "*I believe in . . . the communion of saints.*" Other deaths in the past gave me resources of faith; I can believe in "the resurrection of the body, and the life everlasting." These I could muster to meet the shock of D.'s death. But never before he died had I been truly aware of the almost incredible depth and splendor of the affirmation, "I believe in the communion of saints." This, more than anything else, has taken away the sting of D.'s death, insofar as that is possible. I do no more than record my newfound conviction, given me by the grace of God and by D., that the occasional sense of communion I had with D. in his former life has been replaced by an almost piercing sense of his nearness in his new life. The fact that we are no longer related at particular points in time somehow means now that we can be related at every point, at all times. I used to be conscious of him in his office, or his classroom, or as he sat in chapel—now I am conscious of him in my office, in my classroom, as I sit in chapel. I do not mean this in any ghostly sense; I lay claim to no visions. I do mean that my relationship with D. has incredible new dimensions.

This I have discovered to be both a terrible and a wonderful thing. It is terrible in the sense of the poignancy and bereftness with which it invests almost every moment of the day and night, since this new relationship is (at least so far) too intangible to have the same kind of total meaning as was possessed by the relationship we used to have. But it is a wonderful thing also, and in this very important sense, that it invests every moment of time with a sense of the dimension of eternity. I am simply not alone. I am surrounded by "a cloud of witnesses," D. most preeminently among them. D.'s death brings me into an awareness of eternity that makes eternity (for the moment at least) wonderfully real. This is true on several levels.

On one level it means that certain specific times and places will always have special meaning—here a joke was told, here a pipe was lighted, here Berdyaev was explained, here a child was kissed. But it means much more than that. For it also means, on another level, that when another joke is told, another pipe lighted, another philosopher explained, another child kissed, this is somehow related to, and done in the presence of, eternity. D. is now "present" in a way he never was before. I have the strange and wonderful feeling that I get to know him better each day, and that far from his death diminishing his influence over my life, his death means that his true and lasting influence has just begun to be felt. So that whatever the communion of saints means, it means at least this— that the fellowship of believers in Christ is not limited to time and space, nor do those believers in time commune only with believers in time, and those believers beyond time commune only with those beyond time. For me such distinctions have now become quite inadequate—a new dimension has entered into my life, making every moment momentous with sacramental quality.

I am told that this sense of the immediacy of the presence of one who has died will fade or diminish with the passage of time. And I rather imagine that the *intensity* of the experience will suffer some diminution. But if in any really significant way I lose, or become dulled to, the dimension of eternity in my heart which D. by his very act of dying has introduced, then, hard as it is to say it, I will have to ask God through some other experience of pain to make me aware once more of his "terrible goodness," and I will have to look upon that pain, as I have tried so desperately to look upon D.'s death, as "the pain God is allowed to guide."

What I am so gropingly trying to express has been put in better words by C. S. Lewis in an essay in which he describes the impact that the death of Charles Williams had upon him. (Williams, like D., cast his influence over many lives; he was the kind of gay, sparkling conversationalist that D. was. And I am just unsophisticated enough to rejoice in what I feel sure is the joyous acclaim with which Charles Williams and D. have recently "discovered" one another.) Lewis talks about "the ubiquitous presence of a dead man," of whom one is constantly reminded by almost everything that happens, with whom in a real sense one shares everything that happens; and he concludes: "No event has so corroborated my faith in the next world as Williams did simply by dying. When the idea of death and the idea of Williams thus met in my mind, it was the idea of death that was changed." [1]

I first read those words five years ago. I thought they were very interesting, and rather stirring. Now, substituting for "Williams" the name "D.," I know that they are true. No event has so corroborated my faith in the next world as D. did simply by dying. When the idea of death and the idea of D. thus met in my mind, it was the idea of death that was changed. He, by dying, has taught me that.

There is another level still. The "communion of saints" is now real for me not only as something that bridges and in fact destroys the distinction between eternity and time, or to put it another way, invests every moment of time with the splendor of eternity. The communion of saints has come alive for me in the sense of the new bonds of sheer love and tenderness that D.'s death has forged among those who loved him. Never again can I be satisfied to describe this community as a "community of scholars," or "an institution of higher learning." D.'s death has brought to me a realization of the wondrous concern that men and women can have for one another, of the devotion which can spring to the surface in the most unexpected places. When I think of the "bands of love" that I have felt surrounding D.'s family, D.'s friends, D.'s students, my final response, even in the midst of pain, must be one of gratitude to God.

II

A second phrase has come home to me with particular meaning during these days when D.'s presence has been almost as heartrendingly real as his absence. And these words have, by virtue simply of who D. was and what he had been through, helped me greatly to come to honest terms with his death. These are words at the end of the Apocalypse, describing the new heaven and the new earth, *"Neither shall there be any more pain."* (Rev. 21:4.) This was the thing for which I could be grateful, in the first stunned moments when I learned of D.'s death and knew that in a few moments I was going to have to force myself to go downstairs and give a lecture. "Neither shall there be any more pain"—these words told me that the last and most significant word about a human being is always *God's* word. God knows D. had suffered pain of an intense physical sort for almost the last two years of his life. And there had been other pain too, at other times—pain of doubt, pain of tragedy, pain of despair. And D.'s death could be a blessing at least to this extent, that the pain was gone.

It may be that other parts of the total verse are more important: "And God shall wipe away all tears from their eyes; and there shall be no more death, neither sorrow, nor crying, neither shall there be any more pain: for the former things are passed away." But in terms of D.'s particular death, I must assert that the pain he bore became sacramental for me, as his death shouted forth to me the assurance that the writer of the Apocalypse was speaking truth, and that D.'s pain has at last been given up to God, taken away by God, and healed by God. It will always remain a sorrowful mystery to me why the pain could not have been taken away on this side of death, but I will accept that mystery as one that God in his own good time will make plain; and rather than looking in self-pity at my loss, I will try to rejoice with D. in the fullness and freshness of his newfound life.

I must make one comment about the place of pain in D.'s *life*—a fact of which his death helped to remind me. I am sure that one of the reasons why D. was so extraordinarily effective as a pastor and counselor to this community, was because of the pain which he himself had known. I think, for example, of the pain of doubt. At one time, at least, during the years I knew him, this was very real. And it was precisely because he had known for himself in such an agonizingly real way what doubt was, that he helped so many students to work through their own doubts. One friend of mine, after consulting several people about a particularly baffling problem, made the comment later, "D. was the only one who really understood the questions." Of course he understood the questions. For at one time, at least, in his own life, they had been *his* questions.

III

D.'s death has opened up for me another meaning of the gospel. Even to state it may seem to verge upon the sentimental or the idolatrous, but I mean it in a way that I think is safely removed from either of those sins. During the reading of the Scripture lesson at the funeral service, it hit me with almost physical force, that in the most literal sense of the words it was true that D. had *"laid down his life for his friends."* It was precisely because he had given himself so totally and so lavishly to generations of students and faculty, that his body was broken. To the extent that I made demands upon him, D. died for me. One remembers, with a kind of wistful sadness, his efforts finally to guard some time for his family and for a margin of health, and how he was yet always being battered upon from without, as person after person made claims upon his energies. And so the truth that there is no greater love than to lay down one's life for one's friends comes home with a peculiar poignancy in the fact of D.'s death.

I realize that the full significance of this phrase of our Lord's should have long since come home to me as I contemplated and tried to involve myself in the event of his crucifixion. But I shall always owe to D., by virtue of the very fact of his dying, the immediacy for my own faith of this truth which his own life and death incarnated. And I do not fancy that God is ill pleased, if through one of his children we come to see more clearly than we had before, the meaning of what happened to his own Son. In making me aware of the depth of the greatest love, D., by his death, has opened for me one further window into eternity.

IV

Finally, D.'s death has helped to transform from a phrase to a reality *"the peace of God, which passeth all understanding."* Until his death I had always known that there were many things about God which passed particularly *my* understanding, but I did not know the extent to which this peace of God, even though it passed understanding, could be real. And D.'s death has illumined for me at least two aspects of the peace of God.

One of these I have hinted at in writing about his pain. It is clear to me that D. now knows the peace of God in a full and ultimate way. For him the ambiguities are passed, the paradoxes are resolved. He can, perhaps, say, "Why, of course! I should have known all along it was this way!"

But there must surely be more to the peace of God than that. That which D. knows in its fullness must in some measure be a possibility for us as well as for him. There is no thing for which I have prayed more earnestly for those close to D., than that somehow the peace of God which he knows can be increasingly real for them.

And I now know that this *can* be real. I know it, to be sure, only fragmentarily, and I doubt that it is given to many people fully to experience it in this life. The peace is not an easy peace, or a static peace, but it *is* a kind of peace. It is a peace that we find not in the absence of pain but in the midst of pain; not in pure joy but in a joy that is embedded in sorrow; not in unruffled calm but in a calm that rests secure in the center of enormous turmoil. These are not "dialectical statements" for a technical discourse on "the peace of God"—they are only descriptive, *merely* descriptive (one might say) of what D.'s death has taught me about how the peace of God comes to us. It is a peace for which a heavy price is paid; it has cost me D.'s death to find it. To know resurrection, it is quite clear, one must first know death.

And I am quite sure that God somehow also knows *this* kind of peace which he grants *us*, as well as the peace he has granted D. For the most adequate description of it would be found by pointing to the figure of the Crucified One in all his agony, saying in perfect serenity, "Father, into thy hands I commit my spirit." If that is truly the peace of God as men experience it in history, then I have discovered what it is only since, and because of, D.'s death.

> Man was made for Joy and Woe;
> And when this we rightly know
> Thro' the World we safely go.
> Joy and Woe are woven fine,
> A Clothing for the Soul divine.[2]

I am sure that "the peace of God," in the sense in which I know that D. knows it, will gradually become more real for those who love him, and that even though joy and woe will remain "woven fine," some of the woe will be suffused by the deeper joy which D. now has.

V

It may be that in time I will be able to make an act of thanksgiving to God for D.'s death, in this sense at least—that he permitted D. by his very death to bring me closer to God, by dying, than anyone else has or could, by living. I have the strange feeling that the things I learned from D. in his lifetime, important as they are, are not worthy to be compared to the things that he has taught me in the space of one long, terrible, and wonderful week since his death. And I know too that the things he has helped me to learn in that one week are only the beginning of the things which I shall continue to learn from him.

I could never say that this "justifies" D.'s death. But I do say that in these ways, his death, which at first seemed to me totally bad, has become a sacramental means of grace for me, and in that sense at least has shown forth the love and the goodness and the mercy of God, so that I can be filled with gratitude to God for D.'s life, short as it was, and also be filled with gratitude to him that in the midst of the deepest sorrow I have yet known in this life, God has been pleased to reveal to me something of his love and grace.

The moments when I can say this with utter conviction come and go, to be sure, but I know at least that *they* are the real moments, and I can live between them in faith that they will return. I know in an unutterably real way, how true are the words that were sung at D.'s funeral, to the almost unearthly beauty of Bach's music, words that go like this:

My faith is still secure
And still I love my God,
For all my pains and fears
Are chastenings of His rod.
With God I am at peace:
No more will I repine.
God is my strength and shield
Protecting me and mine.

Whate'er my God ordains,
Though I the cup must drink,
That bitter seems to my faint heart,
I will not faint nor shrink.
My tears shall pass away
When dawns again the day,
Sweet comfort then shall fill my heart
And care and pain depart.

And so my God I thank
And love Him truly still.
On earth the only law
Is to obey His will.
In Him I put my trust,
In His I place my hand.
Thru pastures green I'm led
Unto the promised land.

NOTES

1. In C. S. Lewis' introductory article to *Essays Presented to Charles Williams* (Oxford University Press, 1947).
2. William Blake, *Auguries of Innocence*.

Ecumenism Behind Bars

Leon County Jail
Tallahassee, Florida
August 5, 1964

. . . Probably the most difficult thing to cope with is the uncertainty. You unfasten your seat belt to get off the plane and have no idea what will happen when you have gotten to the bottom of the ramp. A rumor is out that you are to be rearrested immediately. If so, will you be allowed to contact counsel? Will you be able to maintain outward calm, no matter how much your stomach is churning inwardly?

There are no policemen at the foot of the ramp but, to your surprise, there are reporters. How did they know you were coming back to face jail sentence? Can you talk to them without committing your fellow ministers and rabbis to some attitude or reaction of yours they may not share?

You walk into the airport terminal, the same terminal where three years before a mob had gathered in the darkness intending to beat you up for being a "nigger-lover"; the same terminal where three years before the city officials had finally arrested you—not the mob—for "unlawful assembly with incitement to riot."

Originally published in *Presbyterian Life*, Sept. 15, 1964. Used by permission.

Much is still the same. The rabbis and the black and the white ministers with whom you had come to test the airport facilities are there. Even some of the reporters who were covering the story three years ago are back. The murals on the wall, though slightly faded, are the same murals.

But there is one important difference. The restaurant, which three years before had refused to serve you because some of your group were black, is now integrated. The issue that had brought you here three years ago is no longer an issue. That battle has been won. But the city officials, three years later, are stubbornly insisting, on a legal and procedural technicality, that you return to face imprisonment.

It is now late at night. You have missed the airport bus into town, six long, dark miles away. Every time you made that trip three years ago you had a police escort, so that the rednecks waiting to get you would be thwarted, even in the dark in which they love to work. A reporter offers you a ride back to town, where you have been told that you will be able to stay in an integrated hotel—a miracle beyond all your anticipations.

You thank the reporter, climb in, and drive off. As you leave, another car pulls out of the parking lot behind you and follows you into the dark void of that six miles of country road to town. The car's headlights stay a measured distance behind you, and once again the involuntary pang of fear makes its way up to your throat. You wonder who is in that car, and how long they will wait before they gun their motor, pull up alongside, and force you off the road.

And then you catch yourself. This is pure fantasy, induced by a sleepless night and a hectic day. That sort of thing might have happened three years ago, but this is 1964, and the civil rights bill has been passed. Things have changed.

You relax, and you do get to your hotel without incident. But you can't help remembering that not so far away, in Mississippi, cars *are* pulling up and forcing other cars off the road, and "nigger-lovers" are being beaten up and killed, and it is

still 1964, and the civil rights bill has been passed. Only things
have not changed.

The next day you go to court, are given brusque and contemptuous treatment by the city judge, and find yourself once
again in the same jail you inhabited three years ago—a step
that had to be taken so that the lawyers could start the long,
weary fight up through the courts again.

Once more, there is uncertainty; though now you are safely
behind bars, the uncertainty is no longer tinged with fear. You
may find your case reinstated and be out on bail in a few
hours. Or a number of appeals may be necessary, and you may
be here a few days. Or, though it is hard to conceive, you may
lose the whole case on a technicality and face the prospect of
a full sixty-day incarceration . . .

What has all this got to do with ecumenism? A number of
things. And the word is one you begin to appreciate in a new
way when you are behind bars. For you discover very soon
that, although the law can keep you in jail, the law can't keep
the church out of jail. You realize that you are not alone. You
do not have a heightened mystical sense of the presence of
God, but you do have a heightened tangible sense of the presence of the communion of saints. The telegrams of support
begin to come—from a Catholic layman in California; from a
white southern Presbyterian couple in Arkansas; from a group
of priests, nuns, lay people, and Protestant ministers on joint
retreat; from a Catholic seminary professor; from members of
the rabbis' congregations; from your own denominational
officials; and, most humbling of all, from Martin Luther King
—humbling because he has been in jail dozens of times more
than you have, and how many telegrams did you think to send
to him?

It's not just the telegrams. It's the fact that almost all the telegrams remind you that the senders are praying for you and
have groups of people praying for you. And you realize as you
sit in jail that Protestants in Hot Springs, Catholics in Menlo

Park, Jews in Springfield, blacks in Newark, "WASPs" in New York City, and many others you know not of are upholding and supporting all of you by a great web of love and concern and intercession.

When one of the rabbis gets a telegram that goes "*Baruch ata adonai matir assurim*" (and how the prison censors must have puzzled over that one), you know as a Protestant that you too are being included in the ancient prayer of the Jewish liturgy that goes, "Blessed art thou, O Lord, who freest the captives." When a priest wires you of "the prayers and penances of many for your group," you are strengthened at the picture of Catholics gathered to pray exclusively for Protestants and Jews.

Not only are there ecumenical "prayers and penances," there is joint ecumenical action as well. The chairman of the social action commission and the vice-president of the Synagogue Council of America join with the director and associate director of the Commission on Religion and Race of the National Council of Churches of Christ in sending telegrams of protest to the city officials. Another official of the National Council of Churches of Christ wires your group that he is willing to enlist clergymen to picket the jail (and that one does rock the prison censors). A Presbyterian denominational official flies down from Nashville just to visit you in prison. Another comes from New York. Later a large basket of fruit arrives in their name. The local Jewish rabbi visits the jail every evening. The black clergy of Tallahassee continue the marvelous public support they gave you three years ago, visiting the jail, bringing writing materials (on which this is being written), reading matter, shaving equipment—vehicles all of an *agapē* that transcends denominational boundaries, and encompasses and destroys interfaith boundaries. For the first time, local white Protestant ministers visit the "nigger-lovers" in jail—three of them, all told, in an act that defies the local mores and brings a further sense of local support to the inmates.

Finally, after a few days of this, one of the rabbis says to you, "It's the black who has brought us all together. Until the civil rights movement, I hardly knew any Protestants, and I certainly didn't know any Catholics." And he is right. You discover that you still have theological differences with the rabbis inside the jail who are living with you, and with the Catholics outside the jail who are praying for you. But you make the even more important discovery that on this particular issue—equal rights for all men—you have absolutely no differences whatsoever. Here you are totally and unequivocally one. Catholics and Jews are not less concerned about civil rights than Protestants. Protestants and Jews do not see the *imago Dei* in the black any less clearly than Catholics. Catholics and Protestants do not have insights into the civil rights struggle that are denied to the Jews—though Catholics and Protestants still have a lot to learn from the Jews about how Catholic and Protestant abuse of the Jews in the past has given the lie to Catholic and Protestant lip-service concern for them.

As you share a deepening ecumenical fellowship in jail—the Jews joining with you when you pray, you learning from the rabbis a grace before meat from the Jewish liturgy—you wish that a priest also were in your midst. In 1961, the occasion of the incident that has prompted your present plight, it was not possible to work out procedures whereby a Catholic priest could accompany you on a Freedom Ride, though you know some who would like to have done so. Would it have been so hard, you wonder, in 1964, when so much has happened to the church and the world in the interval? And you wonder if in another three years, under similar circumstances, a Catholic priest from the locale of the arrest might find his way clear to visit the jail and pray with his Protestant and Jewish brethren.

Ecumenism, you recall, specifically involves the renewal of bonds between members of divided Christendom, with a special concern beyond that arena for the Jews, who are so deeply and uniquely your spiritual brothers. But the concern to draw together, which ecumenism represents, must finally extend beyond ecclesiastical boundaries to relationship with all men, whether ecclesiastically affiliated or not. You discover foretastes, even of this, behind bars. You share the bullpen with a number of men picked up for drunkenness. Early on, one of them makes a disparaging remark about "kikes." Your rabbi friends endure it in silence, but you learn very soon that another of your cell mates, still suffering from the shakes of acute alcoholism, has gone to the offender and threatened, in no uncertain terms, to bash his head in if he repeats the word. The most humbling reaching out across all barriers comes from another inmate, a southerner who has had experience in a good many jails across the land, and who after a meal, shakes hands with you and says, "This is one time I'm proud to be in jail."

Prison walls are high and thick and hard. But they are not impenetrable to love on the wings of prayer. Denominational walls are high and thick and hard too. But they are not impenetrable either. And you realize that it may be a special gift of grace to have lived behind both kinds of walls, in order to make the discovery that neither one is as formidable as you once thought.

Postscript: Released a few days later, our last act as a group was to go to the airport restaurant that had refused to serve us three years earlier, enter it in company with a number of local black clergymen, and have a cup of coffee together—as close to a sacramental experience as I ever expect to have away from the communion table.

When I add up the bus fares, plane fares, taxi fares, and food bills that it took to get that cup, I'm sure no past cup of coffee ever cost as much as that one did. But I'm equally sure that no future cup of coffee will ever taste as good.

The Berrigans: Sign or Model?

Most people writing about the Berrigans make a big point of the closeness of their own relationship to one or both of the men who have become such important symbols of war protest, and who will continue to occupy that role even through their years in prison. I had better begin, therefore, by admitting that I can't score many points that way, much as I would like to claim them as close friends. On a few occasions, I appeared on antiwar programs and platforms with one or both of them; I had the privilege of introducing Dan at his last appearance before the Stanford University student body; I also had the privilege of speaking on a program with Phil one summer at Emory University in Atlanta, and exchanged some letters with him after he was first arrested. Since both of them spoke and wrote so much, however, and spoke and wrote with such unforgettable vigor and moral passion, those of us whose personal acquaintance with them has not been of long duration nevertheless feel that we know them very well. By all accounts, this has been true also of those who have only known the Berrigans through books or television. Since both of them have such skill in communicating, Dan through quiet but com-

Originally published in a fuller version in the *Holy Cross Quarterly*, Jan., 1971, and subsequently reprinted in William VanEtten Casey, S.J., and Philip Nobile (eds.), *The Berrigans* (Avon Books, 1971). Used by permission.

pelling poetic imagery and Phil through his fact-filled and powerful arguments against war, their impact in personal terms has surely been much wider than either of them is aware.

THE POWER OF THEIR WITNESS

Why is this so? Why has the witness of these two men been so widespread and so profound? I think the fundamental reason is because they have served in our war-wracked society as *signs* pointing to some truths we would otherwise forget (and might indeed prefer to ignore) even when they have not always served as *models* whom people have directly imitated. This point came home to me with great vividness after Dan spoke to the Stanford student body shortly after he had been tried and convicted for dropping napalm on draft board records and was awaiting sentence. He described in a very quiet and persuasive way the reasons that led him to take that action, an action that seemed rather strange and perhaps even grotesque to much of his audience. But the morning after his speech, two students with their fiancées appeared in my office, stating that while they were not yet ready to drop napalm on draft board records, they did feel, as one of them put it, that "Father Berrigan has raised the ante for all of us." Both students had been considering requesting classification from their draft boards as conscientious objectors to the war. But after hearing Dan Berrigan, they had to ask themselves whether they could comply even to that extent with a structure that was supplying the manpower to prolong the war. Subsequently, both students decided that they must turn in their draft cards and refuse to be part of the Selective Service System; at this writing they await the inevitable arrest and imprisonment that will come. Dan Berrigan was to them a *sign* if not a model—a sign that things are not well in our society, a sign that each of us is called to move from ordinary to extraordinary action in order to force our society to realign its moral priorities.

Another way in which the Berrigans have served as signs to our society has been by the highly symbolic character of what they have done, creating pictorial images that are uncomfortably difficult to erase from our minds. If their action at Catonsville seemed "grotesque" to some, it also served to dramatize, in unforgettable fashion, the grotesque moral priorities that have been erected in our country: we give medals to men who drop napalm on civilians in Southeast Asia, but imprison men who drop napalm on pieces of paper in southeast United States. If such a statement seems oversimplified, it is nevertheless a vivid and poignant reminder of what has happened to the collective conscience of our nation: we are outraged when paper is burned, and we are not outraged when children are burned. So when people respond that the action of the Berrigans was "extreme," I think the Berrigans are justified in responding that extreme moral insensitivity on a national scale calls for extreme action on an individual scale to challenge such moral insensitivity: "Our apologies, good friends, for the fracture of good order, the burning of paper instead of children, the angering of the orderlies in the front parlor of the charnel house. We could not, so help us God, do otherwise. For we are sick at heart, our hearts give us no rest from thinking of the Land of Burning Children." So wrote Daniel in the preface to *Night Flight to Hanoi*.

I do not think the Berrigans have suggested that their action at Catonsville was a *model* for everyone else. But I think they have demonstrated that their action is a *sign* to everyone else, namely, a sign that our country has dislocated its sense of right and wrong, and that when the rest of us remain insensitive to that dislocation, ways must be found to bring us to our senses and restore our moral sensibilities. If we do not drop napalm, then we must find *our own ways* to get the message across to others. Until we do, the Berrigans will give us no rest.

Another way in which the Berrigans have been a sign to our society is epitomized by the astonishing photograph that appeared in the national press on the morning after Dan's arrest. It was the epitome of the nature of our contemporary society. For here were two men, one of them smiling, free, and clearly liberated, the other scowling, uptight, and clearly in bondage. But it was not the FBI agent who was free; the free man was Daniel. And it was not Daniel who was in bondage; the man in bondage was the FBI agent. So one looked at this picture and asked, "Who is truly free?" And the answer was that the man who was going to prison was the man who was truly free, while the man who was sending him to prison was the man who was truly bound. All the normal assessments of our society were challenged by the spontaneous gaiety of a man about to spend three and one half years in jail.

Let us press the point. What is the power of their witness? Why have we continued to listen to them? Why have we felt a strange wistfulness that they have been doing things that needed to be done even if we ourselves were not doing them? Why is it likely to be the case that when the history of the twentieth-century church is written, the Berrigans, both of them "criminals" in the ordinary sense of the word, may be remembered as the truly prophetic witnesses of our time? I think the answer is found in the remarkably high degree of consistency between their words and their deeds. They said what many of us said, but they then went on to do what few of us were willing to do, putting themselves in total jeopardy for the sake of their convictions. And each acted in his own style. Dan, as many have commented, has something of the pixie in him, and he is a poet, whatever else he may be as a politician and an activist. Phil is strong on well-documented sledgehammer analysis, and yet he does not let analysis go bail for action. Both of them, in other words, converged from different perspectives on the need to do and not merely to say. And it is surely the nature of the prophet that he acts out what he believes, and does not merely talk about it, even when the action will entail the payment of a heavy price. Such commitment is the more compelling when seen within the framework of other commitments already made. I am impressed, for example, by their mutual pledge to one another that they would not leave the Roman Catholic priesthood. It has become far too easy for Christians, and especially Catholics, to "write off" the more *avant-garde* social witness of those Catholics who have subsequently left the church. But the Berrigans are not going to give us such an easy out, and they will be around to haunt those of us who are part of the Christian community for many years to come.

A further factor that gives power to their witness is the fact that their minds—and deeds—have not remained static. Both of them have moved long strides from where they originally started, one step at a time, and each advance a decisive one. They have not been content to "do their thing" in ordinary, conventional fashion, do it over and over again, complain about not being heard, and let it go at that. This, I fear, has been the route for most of the rest of us. Instead, as they have seen one level of protest after another fail to make an impact on the American conscience, they have been willing to move to new forms of protest. As they have moved to higher degrees of protest, they have had a smaller constituency following them in every detail. But each advance in their thinking and acting has forced the rest of us to reexamine our own thinking and acting. They have made it impossible for the rest of us to be content with where we are. They continue, as my student commented, "to raise the ante for all of us." Voices of protest like the Berrigans' have made it necessary for the rest of us to reexamine previously held positions. It is patently clear to me that if the rest of us had been protesting the war with vigor four or five years ago, there would have been no need for the kinds of actions to which the Berrigans were finally forced. It is because the rest of us were not quick enough to recognize the immorality of the war, and because our voices were too muted and our actions too genteel, that the public conscience was *not* aroused until very late in the day. If the Catholic bishops had said forcefully in 1965 what they finally said timidly in 1968, and if we had been listening to voices like Gordon Zahn's a little more carefully than to voices like Cardinal Spellman's, then perhaps napalm would have ceased being dropped on Vietnamese children and napalm would never have had to be dropped on Catonsville Selective Service records.

A final point that must be stressed, perhaps above all others, is that the Berrigans' witness has remained consistently nonviolent. All who were present at the time of the trial in Baltimore will testify that both brothers spent inordinate amounts of time outside of court urging their supporters to cool it, to avoid inciting violence or provoking it, insisting at every turn that the way to make a witness against violence in Southeast Asia was hardly to practice violence in southeast America. Any attempt to equate the Berrigans with the violence-prone activities of the militant far left is surely stretching the facts further than the truth will bear. And if there has been any single point at which the sign-model analysis is to be faulted, it is surely at this point—that nonviolence is an increasingly compelling *model* for producing social change, thanks particularly to the Berrigans, as well as Martin Luther King, César Chavez, Archbishop Helder Camera and a few others. There is a difference between the revolutionary who wants to bomb, burn, and destroy, and the revolutionary who proposes to bring about change through means other than bombing, burning, and destroying. The latter is the vocation the Berrigan brothers have taken upon themselves, and one must hope that even from their pulpits in prison, they can continue to make us hear the reality that, at least for those of us who are white middle-class Americans, a peculiar burden of witness is placed upon us to engage in the changing of our society by means that are nonviolent.

Some Problems the Berrigans Bequeath to Us

A variety of questions can be raised about the place of the Berrigans on the American scene.

1. We must continually ask ourselves why we are so attracted to them when we hear what they say and do not the things they do. There is a terrible temptation to let them go bail for us, to say in effect that because they have done what they did, we need do nothing more. We are tempted to take refuge in the fact that because they have been a sign, we need not be, or to be content with the fact that since they are in jail, the witness has been made (by somebody else, thank God) and we are thus let off the hook. It may be that we are attracted to them precisely because the level of their commitment is so much deeper than ours that we never feel really threatened by their presence into doing deeds that could bring similar unfortunate consequences upon ourselves.

2. Their actions highlight an ongoing perplexity in the realm of ethics: (a) do we act as we do simply because we must, whatever the consequences, or (b) are we called upon to weigh the consequences in deciding what we will do? There comes a point when we simply must act on the basis of the principle, "Here I stand, I can do no other." Dan and Phil clearly reached that point long ago, and they clearly believe also that the consequences of their actions will help, rather than hinder, the cause of peace. But what if this assessment turns out to be incorrect? What if the consequences should turn out to be (as the saying now goes) counterproductive? Some of their critics argue that in doing what they did the Berrigans have made it more difficult to end the war, by stirring up protest not against the war but against the protestors against the war.

The difficulty with this argument is that since one can never be sure of all the consequences, and since baleful ones can always be projected, one may be reduced to such a vapid kind of moderation that no significant prophetic stance is ever taken. No one would be happier than Mr. Agnew or Mr. Mitchell if all those against the war never acted in a way that could produce counterreactions in "middle America." If one does not risk stirring up antagonism, one simply allows apathy or injustice to reign unchallenged. When one recalls the statements that Mr. Nixon, Mr. Agnew, and Mr. Mitchell have made about protest and dissent in the last twelve months, it is clear that they are prepared to allow any kind of "dissent" that does not threaten their own policy in Southeast Asia. Any significant action will carry within it the risk of stirring up antagonism, but it can also carry within it the possibility of creating new centers of support, and (even through the antagonism) helping to join the issue in a way that would have been impossible otherwise. So against the charge that certain types of actions may have unfortunate consequences can be offered the countercharge that inaction may have the most unfortunate consequences of all.

3. An even tougher question raised by the Berrigans' activities is that of the degree of allegiance one is called upon to give to a structural fabric of our society. (I use the words "structural fabric" as a rather awkward circumlocution for "law and order," since the latter has come to be such a code word for right-wing oppression.) When the Berrigans first burned the draft board records, they waited for the police to arrest them, submitted to trial, and indicated that they would go to jail if convicted. But somewhere along the line, they came to the conclusion that it was no longer proper to play ball with the system, and that a corrupt society had no claim over their consciences.

Now *any* Christian must affirm that a point may come when he must refuse to play ball with the system. Many of us who have been far less vigorous in our war-protest activities than the Berrigans have asserted that at certain points we are willing to break the law, but very few of us have challenged the whole legal system to the extent exemplified by the Berrigans' evasion of surrender to the authorities for imprisonment. A sick society needs some kind of order and structure, and one must analyze the social structures very carefully before deciding that a given society is beyond repair from within. Such a point of total defiance clearly arrived for Dietrich Bonhoeffer and his collaborators in their resistance against Nazi Germany, and it has always been a part of Christian belief that in the final analysis "we must obey God rather than men." (Acts 5:29.) Whether we can maintain the minimal structures necessary for social life without allegiance to some system of law, and without courts and punishment for the breaking of law, is a question that the Berrigans force us to consider afresh, and their actions provide a disturbing sign that we must take seriously, particularly if those actions are not yet the model most of us are prepared to imitate. (My existential confusion is symbolized by the fact that I took a kind of unholy glee in the fact that Daniel Berrigan was able to elude the oh-so-efficient FBI for four months, even though I would not be inclined to take that course of action if I myself were arrested, convicted, and sentenced to jail. Perhaps my glee was irresponsibly romantic, the comfortable glee of one who enjoys seeing *somebody else* demythologize an omnipotent power, and is willing to let somebody else pay the price for one's own greater sense of freedom. But Dan has reminded me by his action that there is a kind of freedom that is possible even when one is bound, a kind of liberty that can be exercised even by those who are being hunted and pursued. And in this very up-tight age, that is a lesson all of us need to learn.)

Sign or model? The Berrigans are a legitimate prophetic sign to us so long as we do not let their actions go bail for our inactions, and they will remain an ongoing prophetic sign by continually keeping us off balance, as their very absence from our immediate midst forces us continually to reevaluate the kind of society that brands them criminals. But if they *free* us to make our own protests in our own ways, they also *bind* us to make those protests more sharply tomorrow than we did yesterday, and to face the uncomfortable possibility that what we may be called upon to do next week is of a magnitude we would not even have considered last month.

4. VIETNAM AND THE EXERCISE OF DISSENT: A FRAGMENT OF HISTORY

The Last Judgment Is Now

The parable of the Last Judgment has been put to many uses. I shall not endeavor to extract from it a detailed account of what American foreign policy in Vietnam should be. Let me, however, highlight three things from this parable that furnish a backdrop for our concern about Vietnam. And although the parable deals with the nations, let us not evade its direct word to us as individuals, but hear it rather as addressed to each of us.

1. In terms of this parable, *How is it that we shall be judged?* Let us not worry about imagery or detail or rhetoric. Let us simply ask the hard, clean question, "How is the worth of a man determined?" And we discover that the question before which we will be held accountable is not: "Were you baptized?" or "Did you tithe?" or "Can you distinguish between true and false doctrine?" Those questions may, in various contexts, be important, but they are not, either individually or collectively, the all-important question. The all-important question, according to this parable, is simply: *"What did you do for those in need?"* What did you do for the hungry, the thirsty, the lonesome, the ill-clad, the sick, the imprisoned?

Where are such people today—those in terms of whom the

A speech given at the National Mobilization of Clergy and Laymen Concerned About Vietnam in Washington, D.C., Feb. 1, 1967.

authenticity of our lives will be judged? We have them, to be sure, in Washington, Cleveland, Topeka, Birmingham, Albuquerque, San Diego, and Portland. But we have them also in a special way in Vietnam, and there our responsibility is the greater.

It is our presence that has made them hungry, by defoliating their crops.

It is our presence that has made them thirsty, by befouling their springs and rivers.

It is our presence that has made them lonesome by killing their children with napalm.

It is our presence that has made them naked by destroying their production capacity.

It is our presence that has made them sick by bombing their supply routes.

It is our presence that has imprisoned them by evacuating their civilians to relocation centers and destroying their villages for our military convenience.

The question stands: "What did you do for those in need?"

2. A second emphasis of this parable is surprising and threatening to conventionally religious people. We have been taught that religion deals with our spiritual needs; the constant criticism we hear leveled at our churches and synagogues is that we are meddling where we don't belong: "Reverend, don't talk politics, preach the gospel"; "Rabbi, let's have a little less about acts of charity and a little more about Judaism."

But in the parable, the terms of accountability are not "spiritual" at all. The question is not: "Did you give them spiritual nourishment?" but "Did you give them soup?" Not: "Did you give them peace of mind or peace of soul?" but "Did you give them a piece of bread?" Not: "Did you clothe their spiritual nakedness with sound theology?" but "Did you cover their shivering bodies with warm clothing?" The parable tells us that our concern for those in need will be measured in the *most materialistic down-to-earth terms imaginable:* we are to deal specifically with hunger, thirst, loneliness, lack of clothing, illness, imprisonment.

We are not allowed to pretend that all that is someone else's job, that those are "secular" enterprises, and that we are to deal exclusively with "spiritual" enterprises.

The parable demolishes that pious evasion. For it puts in blunt pictorial terms the truth that is embedded in both Christianity and Judaism—that the two great commandments (which we Christians had better have the grace to acknowledge are no Christian invention but come from the Hebrew Bible) these commandments, to love God and love the neighbor, are one and the same. The parable translates that from the abstract to the concrete: for the Christian to feed the hungry is to feed Christ; for the Jew to feed the hungry is to give honor to God.

Where, then, is God found? Not necessarily in our cathedrals or churches, not in our closed-off religious sectors—but in the halls of Congress where issues of hunger and thirst and illness are debated; in our State Department where men determine who will live and who will die; in the efforts of humble citizens who seek to mobilize their outcry on behalf of those who suffer nakedness and want. We clergy do not "take God" to those places, but if we *go* to those places, it is *there* that we will find him. And if through those places we minister *not* to those in need, we neither minister to God nor in his name.

3. The third thing we learn from this parable is something religious leaders in particular need to hear. For when we ask who are those in this story who have done the will of their Father, we learn a surprising and important thing: *the righteous do not know that they are righteous.* "Lord, when did we see thee hungry and feed thee, or thirsty and give thee drink? And when did we see thee a stranger and welcome thee, or naked and clothe thee? And when did we see thee sick or in prison and visit thee?" (Matt. 26:37-39.) The righteous do not ap-

proach the moment of judgment confident and secure, loaded down with a whole bagful of good works to be dumped on the scale of judgment. They do not say, "We of all people have earned the divine favor." No, confronted by the terms of judgment they feel themselves empty and defenseless. They say in effect, "On the terms you dictate, we have nothing to offer, there is nothing to commend ourselves to you."

These are surely the only terms on which we can face God —not in self-confidence, but in abasement. Let us not presume as clergy that we are righteous because we oppose a foreign policy we believe to be unrighteous; let us not presume as a nation that we are righteous because we oppose an ideology we believe to be unrighteous. Let us put aside the terms "righteousness" and "unrighteousness," which means putting aside any kind of human presumption, leaving to God the disposition of what we offer up to him.

The parable is very harsh. It rises to a crescendo of judgment, with only a grace note of mercy. It can be argued that it is not the whole story of our faith, that it is "one-sided," that it must be seen "in context," and all the rest. So be it. But there are times when we do not deserve a balanced picture, where we need to isolate one harsh note and blare it forth. To many in our suffering world today, the note most needed is the note of grace and compassion. But that is not the note *we* need to hear. The note we need to hear is the note of judgment, the reminder that by what we have done and continue to do, the word that may be spoken to us is simply the word of judgment: "Depart from me, you cursed." Our hope, in the face of that possibility, cannot be that we presume on "cheap grace," or count on benign divine indifference to our deeds, but that we seek, before it is too late, a fresh direction.

If we do not do so, we can be sure that God will judge us harshly, and will hold us accountable for the horror we continue to unleash. But if we turn about, if we seek to undo whatever measure we can of the wrong that has been done, then we can also be sure that as we walk that long and hard and often discouraging road, God himself will be with us, to guide and chasten and sustain us, and that he will deign to use even us in restoring some portion of the divine creation we have so grievously misused.

Protest for the Sake of Persuasion

While I speak only in my own name today, I do speak as a churchman, and I hope there are many within the churches and synagogues who will affirm my words.

I am haunted by the memory of German Nazism in the '30s, and the failure of the church to speak and act until it was too late. I am haunted by the ongoing reality of American racism in the '60s, and the failure of the churches and synagogues to involve themselves until the eleventh hour. But I am even more haunted by the escalating evil of this war, and the timidity of the American religious community in condemning it. In combating those three evils of our day—totalitarianism, racism, and war—we of the religious communities have been tardy opponents, and for that we must first of all ask forgiveness of those who have been manning the battlements of our absence.

But breast-beating is cheap. What is demanded of the religious communities is involvement. Both the pledge and the reality of that involvement have been wonderfully symbolized in recent days by Martin Luther King. His was the probing and disturbing voice of conscience in the battle against racial injustice at home, and his has now become that voice in the battle against international injustice abroad. I only pray that this time we will follow him more swiftly than we did before,

A speech given at the Spring Mobilization Against the War, Kezar Stadium, San Francisco, April 15, 1967.

so that his voice and the voice of his courageous wife will be transformed from a duet into a mighty chorus of concern that American honor is stained by the Vietnamese blood we shed.

You and I share that concern today, whatever the theology or ideology that has brought us here. We may disagree about the tactics of protest—but we agree that this war is immoral. We may disagree about how or why we stumbled into this war—but we agree that there is no problem of greater urgency than finding a way to stop it. We may disagree about the specifics of a negotiated peace—whether it should be based on U Thant's three points or Martin Luther King's five points or Senator Fulbright's eight points—but we agree that there is something brutalizing about using military escalation to solve political problems.

We therefore share a deepening sense of moral indignation and moral outrage, and we must give voice to it. We do so not because we hate our country, but rather because we love our country so much that we cannot remain silent when our leaders commit us to policies of devastation and destruction. We make our protest not only out of love for our nation, but in the name of an allegiance higher than allegiance to our nation. We give that higher allegiance different names. For some, it is allegiance to truth. For others, it is a witness to the inviolability of conscience. Some hearken to it in response to Yahweh's word from Sinai, "You shall have no other gods before me." Others respond with Peter and the apostles, "We must obey God rather than men." Usually when we obey truth or conscience or God, we can also obey our nation. But when allegiance to truth or conscience or God conflicts with allegiance to our nation, then we have no choice—we must follow that higher allegiance whatever the cost. And Vietnam has posed that choice for us.

The cost is not yet great for most of us, although it may become so. Some, indeed, may court the joy of cost too quickly. If you are among them, I beg of you, do not seek a premature martyrdom. Martyrdom is never to be sought for its own sake.

It is only to be accepted if it comes. The immediate need, while we still have a democratic process, while we still have instruments of protest, is not for martyrs but for statesmen. We need to do more than get on record. We need to do more than salve our consciences. We need to change our nation's policy. *Protest must be for the sake of persuasion,* for the sake of swelling the ranks of those who feel this monstrous war must end.

Why does the Government so consistently ignore the petitions, the marches, the letters, the advertisements, the demonstrations? Because it is convinced that we speak only for a handful. Not until we have made clear to our Government that we who oppose the war speak for vast numbers across the land, and not just for the dedicated few, will our voice be heard. And if that sounds hopelessly square, I remind you of one elementary fact of political life—squares have votes.

This means that stemming from our common witness today, different ones of us will have different tasks tomorrow. It means that Republicans must persuade their party to overcome its instinctive death wish in wooing the right wing, and offer the voters a choice in '68—not a Nixon or a Reagan or a Romney, but a candidate who will have the courage to oppose our present policy, and thereby give us a choice. It means that all of us must give every support—moral, spiritual, and legal —to men of draft age who apply for conscientious objection, supporting to the uttermost everyone who says, "No matter what you do to me, I will not kill my fellowman." It means asking our ministers, priests, and rabbis of draft age to forgo their clergy exemption, and request conscientious objector status, and make their witness count more visibly. It means supporting the congressmen who are already on record against our present policy, so that they will be bolder, persuaded that they speak for millions and not a handful. It means most of all creating a climate of opinion in this country so strong, and so articulate, that it will not only be politically feasible for our own government to end the war, but politically suicidal for it *not* to. That, I fear, is the only language the White House presently understands.

I no longer believe we can get the message through unaided. Perhaps only before the bar of world opinion can our leaders be persuaded of the folly to which they increasingly commit us. We must ask the other nations of the world to save us from ourselves. Many nations, ourselves included, daily express outrage at what goes on in Rhodesia or South Africa. Surely the time has come when the searchlight of that sort of international judgment must come to focus on us. So I would plead with the other nations of mankind that through their press, their UN delegates, their trade policies, they remind us of how we look to them.

Let them remind us that when we poison the wells of Vietnamese villages, we also poison the wells of international understanding; that when we drop napalm we not only burn the flesh of women and children in Vietnam, we also incinerate the tissue of human dignity everywhere; that when we support despotic regimes by the force of our arms, we make a mockery of justice; that when we destroy a people in the name of liberating them, we also destroy what little remaining trust the rest of the world can have in us; that when we rewrite history to justify our policies, we debase the word "truth" of all meaning; that when we press for military victory at whatever cost, we not only destroy a basis for negotiation, but also destroy our country's honor; that when we measure progress by "body count" and rejoice in news reports of enemy deaths, we dehumanize ourselves and kill the dream of love.

Let us ask the rest of the world to say these things to us, and let us have the courage to say them to ourselves. Perhaps thereby we may be shocked into repentance and redirection, so that one day it will again be possible for an American to stand within the community of nations, and utter with integrity such words as truth and honor, justice, trust and love.

"We Must Obey God Rather than Men": The Case for Dissent

In the early summer of 1960, I had the privilege of hearing Bishop Dibelius in East Berlin describe the proof-text game he had to play against the Nazis in the early '30s and against the Communists in the late '50s. Whenever the church refused to follow an edict of the state, the authorities would quote Rom., ch. 13: "Let every person be subject to the governing authorities. For there is no authority except from God, and those that exist have been instituted by God. Therefore, he who resists the authorities resists what God has appointed, and those who resist will incur judgment." (Rom. 13:1-2.) On such occasions, the pastor or the bishop or the congregation under attack would respond with the words of Peter, words that became very familiar to their adversaries: "We must obey God rather than men." (Acts 5:29.)

There is no part of our Christian heritage more in need of proclamation today, no part that more clearly defines contemporary Christian responsibility, than the words, "We must obey God rather than men."

The shadow of the war in Vietnam lengthens over the lives of all of us and of the entire world—a war that by deliberate policy our own Government every day makes larger and therefore more brutal and more immoral, and which that same

Originally given as the commencement address at Pacific School of Religion in June, 1967, subsequently published in *Humanity: Critique and Commitment*, Feb., 1968. Used by permission.

Government simultaneously calls upon us to support more and more unequivocally. Those who find themselves unable to give that support must agree that some hard choices are very soon going to be faced. As I survey the almost tragically inevitable direction of our present foreign policy, it becomes clear to me that we must be prepared for a situation in which our freedom to speak a prophetic word may become more and more circumscribed, and that we must take realistic stock of what this means for the future of the church and our own place in it.

I deliberately invoke the analogy to the German situation, for I think there is no period in recent Christian history that says more to us about the American Church in the early '70s, than the situation of the German Church in the early '30s. Germany confronted a monstrous evil, Nazism, and with a few significant exceptions, churchmen did not rise to the challenge by denouncing that evil until it was too late, until the only witness that could be made was the witness of martyrdom. Any speech or action that might have checked the rising tide of Nazi power was muted for too long. Either people did not really comprehend what was happening around them, or else they waited for the "right time" to speak and act—and found out, too late, that they had waited too long. Since the church did not act, the Dietrich Bonhoeffers, the Fr. Alfred Delps, the Franz Jaegerstetters, had to speak their word from prison. And they, though dead, speak to us now, and they tell us, in the face of the evil of our day, which is an immoral war: "Do not wait too long to speak or you will lose the possibility of speaking effectively; do not wait too long to act or you will discover that there is nothing you can do."

In saying this I am not comparing Mr. Johnson to Adolf Hitler, or the Democratic administration to the Nazis. But I am, let it be clear, saying that as the German churches remained silent in the face of the burning evil of their day, totalitarianism, so too the American churches are remaining silent in the face of the burning evil of our day, an unjust war that threatens to engulf the entire world. Let us learn from the

German experience that the sins of silence and inaction are sins for which we too, in our day, may be held accountable.

To some that comparison may sound more hysterical than historical, but I am deadly sober about it, and I suggest two things for the Christian church today that are underlined by the words "We must obey God rather than men."

1. THE RIGHT OF DISSENT

The first of these is the church's responsibility to maintain for itself and for others the right of dissent. Note that I do not say the *privilege* of dissent, but the *right* of dissent. The positive and theological way of putting this is to affirm the sovereignty of God, to indicate that in affirming his sovereignty we are denying similar sovereignty to everyone and everything else save him.

Why belabor such an obvious point? Because it appears more and more likely that the greatest domestic casualty of the struggle in Vietnam is going to be the right of dissent. Although I think that Mr. McNamara and Mr. Goldberg do genuinely believe in the right of dissent, let me be very blunt, in order to focus the problem. I no longer believe Mr. Johnson, Mr. Humphrey, and Mr. Rusk when they give lip service to the right of dissent. Each of them, after paying the expected lip service, goes on to say, "but" and what follows the "but" cancels out what precedes it. Dissent, they say, is costing the lives of American servicemen, or it is encouraging Hanoi to resist and thus prolonging the war, or it is playing into the hands of the Communists, or something of the sort. Dissent in their book always ends up as something unpatriotic. General Westmoreland has virtually equated dissent with disloyalty. Last year Congressman Hébert of the House Armed Services Committee argued that we should, as he put it, "forget the First Amendment," so that people like Martin Luther King and Stokely Carmichael could be put in jail—and not one member of the congressional committee disagreed with him. From more and more quarters we hear the statement, "My country, right or wrong." Whether uttered by churchman or politician, the statement is a blasphemy and must be denounced by the church as such. Any plea for uncritical nationalism is idolatry, and at whatever cost, the church, and churchmen, must insist that dissent is not only possible but honorable; not a mere privilege but a basic right. We must be willing to die for that right before we surrender it up as hostage to a war we cannot support. If we cannot stand up and be counted on this fundamental point, then we have no reason to expect that anything else we say is going to count for much.

With that as foreground, let me now supply briefly the theological background, the positive affirmation, out of which such a claim emerges. To me the evidence is cumulative and overwhelming.

The first commandment is our touchstone: "You shall have no other gods before me." The ultimate loyalty must be to God alone. It cannot be to false gods, whether of nation, church, or ideology. Nothing can be allowed to usurp the final loyalty which we can give only to God. That fundamental affirmation we share with the Jews.

The early Christian community worked its way through to the same affirmation. When the members of the Sanhedrin summoned the apostles and told them to stop this nonsense of preaching about a resurrection from the dead, Peter, speaking for the others, replied, "We must obey God rather than men." If there is a conflict between what men call upon us to do, and what God calls upon us to do, then for the Christian the priority is clear and unequivocal: We must obey God rather than men, whether the men are the Sanhedrin, the local draft board, the House Armed Services Committee, or the White House.

The point is clearly focused in the earliest creedal affirmation of the Christian community. The creed was both theological and political. It was simply: "Christ is Lord"—"lord" being the one to whom I give my ultimate and unqualified allegiance, the one before whom all other allegiances are second-ary and conditional. Theological to the hilt.

But political also, for in the first century each citizen of the Roman Empire had to reaffirm every year a contrary creed, "Caesar, the state, is Lord"; it is to the state that I give my final and unconditional allegiance. So to affirm that "Christ is Lord" was also to affirm that "the state is not Lord," to say "I do not give my highest allegiance to the state, I give it only to the God made known in Christ."

Sixteen centuries later the Westminster Assembly reaffirmed the principle in its Form of Government, with the ringing words, "God alone is lord of the conscience." The ultimate loy-alty of the Christian is not to the king (the seventeenth-century symbol of power), nor is it to the President (the twentieth-century symbol of power), it is to God and him alone. All other loyalties are subordinate, all other loyalties are conditional, in relation to that absolute and final loyalty to God.

The shoe begins to pinch as we get closer to home. My own denomination has recently adopted a new confession of faith which makes the point as follows: "Although nations may serve God's purposes in history, the church which identifies the sovereignty of any one nation or any one way of life with the cause of God denies the Lordship of Christ and betrays its calling." Fair enough. But the confession also spells it out in even more immediate terms. It calls upon the church to for-give its enemies and commends "to the nations as practical politics the search for cooperation and peace. This requires the pursuit of fresh and responsible relations across every line of conflict, even at risk to national security, to reduce areas of strife and to broaden international understanding." It was that phrase, "even at risk to national security" that continues to upset a small but vocal minority.

But actually, of course, that is only twentieth-century lan-guage for an age-old Christian conviction. Yahweh did *not* say on Sinai, "You shall have no other gods before me, except your

own national security as Jews." Peter did *not* say to the Sanhedrin, "On the whole, we prefer to obey God rather than men,
but if you're really insistent we'll make an exception this time."
The creedal affirmation of the early church did *not* go, "Christ
is Lord except when the state insists that *it* be Lord." The
Westminster divines did *not* say, "God is lord of the conscience most of the time, but if the state wants to be lord of
the conscience then, of course, we'll bow to its request."

No—we cannot admire first-century Christians for putting
loyalty to God above loyalty to the state, and then say that we
don't have to do likewise. We cannot praise Martin Luther for
saying in the face of demands of both church and state, "Here
I stand, I can do no other," and then revise it in our era to
read, "Here I stand, more or less, until things get too hot."

With all that, I would insist, there can be no substantive
disagreement among Christians. We are called upon to maintain for ourselves and for others the right of dissent because
we place loyalty to God above every other loyalty.

2. THE PRACTICE OF DISSENT

But in addition to championing the *right* of dissent, I believe we are now called upon to be the *practitioners* of dissent.

Dissent exists on many levels. I am concerned that it continue to exist on all those levels, and that each person, within
the church and without, find that level of dissent at which his
conscience insists that he operate, and then operate there with
all his might.

For some people this will mean working within one of the
two major parties for a genuine choice. For others it will mean
trying to launch a protest candidate, serving notice on
whoever is elected, that there is a sizable minority within the
country that insists that we work more actively for peace. Still
others will feel that such goals are far too remote—people are
dying today, and we cannot wait for an election year. These
persons will push for such political alternatives as a cessation

of the bombing, an overall de-escalation, willingness of the United States to recognize the Vietcong at any negotiating table, a greater reliance by our Government on the United Nations and other international instrumentalities of negotiation, and so on.

My own concerns were once almost exclusively of the latter sort. I came away from the Washington clergy mobilization in January, 1967, convinced that our task as churchmen was to articulate the massive unrest among the broad middle group of citizens—those who are not "extremists" but who are increasingly disturbed, and who, since they have the votes, Washington cannot afford to ignore. It had been my feeling that Washington is quite prepared to put up with, and be unmoved by, a minority of dissent from the far left, or from pacifist groups, writing off such protest as a tolerable nuisance. I felt that the voice of the perturbed middle was growing, that it could not be written off, and that what was previously the timid and cowering silence of the religious community was at least growing into a louder and louder whisper of concern.

But I now fear that whispers or even agonized speeches may be too little and too late. For the past year, all we have seen from our policy makers is a harder and harder line of military action, an increasing response from those in high places that dissent is disloyal, a disregarding of peace feelers from the other side, and a sabotaging of their efforts to enter into negotiations, a progressive hardening of the terms on which *we* are willing to negotiate from our side, a series of deliberate acts of military escalation designed on the theory that if we turn the screw a little tighter the increased pain will cause the other side to capitulate, a consequent willingness to risk drawing China and Russia into an Asian land war, a national ethos that is increasingly ready to condone the use of atomic weapons "to get the war over."

I think that this policy of military escalation is a policy of folly and utter madness, that we have become so enamored of our power, so captivated by our own propaganda, that our administration has now committed itself to the belief that a military victory is not only possible but necessary, and is deluding our people into the monstrous conclusion that by destroying a tiny nation we are somehow striking a blow for human freedom.

3. A Time for Civil Disobedience

Now even if you accept only a part of that analysis, then the issue is posed: What are we to do? What, in the name of God, is to be the posture of that body of Americans committed to the Prince of Peace, committed to the God who is Lord not only of the Americans but also of the Vietcong, committed to the God who is judge not only of North Vietnam but also of our own State Department? The genteel protests, I have become convinced, are not going to register where they need to register—at the White House. Let me repeat that even so they must be continued, and that each of us must find his own level of activity and protest and concern. A year ago I would have been content to stop there.

But the time has arrived when some within the churches are being called upon to pay a higher price in order to record indelibly our moral abhorrence of the policy of our nation. It is not a role for all. But it is a necessary role for some.

In the past I have always been timid about civil disobedience, not only because I am as chicken as the next fellow, but also because it has often been strategically ineffective and morally dubious. In the early years of the civil rights struggle, the term "civil disobedience" was usually a misnomer, for it was possible when breaking a local or a state law, to do so in the name of the federal law, to appeal, in other words, to the forces of law and order to bring about the overthrow of unconstitutional laws and insist upon the enforcement of already existing laws.

But the issue isn't that tidy in relation to Vietnam, and the extremity of the present situation means that if we are to obey God rather than men, we must now live with something less than spick-and-span tidiness. I do not think that civil disobedience simply for its own sake is likely to be anything but negative and disruptive. But I do think there are certain things the church may be called upon to do, which, although they may be classed as "civil disobedience," will have a positive moral content, and represent our committed attempt at the present time to respond to the demand that "we must obey God rather than men."

Let me use as an example the kind of pastoral problem churchmen are encountering. A young man comes to his pastor and says, "I simply cannot in conscience fight in this war." The pastor explores with him the position of conscientious objection. But it turns out that he does not qualify. The c.o. form requires him to swear that he is opposed to "participation in war in any form." And he says: "I can't honestly say that. I might have fought against Hitler, but I don't know, I wasn't born then. I might fight in some future war, but I don't know, it hasn't confronted me yet. All I *do* know is that I cannot and will not fight in this particular war. I think it is immoral and wrong, and for me to participate in it would be a violation of all I hold sacred and precious. If this means going to jail, then I'll have to go to jail."

And that is precisely what it does mean. To honor his conscience, such a person must break the law. He must refuse induction, be arrested, and face five years in prison.

Now I think the time has come when Christian ministers and congregations and denominations must stand beside such individuals—at equal risk. It is not enough to warn them, "If you follow your conscience you will break the law and have to pay the consequences." We must also say: "If that is the price you are willing to pay to obey God rather than men, then we will pay that price too. Just as it is against the law for you to refuse induction, so too it is against the law for us to 'counsel,

aid or abet you in a decision to refuse service in the Armed
Forces. But since God alone is lord of the conscience, and not
the state, we *do* counsel, aid and abet you in your stand."

I have worded that response very carefully so that it vio-
lates the terms of the present Selective Service Act and opens
the one who utters it to the possibility of up to five years in
prison and up to ten thousand dollars in fines. If Congress
should, at the behest of President Johnson, declare war on
North Vietnam, such a response would not only be illegal, it
would also be considered an act of treason.

That nevertheless seems to me a type of action that the
times and our faith are calling upon some of us to risk. I believe that rather than being merely negative and disruptive, it
has a positive moral content, and that it says and does something affirmative. I am sure that there are other acts by means
of which we could individually and collectively demonstrate
that we have a loyalty higher than loyalty to the state when
the state demands that we act contrary to conscience, and that
if we are not to deny the whole heritage of our faith, summed
up in the statement, "We must obey God rather than men," we
must be prepared to move in such directions, even when they
are called "civil disobedience."

I realize that to many, perhaps most, the notion that the
church not only condone but encourage what are defined as illegal acts (and may later be defined as treasonable acts)
sounds like the height of betrayal. But if we believe that what
we are presently doing in Southeast Asia is wrong, can we permit ourselves the luxury of escaping from that dilemma by silence or by more token gestures of disapproval? Can we turn
our backs while our Government brings us closer and closer to
the threshold of World War III? Can we ignore the fact that
every day not only are the lives of Americans being lost, but
also the lives of North Vietnamese, lives of South Vietnamese,
lives of Buddhists, lives of people who are one and all children
of God? I believe we are now at one of those crucial if exceed-

ingly uncomfortable points of human history, where God is
forcing upon us some kind of ultimate choice—where he is
saying to us, "Either by your silence and inaction you condone
terrible evil and thereby assume responsibility for its contin-
uance, or, at whatever cost to yourself, by speaking and acting, you try to arouse people to stop that evil."

Let us face the further possibility that even these alternatives may be too hopeful. It may be too late to arouse enough
people so that the evil is stopped. It may be that all that is
really left to us is the obligation to get on record; to speak—
knowing that it may make no apparent difference; to act—
knowing that it may have no discernible consequence; to risk
the charge of disloyalty in the name of a higher loyalty to
which we are bound; to risk the charge of treason in the name
of a divine constraint placed upon us; to risk the loss of job,
prestige, comfort, security, and personal safety, in the belief
that when the choice is forced we have no choice but to obey
God rather than men.

The German Church waited too long. Perhaps if it had spoken sooner it could have averted the death of six million Jews
and countless other Europeans, Americans, and Asians. It
finally had only the voice from the prison cell. The American
Church has waited too long. Perhaps if we had spoken sooner
we could have averted the death of thousands of Americans
and hundreds of thousands of Asians. If we do not speak and
act decisively, we too may finally have left only the voice from
the prison cell.

Difficult times, hard choices, and agonizing decisions face
the church—but times, choices, and decisions that are likewise
glorious because they offer us the chance to respond with our
whole being to the divine mandate, "You shall have no other
gods before me," with the word and the deed that says, "We
must obey God rather than men."

The late Alexander Miller, reflecting on times in his own life
when he had to make difficult choices, wrote: "I . . . regret

. . . the times when I failed to meet a challenge because the risk was too great, or to meet a need because the cost was too great. I don't regret any of the times I stuck my neck out for what I then thought was right; I do regret the times I kept it in."

In Conscience, I Must Break the Law

"Vietnam? I've got other things to worry about." There was a time when it was easy for me to say that. I was worried about the California battle over Proposition 14, in which the real estate interests were trying to palm off on the California voters legislation designed to discriminate against minority groups, a measure later declared unconstitutional by the United States Supreme Court. I was worried about the plight of the migrant workers in the San Joaquin Valley, who were striking for the right to bargain collectively. I was also, if truth be told, worried about other things as well: getting tomorrow's lecture finished, scrounging up the extra dollars I was going to need when state income-tax time rolled around, finding time to get acquainted with my kids, recouping some of the losses on the writing project on which I was currently so far behind.

In this, I was like many millions of Americans. In addition, also like many millions of Americans, I was probably afraid to face the issue of Vietnam, afraid that if I learned enough about it, I would have to join those radical, far-out types who two or three years ago were saying in such lonely fashion what many middle-class people are saying now: That our pol-

Originally published in the Oct. 31, 1967, issue of *Look* magazine. Copyright, 1967, by Cowles Communications, Inc. Used by permission. Reprinted in Frederick Crews and Orville Schell (eds.), *Starting Over: A College Reader* (Random House, Inc., 1970). Written shortly after the adoption of the Selective Service Act of 1967.

icy in Vietnam is wrong, that it is callous and brutalizing to
those who must implement it, that it cannot be supported by
thinking or humane people and that if one comes to feel this
way, he has to engage in the uncomfortable and annoying and
possibly threatening posture of putting his body where his
words are.

In the interval since I discovered that I couldn't duck Vietnam any longer, I have tried to do my homework, read some
history, examine the Administration's position, listen to its critics and come to a stand of my own. I've come to a stand, all
right. And I only regret, not just for the sake of my own
conscience, but for the sake of the thousands of Americans
and the hundreds of thousands of Asians who have died in
Vietnam, that I did not come to it with much greater speed.
For I have now gone the full route—from unconcern

to curiosity
to study
to mild concern
to deep concern
to signing statements
to genteel protest
to marching
to moral outrage
to increasingly vigorous protest
to . . . civil disobedience.

The last step, of course, is the crucial one, the one where I
part company with most of my friends in the liberal groups
where I politic, with most of my friends in the academic community where I work, and with most of my friends in the
church where I worship. And since I am a reasonable man, not
given to emotive decisions, one who by no stretch of the imag-
ination could be called far-out, one who is not active in the
New Left, one who still shaves and wears a necktie—a typical
Establishment-type middle-class American WASP—I feel it
important to record why it is that such a person as myself
finds it impossible to stop merely at the level of vigorous pro-

test of our policy in Vietnam and feels compelled to step over the line into civil disobedience.

My basic reason is also my most judgmental: I have utterly lost confidence in the Johnson Administration. Those who do not share that premise may shrink from the consequences I draw from it. All I can say by way of reply is that I tried for many months to work from the presupposition that the Administration was genuinely seeking peace and that it was trying to conduct foreign policy in honorable terms. But the record now makes patently clear to me that our Government is not willing to negotiate seriously save on terms overwhelmingly favorable to it and that it has refused to respond to many feelers that have come from the other side. I can no longer trust the spokesmen for the Administration when they engage in their customary platitudes about a desire to negotiate. What they do belies what they say, and at the moment they express willingness to talk with Hanoi, they engage in further frantic acts of escalation that bring us closer to the brink of World War III and a nuclear holocaust. I do not believe that they are any longer reachable in terms of modifying their senseless policy of systematically destroying a small nation of dark-skinned people so that American prestige can emerge unscathed. All of us who have written, spoken, marched, petitioned, reasoned, and organized must surely see that in the moments when Mr. Johnson is not calling us unpatriotic, he is simply ignoring a mounting chorus of moral horror with benign disdain and proceeding day by day, week by week, month by month, to escalate the war far past the point of no return.

This means that if one believes that what we are doing in Southeast Asia is immoral, he has no effective way of seeking to change such a policy, for the policy, in the face of two or three years of increasing criticism, is only becoming more hard-nosed, more irrational, more insane. The procedures through which change can normally be brought about in a democracy are increasingly futile. Mr. Johnson emasculated

Congress in August, 1964, with the Gulf of Tonkin agreement, which he now uses to justify air war over China. Public protests are written off as examples of lack of patriotism or lack of fidelity to the Americans now in Vietnam or even, by members of the House Armed Services Committee, as treasonable. With each act of military escalation, the moral horror of the war is escalated. We have been killing women and children all along; now, we kill more of them. We have been destroying the villages of civilians all along; now, we destroy more of them. We have been breaking almost every one of the rules that civilized men have agreed constitute the minimal standards of decency men must maintain even in the indecency of war; now, we break them more often.

This escalation of military power demands the escalation of moral protest. Those of us who condemn this war, who are repulsed by it, and who realize that history is going to judge our nation very harshly for its part in it, must see more and more clearly that it is not enough any longer to sign another advertisement or send another telegram or give another speech—or write another article. The ways of genteel, legal protest have shown themselves to be ineffective. During the time of their impact, escalation has not lessened, it has increased. (I leave as a purely academic matter the question of whether escalation would have been worse without the genteel protests. Undoubtedly, it would have been. But it is too easy a rationalization to argue that we might have killed 500,000 Vietnamese, whereas, thanks to the protests, we may have only killed 100,000. Howard Zinn has remarked that World War II furnished us with a very convenient moral calculus: it is not permitted to kill six million Jews, but anything short of that number can be justified in comparison.)

Military escalation has become our Government's stock response to every problem, and in its exercise, our leaders have demonstrated themselves incapable of change. Their only response, now no more than a conditioned reflex, is to hit a little harder. They have become prisoners of their own propaganda.

Their rationalizations of their policy become more frantic, their attacks on their critics more strident, their defense of their actions more removed from the realm of reality. In justifying the decision to bomb within ten miles of the China border, Mr. Johnson, in a not untypical burst of omniscience, assured us that he knew the mind of the Peking government and that the Peking government would not interpret our action as a widening of the war. But who, even in Peking, can predict how that government will respond? Such acts and gestures and declarations on our part indicate the awful temptation of using power irresponsibly and the way in which our blithe self-confidence may sow the seeds of our own—and everybody else's—destruction. I do not know which is more terrifying to contemplate: the possibility that Administration leaders really believe the reasons they give to defend their policy or the possibility that behind their public reasons, there lies another set of motivations and justifications that they dare not share with the rest of us. On either count, their right to lead the most powerful nation on earth is faulted.

I have already suggested that history will judge them harshly. But such a statement is a little too smug, however true it may be. History will judge *us* harshly, that is to say, those of us who continue to support our present policy makers, either overtly by echoing their tattered clichés or covertly by our silence. He who is not against them is for them.

In the face of such conclusions, one is counseled, "Work for '68. Wait for '68." I will, of course, work for '68, just as, inevitably, being a child of time, I must wait for it. But I am no longer content to throw all my energies in that direction, and for the following reasons: (1) It seems clear that no Democrat will have either the courage or the power to challenge Mr. Johnson. In the face of his virtually certain nomination, it is important that millions of persons like myself get on record as indicating that under no circumstances whatsoever would we vote for him. (2) There is little indication that the Republican

Party will offer a real choice. Nixon and Reagan are more hawkish than Johnson, and Romney has displayed an indecisiveness about Vietnam seldom matched in the history of American politics. (3) The vacuum within the two major parties leaves voters opposed to our Vietnam policy with rather bleak alternatives. The decision to cast no vote at all cannot be justified by those who believe in the democratic process. All that is left, then, is to vote for a protest candidate who will not win. Several million voters so acting might serve notice on whoever wins that there is a body of opposition that cannot be discounted. But serving notice is a far cry from influencing policy. (4) All of this remains desperately abstract, however, because 1968 is a full year off. What is not in the least abstract is that in the meantime, men and women and children are dying. They are dying horrible deaths, inflicted not only by the Vietcong but also by our own soldiers. As our casualty rate increases in the next twelve months, the casualty rate of the enemy will increase perhaps ten times as fast. Meanwhile, our escalation will be bringing us closer and closer to war with China and possibly with Russia.

In the face of such facts, an informed conscience does not have the luxury of waiting twelve months to see what the political machinery may or may not produce. Therefore, I find myself forced, by the exclusion of alternatives as well as by an increasing sense of moral imperative, to escalate my own protest to the level of civil disobedience. The war is so wrong, and ways of registering concern about it have become so limited, that civil disobedience seems to me the only honorable route left.

I make this judgment, foreseeing two possible consequences.

First, there is always the remote possibility (on which it is not wise to count too heavily) that civil disobedience might make a significant enough impact on the nation as a whole that the policy makers could not any longer ignore the voice and act of protest. If engaged in by significant enough numbers of people (and significant enough people), it could conceivably shock the nation and the world into a recognition that our actions in Vietnam are so intolerable that a drastic shift in our policy could no longer be avoided. There is the further remote possibility that others, not yet ready to escalate their protest to civil disobedience, might at least escalate somewhere in the spectrum and thus produce a total yield noticeably higher than in the past.

I would like to believe that such things might happen. I see little likelihood that they will. Why, then, protest by breaking the law, if such protest is not going to do any discernible good? Because there comes a time when the issues are so clear and so crucial that a man does not have the choice of waiting until all the possible consequences can be charted. There comes a time when a man must simply say, "Here I stand, I can do no other, God help me." There comes a time when it is important for the future of a nation that it be recorded that in an era of great folly, there were at least some within that nation who recognized the folly for what it was and were willing, at personal cost, to stand against it. There comes a time when, in the words of Fr. Pius-Raymond Régamey, one has to oppose evil even if one cannot prevent it, when one has to choose to be a victim rather than an accomplice. There comes a time when thinking people must give some indication for their children and their children's children that the national conscience was not totally numbed by Washington rhetoric into supporting a policy that is evil, vicious, and morally intolerable.

If such language sounds harsh and judgmental, it is meant precisely to be such. The time is past for gentility, pretty speeches, and coy evasions of blunt truths. Evil deeds must be called evil. Deliberate killing of civilians—by the tens of thousands—must be called murder. Forcible removal of people from their homes must be called inhumane and brutal. A country that permits such things to be done in its name deserves to be condemned, not only by the decent people of other countries but particularly by the decent people who are its citizens, who will call things what they are and who recognize finally and irrevocably that the most evil deed of all is not to do bestial things but to do bestial things and call them humane.

In light of this, I no longer have any choice but to defy those laws of our land which produce such rotten fruits. I believe with Martin Luther King that such civil disobedience as I engage in must be done nonviolently, and that it must be done with a willingness to pay the penalties that society may impose upon me. I recognize the majesty of law and its impregnable quality as a bulwark of a free society, and it is in the name of law that I must defy given laws that are an offense against morality, making this witness wherever need be—in the churches, on the streets, in the assembly halls, in the courts, in jails.

Each person who takes this route must find the level at which his own conscience comes into conflict with laws relating to American presence in Vietnam, and the cardinal rule for those engaging in civil disobedience must be a respect for the consciences of those who choose a different point along the spectrum at which to make their witness; words like "chicken" or "rash" must have no place in their lexicon. Some will refuse to pay that portion of their federal income tax directly supporting the war. Others will engage in "unlawful assembly" in front of induction centers. For myself, it is clear what civil disobedience will involve. I teach. I spend my professional life with American youth of draft age. And while I will not use the classroom for such purposes, I will make clear that from now on my concerns about Vietnam will be explicitly focused on counseling, aiding and abetting all students who declare that out of moral conviction they will not fight in Vietnam. I will "counsel, aid and abet" such students to find whatever level of moral protest is consonant with their consciences, and when for them this means refusing service in the Armed Forces, I will support them in that stand. In doing so, I am committing a federal offense, for the Military Selective Service Act of 1967 specifically states that anyone who "knowingly counsels, aids or abets another to refuse or evade registration or service in the armed forces" opens himself to the same penalties as are visited upon the one he so counsels, aids and abets, namely up to five years in jail or up to ten thousand dollars in fines, or both.

I will continue to do this until I am arrested. As long as I am not arrested, I will do it with increasing intensity, for I am no longer willing that eighteen- or nineteen-year-old boys should pay with their lives for the initially bumbling but now deliberate folly of our national leaders. Nor am I willing to support them in action that may lead them to jail, from a safe preserve of legal inviolability for myself. I must run the same risks as they, and therefore I break the law on their behalf, so that if they are arrested, I too must be arrested. If this means jail, I am willing to go with them, and perhaps we can continue there to think and learn and teach and reflect and emerge with a new set of priorities for American life. If, as is far more likely, this means merely public abuse or ridicule, then perhaps a minority of us can be disciplined, chastened, and strengthened by that kind of adversity.

But whatever it means, the time has come when some of us can no longer afford the luxury of gentility or the luxury of holding "moderate" positions. The issue must be joined. Our country is committing crimes so monstrous that the only thing more monstrous would be continuing silence or inaction in the face of them.

Draft Card Actions

A. FROM A MANDATE FOR MURDER
TO A PLACARD FOR PEACE

What does one preach about on an occasion such as this? Not about Vietnam or the draft, for you already have strongly formed convictions on those matters. Instead, I shall preach about those of you who are turning in your draft cards, and I shall preach about ten minutes.

Originally we had hoped to have this service in Grace Cathedral, and we were disappointed that your request to make an act of highest moral commitment was denied such a clear symbolic setting. But as I reflect upon it, I begin to believe that it is a good thing we are not in a cathedral, that the time has come to take our faith out of buildings and express it in the marketplace, not to confine it within cement walls but to express it on cement plazas. So although the church today would not support you with its buildings, many churchmen today support you with their bodies.

Those of you who are going to turn in your cards are engaging in this act from a variety of presuppositions.

For some of you, the allegiance you express is to Yahweh your God, and you are today responding to his first command-

A "sermon" on the steps of the Federal Building, San Francisco, Dec. 4, 1967, in connection with a specific act of civil disobedience.

ment, given to your people on Mt. Sinai, "You shall have no other gods before me," not the god of nation or ideology or war machine or draft.

Others of you are acting out your conviction that, as the earliest Christian confession put it, "Christ is Lord," thereby denying that Caesar is Lord, denying that the state is Lord, denying even that Lyndon is Lord. You are saying by your action, in conformity with another early Christian utterance, "We must obey God rather than men."

Still others of you, who believe neither in the God of Abraham, Isaac, and Jacob, nor in the God and Father of Jesus Christ, nevertheless also affirm your belief in something or someone more ultimate than the whim of General Hershey, or the power of a draft board, or the god of nationalism. You give this allegiance different names—conscience, integrity, honor, decency. It represents for you too an ultimate loyalty you cannot define but which your action affirms, and what you do speaks so loudly that we do not need to hear what you say.

All of you, therefore, are affirming with Martin Luther, "Here I stand, I can do no other," even though many of you may not want to go on to add, as he did, "God help me." Will you be offended if I, from where *I* stand, make that prayer on your behalf and mine?

We have been accused of "anarchy" and "extremism." The President of our land, in tones that border on contempt, calls us disruptive and virtually disloyal. But I believe that we are acting today not because we hate our nation and its processes, or hold them in contempt, but precisely because we love this land, because we love it so much that we cannot remain idle and complacent when we see it destroying its moral fiber, and in the process threatening the destruction of all mankind.

It is because we believe in law that we must challenge a particular law. It is because we trust the body politic that we must on this occasion challenge the body politic. It is because we are committed to justice that we must be prepared to be the recipients of injustice. And if this be "anarchy" and "extremism" then so be it, we must wear that label proudly. But I choose rather to believe that what we do today is not an act of disloyalty but an act of a higher loyalty, an appeal from America ill-informed to America better-informed, an appeal to our national leaders to recover sanity before it is too late, an appeal from the law of conscience, a law that the highest court in the land can never overrule.

Let me address a few pastoral words to those of you who are about to turn in your cards. The deed you do today must be your own. It cannot be a decision someone else has made for you or forced upon you. It must be a deed about the rightness of which you are convinced in your innermost being.

For you make a decision today to endure not only the first event but also the last in a predictible sequence of events—a sequence that will move from turning in the card, to receiving a delinquency notice, to reclassification as I-A, to an induction notice, to arrest, to trial, to conviction, to imprisonment. You must be ready today to follow that course to the end. If you *are* ready, if the decision is yours, then know that your act today is a moral act of the highest consequence and that you make it not alone, but with the support of a community of concern beyond just yourselves—ministers, priests, rabbis, laymen; Catholics, Protestants, Jews, humanists—who by our presence here pledge to you our support, many of us by such action placing ourselves in the same legal jeopardy as you, and, sharing your convictions, offering to share your incarceration for those convictions.

In facing that kind of future, I remind you of the words of a hymn written in a similar situation of great travail, "Ye Fearful Saints" (and I remind you that "saint" does not mean a holy man but simply a believer):

> Ye fearful saints, fresh courage take:
> The clouds ye so much dread

Are big with mercy and shall break
In blessings on your head.

Let's face it. There is no one here today who is not fearful. No
one cavalierly or complacently sets himself against his government, his friends, his family. But let us not only acknowledge fear. Let us also believe that courage comes to the fearful. Let us also believe in the mercy and blessing that the hymn
describes, recognizing that with all the turmoil that precedes
such a decisive step, there can indeed be a strange and wonderful serenity, once the step has been taken.

A newsman asked me a few days ago if it was not sacrile-
gious to use the offering for an act of law-breaking. I could
only remind him that the offering is an offering of the self, and
that it is an offering one makes to the highest he knows. If
there is a conflict between the law and the highest that one
knows, the offering must nevertheless be made, whether to
Yahweh or Christ or conscience, or all three. You are saying
through your act that even though your government orders
you to kill dark-skinned men seven thousand miles away, you
will refuse to do so, whatever the cost to you personally, that
in the face of a terrible evil, America's war abroad, you will
here and now seek to wrest something good out of that evil—
a witness to an ultimate loyalty that no man and no government can coerce.

Your depositing of your draft card in the offering plate can
be a powerfully symbolic expression of wresting good out of
evil. The card you now hold has become for you a symbol of a
system of coercion and force, of killing and destruction. But
the moment you place it on the offering plate it becomes
transformed into something else; it is transformed by that act
from a mandate for murder to a placard for peace. It will immediately go in the mail to General Hershey's office, there to
be transmitted to the FBI, and thence perhaps to your local
draft board. At each stage on that journey it will be a messenger of peace. It will say to Selective Service, to the FBI, to the

local draft board, to the whole country, that there are those who believe that they may not kill their fellowmen, and who are willing to pay a price in order to recall our nation from a policy that forces men to do just that. It will be a messenger proclaiming that a man must follow his highest loyalty, openly, cleanly, and without equivocation. The card remains a card, but your act endows it with a message. It becomes a messenger of peace.

Dietrich Bonhoeffer, the German martyr executed by the Nazis, who once said, "Only he who cries out for the Jews has the right to sing Gregorian chant," thereby tieing religion and politics together indissoluably, also said, in words I likewise wish to make my own:

> One asks: What is to come?
> The other asks: What is right?
> And that is the difference
> Between the slave and the free man.

God be praised that today you are not asking the enslaving question: "What is to come?" but are asking the liberating question: "What is right?" and are offering your own unequivocal answer.

B. A NATIONAL CALL TO CLERGY
IN SUPPORT OF COFFIN, SPOCK, AND COMPANY
(with Fr. Daniel Berrigan, S.J.)

One of our number, Rev. William Sloane Coffin, along with four other citizens, has been indicted by a federal grand jury, on charges of conspiracy, based on "counseling, aiding and abetting" those who in conscience refuse to fight in Vietnam.

There are many of us who believe that the war in Vietnam is immoral and that men should not be forced to participate in

---

A response to the decision of the United States Government to indict five men for conspiracy.

it. There are many of us who believe that it is therefore a moral act to refuse in conscience to cooperate with the system that involves men in that war. There are many of us who have been engaged in "counseling, aiding and abetting" such men. We have counseled them to find whatever level of moral protest is consonant with their consciences, and when this means refusing service in the Armed Forces we have supported them in that stand.

Now that indictments have been issued against a few of us, no one must conclude that the rest of us are going to be dissuaded from our ongoing pastoral task of giving moral guidance and support to young men who have made the decision of noncooperation.

Therefore, we call upon all clergy—Protestant, Catholic, and Jewish—who in conscience can do so, to join with us and other citizens in acts of public support on January 29, 1968, the day of the arraignment of the five indicted men. On that day we will give our support not only by word, but also by deed, to young men who find that in conscience they can no longer cooperate with the Selective Service System. We will do so by personally receiving their draft cards at an ecumenical service of worship, and transmitting them to the Selective Service office in Washington.

We recognize that this act opens us to the possibility of indictment. While we do not seek indictment for the sake of indictment, we must, however, be willing to risk it for the sake of an ongoing witness to our belief in the integrity of conscience.

By this act, we will demonstrate our support of all the men under indictment, our support of all young men of conscience, and our ongoing belief that the right to give counsel and support and help is a constitutional and moral right we cannot relinquish, even under intimidation, without destroying our own souls and further tarnishing the moral fabric of the nation we love.

C. WHY ARE WE HERE?

Why are we here?

We are here tonight because five of our fellow citizens were in a federal court this morning—where they ought not to be.

We are here tonight because William Sloane Coffin has said: "The clergy cannot educate young men to be conscientious and then desert them in their hour of conscience"; because Benjamin Spock has laid his body on the line to defend the notion that war is unhealthy for children and other living things; because Marcus Raskin has insisted that what we are doing in Southeast Asia is indefensible; because Michael Ferber has urged that men who oppose the war have a right to oppose it openly and publicly and cleanly; because Mitchell Goodman has had the temerity to suggest to young men of draft age that this is a time to say "no."

We are here tonight because such men must be assured, and the Government that indicted them must be assured, and the country that is watching these proceedings must be assured, that those of us who share their convictions have no intention of going into hiding just because the price of public utterance and action has been upped. We who share their conviction are also prepared to share their vulnerability.

We are here tonight because five of our fellow citizens were in a federal court this morning—where they ought not to be.

We are also here tonight because 500,000 of our fellow citizens are in Vietnam tonight—where they, too, ought not to be. We probably have many different reasons for feeling that they should not be there—political, tactical, moral, and even military. But it should be crystal clear that our action tonight is a

A speech given at a rally in Glide Memorial Church, San Francisco, on the evening of the arraignment of "Coffin, Spock, and Company," at which draft cards were received and forwarded to the national office of Selective Service.

supportive action for them also. We feel that they are wrongly there, and that unless our national policy is changed, not only will they remain there to kill and die, but that hundreds of thousands of others will be sent there likewise to kill and die. At the moment, the only way men of draft age can affect our policy is to refuse to go to Vietnam at heavy price—arrest, trial, imprisonment, and fine.

We are here tonight also because thousands of young men on whose behalf five indicted men are charged with conspiracy, must also be assured that if the price of freedom of conscience to protest an immoral war is increasing, there are many of us who are prepared to ride that whole inflationary spiral with them, and who do not propose to be intimidated into leaving them alone in their moment of decisive witness, whether the cost be misunderstanding or ridicule or scorn or contempt or indictment or imprisonment. When our society believes that it can silence dissent by intimidation, then it is very late in the day and the time for speech and deed can no longer be postponed.

We are here tonight because we tremble for what would be happening to our nation if we had been intimidated into *not* being here, and because we fear what is happening to our nation even though we are here—a growing moral paralysis that is content to say to the finest of our youth: "You may have conscientious convictions—just so they do not clash with the convictions of the White House. You may speak publicly—just so long as you say nothing of which we do not approve. You may act as you feel morally bound to act—just so long as we decide that your actions conform to *our* definition of 'the national interest.' You may be for peace—just so long as you do not inhibit us in the waging of war." We are here tonight because notice must be served that we do not accept such limitations as consistent with the American vision or with the moral stature of free human beings.

We are *not* here tonight to act spitefully toward our country, to thumb our noses at the Attorney General of the United

States, saying no more than, "Some of us will now break the law, arrest us if you dare." But we *are* here to serve notice, with desperate earnestness and resolve, that if to stand in full support of the five indicted men, and in full support of all men who in conscience cannot cooperate with the draft—that if to do so means that we are breaking the law of the land, then such a law must indeed be challenged, and we are prepared to do so, and suffer the consequences, with them and for them. Thus our intention tonight is positive; to give witness forthrightly and without dissimulation to our convictions, not for the purpose of seeking legal entanglements, but with the willingness to risk legal entanglements, if that is the price that must be paid, so that, in the words of Albert Camus, our words and deeds will "speak out loud and clear," and that we thus voice our condemnation "in such a way that never a doubt, never the slightest doubt, could rise in the heart of the simplest man." For, as a recent Supreme Court decision put it, "The greatest menace to freedom is an inert people."

What Kind of "Patriotism"?

In July, 1939, Dietrich Bonhoeffer, having come to the United States to avoid the war that was about to break out in Europe, realized that he had made a mistake. He wrote to Reinhold Niebuhr about his decision to return to Germany:

> Christians in Germany will face the terrible alternative of either willing the defeat of their nation in order that Christian civilization may survive or of willing the victory of their nation and thereby destroying our civilization. I know which of these alternatives I must choose, but I cannot make that choice in security.

Although we may cringe in the face of words like "Christian civilization," we know what was at stake for Bonhoeffer. He returned to Germany and gave himself through the resistance movement to working for the defeat of his nation. It cost him his life.

During a brief visit to Zurich in the autumn of 1941, Bonhoeffer was asked by Visser 't Hooft, "What do you really pray for in the present situation?" Bonhoeffer replied: "If you want to know, I pray for the defeat of my country, for I think that is the only possibility of paying for all the suffering that my country has caused in the world."

Written after the invasion of Cambodia in May, 1970, and published in *Christianity and Crisis*, Vol. XXX, No. 11 (June 23, 1970). Copyright June 23, 1970, by Christianity and Crisis, Inc. Reprinted by permission.

And in the summer of 1970, we American Christians, reacting to the American invasion of Cambodia, have to ask ourselves whether we have not come perilously close to the position in which Bonhoeffer found himself, and whether we, too, may not have to will and to pray for the "defeat" of our country.

There is an irresponsible way of raising this question that assumes in advance that there is nothing worth saving in the American experience and that the sooner the whole thing is destroyed the better. But the question can also be raised in a way that assumes there is still so much potential good in the American experience that it must at all costs be saved from destroying itself, even if the cost of that salvation is now going to be the "defeat," or at least the "humiliation," of America in the President's attempt to extricate us from Southeast Asia under guise of some supposed military "victory."

It is desperately important to avoid irresponsible rhetoric here, but irresponsible rhetoric has surely been employed by Mr. Nixon in justifying our invasion of a neutral nation on the grounds that America must not endure the first defeat in its proud 190 years of history. As long ago as 1967, Robert McNamara, then Secretary of Defense, said that words like "victory" and "defeat" had no meaning in our involvement in Southeast Asia. However, if the terms of discussion are to be those of Mr. Nixon, we begin to wonder if such intoxication with victory can be overcome by anything short of "defeat." If our present foreign policy is going to be predicated on the assumption that our military prestige must remain untarnished, then surely we are called upon, with Bonhoeffer, to will and to pray for the defeat of such a notion.

What Mr. Nixon's rationale demands in the name of "patriotism" must be attacked on precisely the grounds on which he defends it. For it is a diabolical kind of patriotism that is willing to shore up our own national self-esteem at the cost of invading another country and is willing to let the domestic scene go up in smoke to preserve the military image. We must surely

insist that the true "patriotic" stance for our time is to insist
that we love our country too much to let it escape from Southeast Asia without having learned some very hard and searing
lessons. If our pride can be chastened only by humiliation and
only by the "defeat" of many things that presently characterize
our national and international posture, then surely we must,
with Bonhoeffer, will and pray for those things as precondi-
tions for the recovery of national health and sanity.

In these ways, at least, we must will and pray with Bonhoeffer for the following:

the defeat of all in our national life that enables men to
make political decisions in the light of military criteria, instead
of the other way around;

the defeat of the attitude that says that saving face is more
important than saving lives;

the defeat of all verbal tricks that lull us by telling us on the
occasion of an invasion that there has been no invasion;

the defeat of the mentality of those in public life who ignore
and scorn peaceful protest and then profess to be astonished
when subsequent frustration moves the protest to more dramatic expression;

the defeat of those who use "law and order" as code words
for repression against minority groups and minority opinions,
and cannot tolerate the notion that justice means a radical
reordering of our priorities.

Our times will not enjoy many victories for justice; perhaps
the most we can hope for is the defeat of certain injustices.
But that in itself would be a nobler banner for patriotism than
the White House cry for an American victory in Southeast
Asia.

Draft Board Actions

A. TO SAVE LIFE RATHER THAN DESTROY IT

For over five years my major activities against the war, both as a professor and as a clergyman, have been related to the young men who are drafted to kill and be killed, ordered by their Government to commit crimes against humanity. I have sought through speaking, writing, counseling, petitioning, and marching to raise a voice against that illegal, immoral, and now increasingly racist war, and against the laws and structures that force young men to participate in it.

I have come to the place where the words I have spoken with my mouth must now be spoken more loudly with a deed. I feel that it is wrong for young men to be forced to enter draft board offices and be enrolled in organized murder. I feel that it is wrong for such offices to enroll them. And I now find no other way open to me to say *that*, than to engage in this symbolic act of impeding entrance to the draft board office. I can no longer stand idly by while young men are forced to do things that the consciences of all good men abhor, nor can I stand idly by while members of minority groups are increasingly drafted to take up the burdens of the fighting.

A statement read in front of the San Mateo draft board on Ash Wednesday, 1971, prior to linking arms with eight other citizens in an act of civil disobedience.

I can no longer avoid the conviction that I must engage in a small corporate act designed to *save* lives, rather than engage in ongoing complicity in huge national acts designed to *destroy* lives. I do this in a spirit of nonviolent love, hoping thereby to show that the violence we are committing abroad must be stopped by nonviolence at home.

I hope that others will engage in similar acts, or in acts consonant with their own consciences, in order to heighten our nation's awareness of the immoral nature of the war we are forcing our youth to wage, so that our moral abhorrence will be expressed in ways the Administration can no longer ignore.

It is important to me that we engage in this act on Ash Wednesday, since Ash Wednesday is the beginning of a season of penitence. I engage in this act penitent for the weakness of my own protest in the past, and penitent for the sins of my nation against its own sons and against the peoples of Southeast Asia. I do so hoping that for others as well as myself today will mark the beginning of a new direction—a turn toward a world in which "nation shall not lift up sword against nation, neither shall they learn war any more."

B. THE POWER OF LOVE IS STRONGER
THAN THE LOVE OF POWER

I am a citizen, a clergyman, a professor. I am also a father, and on this occasion I am proud to be blocking the entrance to this draft board in the company of my draft-age son. As a clergyman, I choose to preach my Good Friday sermon not in a church but on a pavement, not with words but with a deed. I do so grateful that today is not only Good Friday but also the beginning of the feast of Passover, the time when Jews reenact the liberation God gave his people.

A statement read in front of the Berkeley draft board on Good Friday/ Passover, 1971, prior to linking arms with sixteen other citizens in an act of civil disobedience.

The sermon I seek to do instead of say is very simple. It goes like this: "It is wrong for young men to go through these doors and be enrolled to kill. Since it is wrong it must be opposed. And we today are opposing it by blocking these doors in a spirit of nonviolent love."

Nonviolent love didn't work too well against the state that first Good Friday. The state won. Or so it seemed. But Easter turned the apparent defeat into victory, and showed that love can defeat fear and hate, that freedom is not finally held in bondage. At that point the message of Good Friday/Easter and the message of Passover are the same—love is conquering even when it seems to lose.

We, too, will seem to lose today. Once again the state will seem to win; we will be taken off to jail. But we affirm by our presence here that the power of love is stronger than the love of power, that no jail need imprison the human spirit, that Good Fridays can turn into Easters, that Passover triumphs can be repeated, and that as long as good men are being drafted to fight evil wars, we (or others like us) will return to this spot.

C. THE MORAL NECESSITY
OF CIVIL DISOBEDIENCE

Your Honor: We appreciate the court's willingness to let us make a statement concerning our reasons for blocking the entrance to the Berkeley draft board on Good Friday/Passover, April 9, 1971.

While the seventeen of us acted for a variety of reasons, we were united in a belief that the war in Southeast Asia is wrong, that Americans should not be destroying Asian lives and Asian countries, and that as long as men go through the doors of draft boards, the manpower for waging that war or

---

A statement read in the Municipal Court at Berkeley, April 19, 1971, before being sentenced for impeding entrance to the Berkeley draft board.

similar wars is assured. On Good Friday/Passover we chose to engage in a symbolic act of stopping that flow of human lives heading toward destruction. What we have said for years with our words we chose to say this time with our bodies as well. We tried to say that as long as we stand here, no man will be enrolled here to kill or be killed, no work will be done here to widen the war, no one will receive orders here that make him a potential war criminal, no action will emanate from here that will lead to the dropping of napalm on children, the shooting of women, or the destruction of villages.

In doing what we did, we broke a law. We did so knowingly. We did not do so lightly. Before that morning all of us had decided that we must up the ante of our protest, risking whatever charges might be brought against us (whether five years in jail, or five days, or less), believing that the crime we committed pales to insignificance before the crimes our nation orders young men to commit once they have walked through those doors.

Any of us, seeing a defenseless child in Berkeley, and standing between that child and someone ordered to burn the child, would break a law, whether local ordinance or federal statute, in order to save that child from burning. Your Honor, without seeking to be melodramatic, I say as soberly as I can that each of us sees burning children (and many other horrors) as the ultimate end of what begins in a draft board office. So to prevent such deeds, even at the cost of breaking a law, seems to us not only morally defensible but morally necessary, not simply to purge our consciences but to sensitize the consciences of others as well. We hope that our act will force you and others in this court, and those on the street outside, to ask again and again and again, "What am *I* doing to end this war?" We do not say that you must do what we have done, but we do hope that, acting in a spirit of nonviolent love as we have tried to do, and in whatever ways are most consistent with your own consciences, you too will insist that not only must the killing stop, but that it must begin to stop right here.

I think there was a kind of intuitive feeling on the part of those arrested, whatever their religious convictions, that Good Friday/Passover was an appropriate time to do what we did. Good Friday is the day when nonviolent love appeared to be defeated by a powerful state. But for Christians the seeming defeat became a victory on Easter when love rose triumphant out of apparent defeat. The feast of Passover is the time when Jews recall their liberation from the tyranny of a powerful state. Again, the triumph appeared to be a defeat, for there were forty years in the wilderness before the Promised Land was reached. In both cases hope was deferred but not extinguished, and so those two events, Good Friday and Passover, help to illustrate our trust that in the midst of the seeming defeat of our own act of nonviolent love, a victory is being worked out.

For we believe, whether Christian, Jew, Zen, or agnostic, that what we stood for on that pavement will triumph over what the draft board stands for, and we believe that the vulnerable love of a single human person is stronger than the apparently invincible power of an entire state. So we are here not in frustration or anger or resentment, but in hope. For we also believe that no arrests, no police stations, no courts, no governments, and no prisons, will finally prevail against the quiet but growing movement that is the conquering power of love.

Epilogue: "We Must Love One Another or Die"—A Christmas Meditation for Every Day of the Year

Christmas is a time when we indulge our sentimentalities. We see pictures of the helpless "Babe of Bethlehem" and are charmed, forgetting that the helpless Babe ends up on a cross, the first-century equivalent of an electric chair. We read about "gentle Jesus meek and mild" and forget about what T. S. Eliot called "Christ the tiger." We enjoy the rich pageantry of the visit of the Magi in the first part of Matt., ch. 2, and overlook the sequel, the slaughter of the innocents, in the latter part of Matt., ch. 2, where it is reported that Herod, in a fit of rage, killed all the male children under two years of age, because the Magi had tricked him.

We extend the sentimentalities into the later events of Jesus' life. We become so innoculated by paintings of an effeminate, golden-haired nineteenth-century Nordic Jesus, that it is almost inconceivable to us that such a one used a whip, in a spirit of righteous indignation, to drive loan sharks out of the Temple. We are so used to thinking of him as mild and milquetoast, that we find it hard to think of him excoriating the Pharisees for their hypocrisy, repeatedly referring to them as "blind guides" and "blind fools" (check the handy collection of imprecations in Matt., ch. 23). We move easily to visions of Easter Sunday morning (presented to our minds in widescreen, living Technicolor), forgetting that resurrection is

Published in *California Living*, Dec. 24, 1967. Used by permission.

preceded by death, and that in this particular case the death was a grisly one, enacted on a city dump heap under barbaric conditions that can disturb the stomach even of one who has seen a freeway accident.

But at one point we refuse sentimentality. We never allow it to intrude into our interpretations of Jesus' teaching. At that point, we become hard-nosed. At that point, we remind ourselves that all the love business has to be understood metaphorically, or viewed as an instance of Oriental hyperbole, or pruned away so that it won't make unpleasant demands upon us. At that point, reversing our field, we declare Jesus to be the sentimentalist, and dismiss him as visionary and impractical, so that we can get on with the business of living in the hard world his love commandment fails to understand.

This betrayal of love is the ultimate betrayal. Because of it, men have slaughtered their fellowmen in the name of the Prince of Peace. Walls of unscalable height have been erected between men and between nations. To the early Christians, the cross was a symbol of the love of God for man, but later Christians did things under the sign of that cross that made it to Jews a symbol not of the love of God for man, but of the hatred of man for man. Of the instrument of their own liberation, Christians fashioned an instrument of others' persecution. In the name of the God that cross revealed, German soldiers inscribed "Gott mit uns" on their army uniforms and went into bayonet battle with French soldiers whose priests had assured them God was on their side. A vicar of Christ on earth praised Mussolini for his invasion of helpless Ethiopia. "German Christians" hailed Adolf Hitler as a new messiah and acquiesced in his systematic liquidation of the Jewish people.

These things, and many more, we Christians have done in our disavowal of sentimentality, and yet every Christmas we turn to the trees and the crèches and the carols (tremolo, please, on a Hammond organ), and for that one day become sentimentalists once more, after which we resume the hardheaded role from which our sentimentalized Jesus would presumably lead us, were we not on our guard.

It would appear that we have things exactly backward. For his teaching, which we dismiss as sentimental, is actually the most hardheaded kind of realism. And his life, which we sentimentalize, is almost brutally realistic.

In his *New Year Letter*, W. H. Auden remarks, "We must love one another or die." Surely the options are that stark. Auden wrote his line shortly after the beginning of World War II, when Western man seemed about to enter a new Dark Age. In the 1970's we are, if anything, closer to a Dark Age than even Auden could have supposed in 1939. There is the realistic possibility that this has happened to us not due to an excess of love but due to a deficiency of love. Our history has not been a record of practicing love and thereby showing our sentimentality; it has rather been a refusal to practice love, thereby unmasking our brutality.

All of which, in turn, can be sentimentalized. In a day when churches are accused of becoming "too involved in political issues," it is clear that the charge is not only trivial but inaccurate. If the churches are to be faulted, it is not from overinvolvement in the political arena, but from underinvolvement.

It is one thing to say, as followers of Christ quite glibly say, that love should be operative in human relations, both individual and corporate. This can be said with little pain and produce equally little response. But it becomes desentimentalized when it is spelled out in concrete terms. And we resent such rude intrusions. Love in the abstract, confined to the churches and pulpits, is fine. But let love be translated into a specific attitude toward, let us say, fair housing legislation, and howls of protest result. Or let it be suggested that love must be extended to dark-skinned peoples not only in East Oakland and Watts, but to dark-skinned peoples in Vietnam, and this makes love so specific and so demanding that people wince.

In such situations, love is no longer vague and pious. It is a crushing demand. Whatever else it may be, it is no longer senti-mental.

Is peace on earth just a dream? It will be a dream as long as people insist that love is just a dream, as long as they insist that it be kept isolated from where men live their lives and make their decisions, as long as they pretend that it is only an "ideal," as long as they are afraid to translate it into justice, as long as they refuse to understand it as a simple description of the terms on which life must be lived if men are to survive, and life is to be more than a way station on the path to self-destruction.

We have reversed our priorities. Our sentimentalities have blinded us to the fact that behind the manger lies the shadow of a cross, and that in front of the love commandment lie a host of obligations that must be embraced, if we wish to live in love. For if we refuse to embrace them, we will die in hate.